# Gwen took his face in her hands…

Her mouth came down on his, hair tumbling free to surround them. Her leg twined between Mac's thighs, her breasts pressed against his chest. One hand left his face to creep down his chest, lying flat against his stomach and reaching lower.

And all of it, *all* of it, was his to feel. His…and hers. The swell of sensation, the rush of heat. The groan in his throat born of wanting, the wicked hard thump of his heart pounding in his chest and ears.

She froze, however briefly—and then tipped her head back and laughed.

"Ha, ha?" he said, breathless and bemused.

"Ha," she said. "Do you see us? Rolling around on the floor a day after we first saw each other?"

He cursed, and crushed her close and forgot he was supposed to be kissing her—straining against the cuff, straining against her hand, straining against sanity in the very best kind of way.

# CLAIMED BY
# THE DEMON

## DORANNA DURGIN

First published in Great Britain 2013
by Mills & Boon, an imprint of Harlequin (UK) Limited,
Eton House, 18-24 Paradise Road, Richmond, Surrey TW9 1SR

© Doranna Durgin 2013

ISBN: 978 0 263 90416 1
ebook ISBN: 978 1 472 00680 6

089-1013

Harlequin (UK) policy is to use papers that are natural, renewable and recyclable products and made from wood grown in sustainable forests. The logging and manufacturing processes conform to the legal environmental regulations of the country of origin.

Printed and bound in Spain
by Blackprint CPI, Barcelona

**Doranna Durgin** spent her childhood filling notebooks first with stories and art, and then with novels. After obtaining a degree in wild-life illustration and environmental education, she spent a number of years deep in the Appalachian Mountains. When she emerged, it was as a writer irrevocably tied to the natural world and its creatures—and with a new touchstone to the rugged spirit that helped settle the area, which she instills in her characters.

Doranna received the 1995 Compton Crook/Stephen Tall Award for best first book in the fantasy, science-fiction and horror genres; she now has fifteen novels in eclectic genres, including paranormal romance, on the shelves. When she's not writing, Doranna builds web pages, enjoys photography and works with horses and dogs. You can find a complete list of her titles at www.doranna.net.

To my Arizona friends Judy Tarr and
Jennifer Roberson—because some things
change, but some things never will.

# *Prologue*

*Someone's coming.*

The demon blade told Devin James as much, drawing him to the expansive window of the old Rio Grande bosque estate just southwest of Albuquerque. It was a primary blade...a powerful blade. It claimed this entire region for its own, and it kept track.

It whispered to him of encroachment. Of changes. Of danger.

It suggested it should take control.

"Go to hell," he muttered at it, arms crossed and scowling out into the early morning darkness.

A quiet step from behind; arms wrapped around his. A slightly sharp chin pressed against his shoulder. He shrugged against it, briefly increasing the silent contact.

*Some*thing's *coming.*

The demon blade was named Anheriel, and it had changed everything.

It had killed his brother, threatened his sanity, remolded his life.

It had given him Natalie.

And now it had given him responsibility. This estate, inherited from the man who would have killed him—who would have taken Anheriel, combining their blades to create of himself an invincible creature—not so much possessed as in collusion with the demons within. Demons turned to trapped entities who craved redemption...but who could find it only through those wielders strong enough to resist their insidious corruptive influence.

The endless battle within.

And the estate's library was giving him the means to fight that battle, providing information about those demons. Natalie was giving him the means to fight it.

Devin James, back from the brink.

Just in time, it would seem.

# *Chapter 1*

*Coulda, shoulda, woulda* been in Vegas.

It wasn't the first time the thought flashed through Gwen Badura's mind, but this time might have been the loudest. She sat in her tough little VW Beetle along the side of quiet old Route 66, looking west upon the dark bulk of the Sandia Mountains and knowing she'd just about reached destination on this strange walkabout.

*"What do you mean, you're not coming?"* Sandy's voice still rang with wounded disbelief in her mind.

No little wonder. They'd had the vacation trip planned for months. And boy, had Sandy planned. After a year of urging Gwen to lighten up and have some fun before she hit thirty, her friend had targeted Vegas for the big moment—shows and casinos and plenty of role modeling. Time for Gwen to let her hair down.

It had to be said, Gwen had a lot of hair to let down. Unruly, tangled curls that passed as brunette as long as she didn't take her head out into the direct sun or expose the coppery cast of the freckles on her arms. Stealth redhead, that's what she was.

Stealth redhead with an attitude.

Stealth redhead looking at the Sandia Mountains and its windward foothills spread out before her, imagining Albuquerque beyond.

*"I can't,"* she'd said to Sandy. *"I have to do this thing..."*

Right. Because there was no real explanation, was there? *I have to follow this sudden salmon-swimming-upstream urge to head somewhere else.*

She hadn't even known where. Not until this evening.

Not until she'd pulled over to the side of the road, looked out over the mountains, and suddenly known... this was where she'd been heading. Following the inner voice that had been her companion since the night her father had died—warning her, chivvying her, getting her in trouble.

But never like this, driving her right out of her home and onto the road and here—to the city beyond the mountains. But she'd listened anyway. So yeah, she was here.

She just didn't know why.

Michael MacKenzie sat on the hood of his Jeep Wrangler and contemplated the Albuquerque city lights, wondering what the hell he was doing here in the first place.

Restless feet, he was used to. Driven feet? Not so much.

*Herded.* But by who?

More likely, by what.

Even the demon blade couldn't explain it—although the damned thing usually did leave him with more questions than answers. Left him wary, too. Of himself...of others. Of the moment-to-moment byplay with the world outside of himself that most people took for granted.

He hadn't been *most people* for a while now.

Well, he was here; he'd get the lay of the land before he settled in. That meant driving the informal circuit around the city, from the highway to the big north loop around the reservation end of the city and feeder streets back south again. Not many people on the roads, easing toward midnight—now was the time to do it.

Mac tossed his map in through the open passenger window—under this moon, his blade-given vision had no trouble following its detailed streets—and pushed off the hood. The sooner he did the circuit, the sooner he could crash at the little hotel just off the airport cluster.

The sooner he could figure out what had brought him here and how hard it might try to kill him.

He stretched, rotating his shoulders...breathing deeply before he slipped in behind the wheel. Quiet, hearing his own breathing in the darkness, perched on the south-side berm with his nose full of sharp, dry dust and the fading scent of sun-warmed cactus.

The slam of the Jeep door rang loud in the night; the engine was only a secondary insult. He rocked the gear stick into place, nursed the clutch past its chronic initial sticking point and headed out to drive the city.

The blade sat quiescent on the passenger seat, half-covered by the map and an empty pretzel bag. The passenger foot well was crammed with his smaller duffel and netbook case and a jacket stuffed beside a carelessly jammed shave kit. The cargo area had been done on auto-pack—the sleeping bag, the air pad, the big duffel, a gallon of water, the cooler…all of it and more, everything in its place. Everything always ready to go.

Especially Mac.

He drove into and around the city. At first, he felt little of it through the blade—just a smothering kind of darkness, trickling in only because the knife was thirsty enough to bother. Going past the hospital, that was a biggie. And there—a hotel, close to the highway and hosting some sort of convention.

Nothing worth lingering over. The knife—an inexplicable impossibility of living metal and unrelenting demand, literally thrust upon him in the dark—had its standards.

It wanted the good stuff. The intensities of grief and fury and fear and love. It found the violence of the night and drove him there—where he'd end up in the middle of it, battered by echoes of outside feelings and usually battered by fists and pipes and the occasional bullet.

A few years ago, before he'd seen how miraculously the blade could heal him, he would have worried more about those dangers. Now, at thirty-six, he knew more about pain and miracles than he'd ever thought possible.

Now, he just worried about his sanity.

He drove the vast curve north of the city, past the gas station beyond the overpass. It was the only visible building in this unsettled area, just outside the Sandia Pueblo reservation bordering the north side of the city and past the dark lumps of somnolence that, after a double take, he identified as bison.

He might have hesitated there, slowing to enjoy the grin of it—but the *knife*—

It spiked into action, flinging out *alert-beware-fear.*

*Fear,* racing along his spine and the back of his legs; fear, sending his pulse into overdrive.

Grim experience kept his foot from punching the accelerator in reflexive flight; it allowed him to push away everything but the merest thread of feeling— *not mine*—to pretend he didn't feel it at all, even as he heard the rasp of his own sudden breath.

*To pretend.*

Instead of giving in to it, he followed it.

And then he saw them—also dark lumps at the side of the road. One stopped compact pickup truck, three figures, struggling—no. One figure struggling and two attacking.

*Beating.*

He skidded the Jeep right to the edge of the shoulder, close enough to sling gravel on the grappling figures, and reached for the blade without looking—knowing it would find his hand just as much as he found his grip on it.

Whatever form it chose.

It had favorites; it had surprises. Tonight, a familiar feel—square handle of cool wood—and he knew the rest of it without even looking. Dark maple, brass pins, a five-inch blade of moderate width with a wicked clip point, polished metal showing a residual scale that wasn't Damascus but looked it.

The Colonial expedition trade knife. The one that meant no bluster, no nonsense...all confidence. *Deal with the situation.*

Two men standing, one on the ground. Mac got a glimpse of bloodied face and desperation, broad features and a strong nose. A man weathered and worn and, from the surge of new fear coming in through the blade, figuring the odds just got worse.

Of the two men standing, one held a wallet; the other held a worn satchel.

Oh, the blade wanted to scare them, too.

Mac stuffed the feeling deep. That's not what he was about. It wouldn't ever be what he was about.

*—yes yes yes—*

No, dammit!

"Find your own," one of the men said, yanking money from the wallet and tossing the worn leather at his victim. "We're not done here."

"Yeah, you are," Mac said. "Once you put that

money back. And add what's in your pockets while you're at it."

The blade gave him their every intimate flicker of reaction. Their annoyance—and then, with their exchanged glance, the cruel glee of two bullies with a new victim.

*They're not my feelings. Not who I am.*

Those first days after the blade had attached itself to him, he'd almost lost himself in the flood of invading sensation—and woe to the man he'd been, trying to calm a bar fight that had spilled out into the night. But once he'd realized the impossible connection to the blade, the truth of it…

*Not my feelings.*

All the same, the flickers gave him warning—telling him that this wasn't about the money. Their faces—and their body language—gave him warning, too. Young, buff, tightly shorn, they had amateur tattoos and a certain fervent glint of expression. One white, one Latino—but their features didn't really matter. Their faces were filled with hate.

"Gotta knife, boys," he said, in case they hadn't noticed. He couldn't remember, sometimes, how much he'd been able to see in the darkness before the blade had found him. "Gotta helluva left hook. And you need to return this gentleman's money."

The older man looked up from the ground in disbelief—the blade sucked that up, too—and moved away by inches as he groped for the emptied wallet.

"And his gear," Mac added, nodding at the ragged satchel.

The young man holding the satchel threw it at his victim without looking. "This," he said, grinning at Mac, "is more like it."

He'd been bored, beating on the Pueblo man. Now he saw opportunity for more savage satisfaction.

The blade told Mac as much.

But Mac needed no warning. Not after so many confrontations like this one. The young men gave themselves away with a glance, a shift of weight, a sneer of lip. They rushed him without finesse, without training or style.

Bullies too used to their own strength and so highly aware of their own balls.

*—hurt them scare them do it do it—*

"I don't think so," Mac muttered—but he stayed quick with the blade, ducking, whirling, slashing lightly down an arm, jabbing sharp and fast into the back of the hand that snagged him on the other side. It was only a warning: *This is what I can do.*

Faster than anyone ought to be, the blade sharper, the moves more precise.

*This is what I will do.*

They cried out almost as one; they turned in fury. They had nothing but fists and boots, weapons for use on the weak.

*—fear fear leap of hope ESCAPE!—*

The older man ran for it—his satchel snagged, his empty wallet in his hand. Lurching in the darkness, hurting and bruised but safe.

And that, after all, had been the point.

"Hey," Mac said, stepping back and opening his

arms, a peacemaking gesture even with the blade in one hand. "We can rethink this."

—*fury humiliation pain mine mine mine*—

Mac winced at the onslaught from the blade… pushed it away. But it left him ready for their two-pronged attack—a combined rush of brute force, this time wary of the blade. A duck, a feint, another slash—the thin blade so preternaturally sharp.

Deeper this time.

"Seriously," Mac said, his body balanced and ready, his breathing still light and his voice casual. "I've got what I want. And your fun is *way* over—"

Until the blade spasmed, heat in his hand; a sudden glare in the night, hot metal invading his mind.

Inexplicable emotion surged up through the metal to reach Mac, an incomprehensible swamp of pure black tarry hatred slamming into him with vengeance. He grunted; he staggered back.

The men struck.

First with fists and then after he went down—staggered not by their blows but by a retching malaise—they added booted feet. He took the hits, rolling with the impact—over dusty desert ground, over the flat pad of a young prickly pear.

The young men who'd seen and wanted the blade now scrambled for it. Mac had just enough presence of mind to palm the thing—an old Barlow pocket knife now, changed in a swift retreat and with only the briefest strobe of light.

In the end, the change saved him. They thought

him down—they looked for the trade knife they expected to find.

They forgot to look for him.

Mac knew better than to stay down. Even striking blindly, even staggering from the assault on his body and soul—hell, yes, he knew better. He came up swinging. No finesse, no holds barred—the blade flaring to life with its own sparking fury.

Steel and leather, fighting back—a wash of flickering energy and light and suddenly an old cavalry saber filled the sweep of Mac's movement. For the moment, making a team of them.

*Metal, tasting flesh.* That sharp blade barely hesitated in its arc—but it left a scream in its wake.

"Son of a motherfu—" The voice grew muffled, the two men grappling as one tried to support the other. *"—bitch!"*

"Seriously," Mac said—back on his feet now, wavering in a wide stance but still full of snarl. "How about you just call the night over?"

They staggered away, one supporting the other—clumsy enough to ram right into the side of the truck and slide along until they reached the passenger door. The white guy stuffed the Latino inside and threw himself into the driver's side, spinning dirt and gravel until the tires grabbed pavement and squealed around in a tight U-turn back toward the interstate.

Mac thumped down to his knees in the darkness, letting the blade rest against dirt. The surging hate had faded, lapping around them in sticky waves of harsh pain. Fading hate that had fueled the initial assault; fading hate that had then driven it far past first blood. "What," he asked bluntly, "the fuck was that?"

But the blade was silent.

Choosing the hotel went just like the rest of Gwen's trip. Following her nose without realizing it, finding herself where she knew she needed to be. Salmon, swimming upstream.

Clueless salmon at that.

She slung her teardrop back-saver bag over her shoulder and pushed the Beetle's door closed, double-checking the lock before she headed for the hotel entrance. They would, she hoped, have a vacancy. It was a weekday; it wasn't any particular tourist season. Just early spring in Albuquerque.

She stopped short just beneath the lighted entry. Like so many other moments lately, without thinking much about it. Just doing it. To stare.

Like a complete idiot.

At a stranger.

At first glance, he was all distracted grey eyes, a faint frown between dark brows, tension along high cheekbones and lean jaw and with a mouth that looked as though it was crafted to carry a wry smile. Glossy dark hair was as scruffed as the rest of him, his one shoulder carried slightly higher than the other, with his movement not quite even and yet still full of its own strength.

On second glance, she saw his torn jeans and the scruffy ribbed crew-neck shirt, the dust-smeared jacket with sporadic dark splatters and stains that could only be blood. But by second glance, he'd seen *her*.

In point of fact, he was trying to get past her in this limited space—if only she hadn't stopped to fill the space between the oversize potted shrubs flanking the entry walk.

But she had.

He glanced at her, and his polite distraction vanished; everything in those grey eyes focused in on her—*targeted* her. His shoulders straightened; his tired posture transformed into something more alert. Something more powerful.

Her mouth went dry.

His eyes narrowed. "Who are you?"

She'd lived her life with the uncanny ability to see through people, to anticipate them. To ignore the jerks and beware the bullies and step slowly back from the crazies.

From him, she felt nothing.

No, not true. She felt that which she couldn't unravel—only a discordant and tangled duality, a slow humming throb that both called to her and terrified her.

"Who—" he said.

"I don't know you," she snapped, suddenly breaking free of that spell. "I want you to stay back, please." Blunt words, straight to the point. She'd learned that, too, over the years. To listen to the voice that whispered within her—and to act on it.

She wouldn't be here if she hadn't, wandering the highways on her walkabout. Amazing how much trouble her young self had gotten into, reacting to the sudden awareness of another's bad intention.

So yeah, she knew where and when to draw the line.

He only frowned at her. "It's been a long day. Whatever you're up to…don't do it where I have to deal with it."

"Are you crazy?" she blurted, losing her sense of balance with her astonishment. "What are you even talking about?"

Tempting to think he was on drugs. Or off his meds. Or some combination thereof. But those eyes—even in this uneven illumination—were perfectly clear. Perfectly focused. Shadowed not by lighting but by expression and mood, and so pinned to her—

*I'm not breathing.*

No wonder her lungs ached.

Or that her voice sounded not quite so assertive when she said, "Please get out of my way."

She'd been right. That mouth…born for a wry smile. He said, "As soon as you stop blocking the only way out."

*Oh, hell.* She took a sharp and hasty step aside—clearing the path, leaving as much room between them as possible.

He took a moment—she wasn't sure if she'd ever felt so *looked at*—and then he strode away—not so much as a glance back, that wry smile lingering. Whatever stiff effort she thought she'd seen in his movement, nothing of it remained.

Gwen touched the fine platinum rope chain that was always, always at her neck. Her fingers ran to the flat disk hanging beneath her shirt—the familiar shape of it a comfort, the habit of touching it so instilled that she rarely did it consciously. *Her father's gift.*

Now, she found her fingers on it—through her shirt, closed her hand around it. Looking for…

She had no idea. But she thought maybe something had already found *her.*

Mac reached the parking lot on overdrive—made himself stop, feeling the aches of a beating and the burn of the unnatural healing pushed by the blade. Made himself breathe deeply—once, twice.

*Not mine. The feelings aren't mine.*

But they were.

At least, some of them were. The part of him that responded to an abundance of red-glinting hair and copper freckles and wide, pale blue eyes; the part of him that tightened into awareness at fit curves beneath travel-wrinkled clothing, undeterred by her stark reaction to his presence.

Those feelings…they came very much from within.

She'd stood him down without blinking.

To some extent, without breathing—he'd taken her by surprise, no doubt about it. But nerve…

Oh, yeah. She had it.

She also radiated trouble like a beacon. There'd been no denying the way her presence had slapped at him—*warned* him.

And simultaneously beguiled him.

The blade had absorbed her like a sponge. Her shock at the first sight of him, her frisson of stark, startled response—her feelings, filtered through living metal with more subtlety, more layering...

The blade, Mac would have said, had a crush.

If such a thing were possible. But a true crush... that meant giving.

And the blade only knew to *take*.

Mac rubbed his chest just to the left of center...just a little lower than his heart. There, where the tattoo had appeared overnight. The night he'd thought he'd died, only to find that he hadn't quite.

The night he'd changed from casually footloose—catching up with family here, visiting friends there, working a vague path along the way—to grimly driven from one place to another, never quite comfortable where he was or who he was.

Beneath the thin ribbed shirt, the tattoo's complex design ran raised beneath his touch. No ordinary tattoo at that. He ran his fingers over it, not sure what he was looking for. Never sure what he was looking for.

But he thought, this time, maybe something had found *him*.

## Chapter 2

Gwen should have gone right into that hotel and grabbed a room. Instead she found herself too shaken to handle the transaction. She stood at the double-door entry for a moment, and then turned on her heel, heading for the sidewalk.

Not the best part of town for a midnight stroll. But she'd spotted the all-night diner on the way in—a block away, well-lit—and her stomach had growled at the sight. At the moment it was still a little too clenched to countenance the thought of food, but that's what the walk was for. A block of dark privacy to collect her thoughts.

Besides, she was safer than most in this darkness. She'd know if anyone around was considering mayhem, thanks to her strange unwelcome legacy.

Her father's pendant shifted with her long strides; she rotated the chain, wondering that she noticed it at all. It had been so much a part of her for so many years...never aging, never wearing, shedding soap, shampoo and sweat as readily as it did the tarnishing air.

*I am nine years old, and my father gave me a pendant...and then tried to kill me for it.*

But tonight her skin tingled slightly beneath it, and she briefly cupped her hand over it. "Behave," she murmured.

She couldn't remember when she'd started talking to it. When she'd been a girl and her father had nearly killed her before he disappeared, leaving only this behind? Or somewhere along the way? She only knew that it gave her strange comfort.

She smiled, no matter how briefly. For here she was, a dark city block from where she'd started—breathing deeply of the night air and feeling calm again. With food waiting before her. Just as planned.

Her stomach growled again. Right on cue.

The place looked used but clean, and the food smelled wonderful. A young couple in the far booth played a constant game of touch-and-flirt, mutually afflicted with bad tattoos and poor personal hygiene. A ragged man pushed a coffee cup around his little table, giving her no more than a desultory glance. The midnight clientele.

Including her hungry, travel-worn self.

Gwen grabbed a seat at the counter, snagged a plastic-encased menu, and flipped it open to a picture of the best breakfast burrito she'd ever seen—here in the state that claimed to have invented them. As the waitress approached, she pushed the menu away with her finger on the picture. "And decaf."

Nice to be decisive. In this, at least.

The man with the coffee made a juicy throat-clearing noise, threw change on the table and left. As the door closed, several young men slipped in; the flirting couple drew back from one another to greet them.

Gwen sighed, fingers straying to the pendant.

She knew. She always knew. It had taken time to learn the hard lesson of when to react, when to stay silent, when to run away.

It had taken too long, actually. An emergency room visit or two.

But once upon a time her father had tried to kill her. Once upon a time, he'd nearly succeeded. And when she'd healed, tender young muscle and bone knitting back together, she'd discovered that now, she always knew.

They had weapons. They had intent.

She must have tensed. The waitress, a Hispanic woman with wiry grey at her temples and a tired smile at her eyes, flipped over her coffee cup, filled it and said, so casually, "Whatever they're up to, they won't do it in here." And then a half shrug. "Mostly that crew is just figuring out how to grow up."

They looked plenty grown up to Gwen.

"Thanks," she said, picking up the coffee cup… meaning the reassurance. *Extra tip for you.*

But when the door opened again, she fumbled the

cup, nearly dropping it. *High cheekbones, strong jaw, scruffy dark hair, body by lean and mean.* Her eyes widened, deer in the headlights—already off balance from her awareness of the weapons and the intent right here in the small diner behind her. *Not subtle, Gwen.*

Not subtle at all.

And that mouth, made to carry a wry smile, proved once again its proficiency at just that. "Not," he told her from just inside the door, "following you." His gaze flicked briefly to the young men in the background, noticing them—the low but intense conversation between them, the young woman impatient and defiant.

In this light, she could see the blue in his grey eyes, the exact cast of his mouth, the confidence in his movement. Up went his eyebrows—a bit of a natural brood in them—and he asked, "Okay?"

Belatedly, she realized the courtesy he offered: *If you're not comfortable with my presence, I'll leave.*

"Um, fine," she said. "Eat, drink…whatever."

The waitress appeared with her breakfast burrito, plunking down both ketchup and salsa, and slid the plate neatly into place before Gwen. No mean feat, considering that whereas she had ignored the young men from the get-go, now her gaze never left the man who had just entered.

She, too, had her own sense of things.

*Dangerous things.*

The man nodded at her plate as he sat beside her at the counter. "That looks good. And juice, if you have it."

The waitress nodded, scribbled on her order pad and

stuck the sheet on the counter behind her, a wall-cutout
through which Gwen had gotten occasional glimpses
of a cook. At the far table, voices rose in crude dis-
cord, then abruptly cut off. The young men trooped
out, clomping for effect—leaving the couple at their
table. No more touch-and-flirt…now it was an argument, swift and low.

"Don't do it," Gwen murmured.

But she could feel it. Before the young woman's
face closed in frustration and fear, before the young
man pushed away from the table with a scrape of chair.
She could feel it, and she winced and turned her back
more completely.

Only to find Mac watching. Not only watching,
but aware.

She'd reacted before the young man had moved.

*Get over it,* she thought at him. That was something
else she'd outgrown—the need to explain herself. Herself or her travel-wrinkled clothes or her footloose,
late-night arrival here.

Or even what it was about this man that made it
hard to breathe.

She dug into the burrito. Deliberately.

Besides, if anyone should be answering questions…

He was more than scruffy, here in the café lighting.
He was downright messed up—beyond the worse-for-
wear jacket and the obvious stiffness of utterly sore
ribs. A confusing road map of injuries marked his face,
his hands—abrasions across his knuckles, one hand
swollen throughout. Fresh blood but older cuts. Bruising fading to yellow in some spots but starkly purpled

in others. The careful way he took a first bite of his newly delivered food.

Of course he caught her looking.

Without thinking, she gestured, reaching toward the freshest of the blood, a trickle from just inside his hairline, an unspoken *you've got a little—*

His polite disengagement vanished. His hand flashed out to snatch hers, a block and parry and *grab,* trapping her just tightly enough to verge on pain— stopping short of the follow-through that would have twisted tendon and bone.

She gasped, fought the impulse to yank away. Realized in surprise that she hadn't seen it coming. And voiced, nonsensically, the final piece of the gesture, a single strangled word. "…Blood."

His mouth twitched; the muscles of his jaw worked. Gently, deliberately, he released her hand. "It's been an interesting evening," he said, and it seemed to be meant to cover all of the moment's circumstances. The bruises, the blood and the grab.

Slowly, she withdrew her hand.

The young woman from the corner stifled a frustrated noise, oblivious to them all, and stomped out into the night.

The waitress left them alone.

He ate faster than she did…but she found she couldn't finish the meal, and she set aside her fork even as he dropped his napkin on his plate and fished for his wallet. To her surprise, he also dropped a few worn bills at her plate. "An apology," he said simply.

"That's not—" she started, but she looked at his

face, at the tired expression waiting behind his eyes, and she only shook her head—*that's not necessary* combined with acquiescence.

The smile that took the corner of his mouth had nothing to do with wry. "Thanks."

"Listen," she said, not sure what was going to come next.

He didn't wait for it. "Let me walk you back to the hotel."

Not what she'd expected.

"I'd have to go widdershins around the block to avoid you," she told him, which was apparently not what *he'd* expected because the smile grew into a quick grin, there and gone again, and a duck of his head she wouldn't have guessed of him.

The waitress, scooping up the money, kept her own smile mostly hidden.

As if Mac would have let her walk the single block alone, with the unsettled air this city had tonight.

Whoever she was, and whatever tension had sprung instantly to life between them.

The first slap of her presence had faded to a trickle of warning and awareness, the blade warm in his pocket...silent but smug, and more interested in tasting her reactions than heeding the obvious trouble brewing at the back of the café.

As long as it didn't spill over on him. Not again tonight.

She pulled her thin cotton jacket closed and fastened it with crossed arms, ducking out into a night gone past brisk and right into chill. She paused in the parking lot just long enough for him to catch up, just as aware of him as he was of her.

"Business?" he asked. "Or walkabout?"

She faltered, brows arching, a flash of startlement on that heart-shaped face. "Funny," she said, "that you should put it that way. Walkabout."

"It's a familiar state of being," he said, dry in a way he knew she couldn't understand.

"Are *you*?" she asked and tucked back hair breaking free of restraint—a careless knot at the back of her head, the ends tumbling loose. "On walkabout?"

He rolled his shoulders, breaking free from the stiffness and pain; he could just about take a deep breath again. The blade burned its healing through him—making him pay, rewarding him with an impossibly swift recovery.

Then again, everything about the blade was impossible. From the way it chose its own shape to the way it invaded his mind to the way it healed him of everything from the worst of injuries to the common cold.

The way it whispered to him, pulling him into other peoples' insanities.

*Walkabout.* He said, "Not this time. I've got work waiting." In a week or two. Best he could do, working for a contractor friend of a friend from Colorado who had an assistant going on family leave.

"Temporarily at loose ends," she deduced, moving out for the sidewalk—arms still crossed, shoulder bag tucked under her arm, a frisson of her tension coming through the blade to reach him. Not truly comfortable.

Nor should she be.

"It's a decent hotel," he told her, striking out beside her—out of the parking lot illumination and into a brief pool of shadow before the next streetlight. "But it's on the edge when it comes to the neighborhood."

She slanted him a look. "Do you do that often?"

*Um.*

"Do—" he asked—but didn't finish the question, wincing slightly instead. Normally—when not distracted by the burn of broken ribs on the mend, the twist of muscles in recovery—he'd know better than to respond to unspoken concerns.

"I was just thinking that I'd gone one hotel too far north from the airport."

"Body language," he told her. "Has a lot to say."

This time her look wasn't slanting at all. It came straight on—a quick sweep of his form that held more than obvious appreciation. "You mean like, *'Wow, did I get beat up today or what?'*"

He stifled a snort. "That, too."

"Aren't you even going to say I shoulda seen the other guy?"

"Guys," he told her, hesitating at the curb to make sure the approaching car wasn't going to turn in front of them. "Check the news. We'll see if they both made it."

She modeled mock awe for him. "That's *much* better than my line." And then her brief levity faded. "Except…you aren't kidding, are you?" And she moved a quiet step away.

He couldn't help his irritation. "Their choice."

But she'd stopped him, there in the brightest light of the next streetlight, and turned him directly into it—grasping his arm with a familiarity that seemed to surprise her as much as it did him. She stepped back to narrow her eyes, the light flashing off pale blue as she raked her gaze over him. "It *is* blood. And it's not yours, is it? But you don't have a weapon—"

She said it with such certainty that it took him aback, even as she cut herself short. She stepped back, releasing his arm. "I'm sorry. I'm tired. And I still need to check in."

He thought about telling her how they'd had to search to find him a room, decided against it. Either they'd have something for her or they wouldn't.

He thought about asking her name. Her number.

The knife spiked at him, a brief flare of warmth in his pocket. More of a weapon than she could ever imagine, both for and against him. *—alert!—*

*No,* he told it. Too tired, too hurting, too *done* for the day.

*—alert!—*

"Let's get you back to the hotel, then," he told her. *And damned fast.*

*—alert! fear!—*

But she was the one who stiffened, looking off across the street to the closed zapateria and beyond. "We'd better—"

The knife struck out at him—hungry, insistent. Mac faltered; he shook it off. He shook off her hand, too, as she tugged at him, alarmed and surprisingly assertive, telling him, "We have to go!"

In the darkness, a woman shrieked.

—*yes yes yes!*—

"You're half a block from the hotel," he told her. "Go."

She bristled at the command in his voice—but he didn't hang around for it. Across the empty traffic lanes, the knife prodding him on—lending strength, where he didn't quite have any left of his own. Into the darkness beside the zapateria, his blade-borne sight leaving a stark outline of the barred windows and door, the alley clearly revealed before him.

The toughs from the diner. Of course. And the reluctant young man who'd been there first—and his girl, come to interfere with whatever trouble he'd gotten into and only turning the pack of them back on the couple. Harassing, a push, a shove, a hand twisting in the girl's hair.

—*stop them!*—

And the blade would get what it always wanted—the experience of it, the emotion…the spilled blood, in a most literal way.

"They're punks," he told it—told himself. "No edges."

The knife came out of his pocket and flashed in his grip, a sulky change to a sweeping wooden handle, a ball carved at the end, the glint of a blunt metal spike. Iroquois war club. Deadly if it had to be…persuasive in all ways.

And for the second time that night, he put himself into the middle of it. Dispensing with the small talk, forgetting the rational…just blowing through them so the kid in trouble could grab his girl and run.

Until the blade suddenly spasmed and wailed and sung of hate—the same putrid swamp of it that had nearly claimed them at the edge of the desert. The gang descended upon him. Mac swung out wildly, blindly—connecting with flesh, driving them back, sending gun and blade and chain clattering away.

Until the black pit of hatred rose up for the second time that night and took down man and blade both.

On his knees, but not for long. Mac could run, too.

But he ran just as blindly, slamming into one wall, then two, then the corner of a building, grabbing for purchase as he swung around to find himself—

Wherever the hell he was.

*Whatever the hell had just happened.*

The hatred lifted, leaving him with leaden limbs and heaving lungs that couldn't catch enough air. His ribs shot through with pain, molten bones both liquid and brittle.

The knife returned in a smear of movement, tucking itself away in the palm of his hand, a shaken retreat. Still hungry—still without the victory it craved.

They weren't coming after him. He'd dealt too many of his own blows; he'd left them too confused—at least for the moment.

They'd carry a grudge, all right.

He straightened, one steadying hand against the building—but swore and instantly bent over again. This time, he moved more slowly—pushing away from

the whitewashed cinder block, moving carefully…
keeping the knife to hand.

Twice. Twice in one night. The swamping hatred,
the confrontations so quickly escalating out of control.

He knew, now, why he'd been drawn to Albuquerque. He just didn't have the faintest idea what to do
about it.

*Run. I should be running.*

Right back to the hotel. Everything in her screamed
it.

But Gwen found herself still there when he emerged
from the darkness on the other side of the street, six
lanes of empty pavement between them.

She saw right away the difference in him. Not so
much in what he did as what he *didn't* project—the
confidence, the strength…a certain grim intensity. All
missing. And although she was so certain, now, that he
was armed—and that he'd had a willingness to act that
felt natural in his world and terrifying in hers—she
nonetheless caught no sense of it. Not now, not before.

Just the same instantly compelling response that
had riveted her outside the hotel.

*Yeah, I should've run.*

*I should have gone to Vegas.*

And then he faltered in midcrossing, and she forgot
all that and sprinted from the curb to meet him, slipping beneath one shoulder to take the burden of unfamiliar bone and muscle.

The heat of him shocked her. "You're burning up!"

In response, his eyes rolled back; his knees buckled.

"Oh, no no no," she said, knowing she couldn't keep them both upright. "Middle of the *street,* mister! Move on!"

He muttered a breathless curse, put one foot in front of the other and, as far as she could tell, made it to the curb on determination alone.

She tried to make his landing a soft one.

He rubbed his hands over his face—fresh blood on those hands, dark under the streetlight. "It shouldn't have…" he said. "It wasn't…" He blinked, a deliberate thing, and looked at his hands. "This isn't…"

"Yeah, yeah, I get the idea." Gwen huffed out an impatient breath. Stupid, stupid, to have gotten in the middle of this.

Then again, what else was she here for? To get in the middle of something, it seemed. And she wouldn't know what until she'd done it.

"You're screwed," she told him. "You have a temperature up in the something-fierce range, plus whatever else happened out there. You want to go to a clinic?"

"God, no," he said, as emphatic as anything he'd said yet—maybe even said with a little bit of outright panic.

She laughed. "How to tame the beast," she said and sat down on the curb beside him, his warmth radiating against her. Maybe if he had a moment, he could walk to the hotel. Or intelligibly tell her what he *did* need. And then she could go check in, and—

"What is it about you?" he asked, surprising her. She jerked her gaze around, finding the dark grey of his eyes. Not guarded, as they'd been in the diner. Not wary, as they'd been outside the hotel. Looking right at her as if he *could* look through her. He took her hand, twined his fingers through hers, and examined the arrangement as if it could tell him something. "Doesn't make any sense. You."

She shivered. Inexplicable impulses and gut feelings, every decision she'd made since she'd seen him outside that hotel...since she'd walked away from her Vegas vacation at that. No, it didn't make any sense at all.

And she'd learned better. She had a lifetime of understanding that true intention rarely showed on the surface. She knew how to protect herself.

Or she *should*.

She gathered her wits and gently disentangled her hand. "I make perfect sense," she said. "And I'm not the one who almost fainted in the middle of the road. But I *am* the one who doesn't have a room yet. So let's go back to the hotel. If you need help, we'll get it there. If you don't, you don't."

He sucked in a sharp breath; a certain startled awareness crossed his features, an expression made sharper in the shadows. "I'm sorry," he said. "You're right. Let's get you back to the hotel."

Amusement rippled through her as she stood. Suddenly he was all *Mister I'm back in charge,* was he? Well, that was fine, too. "What was that all about, anyway?" she asked, holding out a hand to help pull him up from the curb.

Whether from pride or wariness, she wasn't sure,

but he hesitated before taking it. "Hazing gone wrong."
Back on his feet, he loomed more than she'd expected.
Gwen Badura was no tiny figure of a woman, and he
hadn't struck her as a particularly large man…but there
it was. Looming.

She resisted the impulse to brush the street dirt from
his particularly fine posterior.

He frowned, striking out beside her; the hotel
loomed darkly a block away. "It wasn't that serious—
didn't have to be. I don't know what—" He stopped
short, dropping entirely back into the man he'd been
before he'd run off into the darkness—the same man
who had faced her at the hotel entrance. The wary one.
The utterly prepared one.

She didn't at first see why—not until a dark figure
emerged from the shadows of the hotel lot landscaping. Then she stopped short on a gasp—one that turned
into a squeak as her erstwhile escort snagged her arm
and jerked her back, putting himself in front of her.

*You must be kidding.*

The newcomer stood in clear challenge mode, legs
braced, chin tipped at an arrogant angle.

He held a sword.

*You. Must. Be. Kidding.* Gwen's fingers clamped
down on the back of her guy's jacket, knowing it was
hardly helpful. *Hide. Yes, I will gladly hide. Right here
behind you.*

The sword glimmered in the light—no, not in the
light. More as if it had light of its own, rolling liquid
along the lines of steel. "My name is Devin James,"

he said. "This is my turf. My *city*. Whatever you're doing, it had better stop."

And Gwen's guy muttered eloquently, "What... the...*fuck?*"

"That's telling him," she said, not a little desperately.

"It's my city," James repeated. "I can feel what you've done here tonight. No one died, which means you get another chance. But I'm watching."

And, very much just like that, he left.

Gwen realized how close she'd gotten to the back of that battered jacket. She pushed herself away, wiped her hands off on her flimsy stretch jacket, and tucked her purse back into place. She pointed at the hotel. "I think you can make it, don't you?"

"No problem," he said, as dryly as a man could.

She stalked away, only belatedly realizing that she still didn't sense the weapon on him—that she hadn't even felt warning of James's big honkin' real-life *sword* for God's sake. Only the same unbalanced push-and-pull that had been tugging at her since the moment she'd set eyes on the man behind her.

She almost didn't hear him say, "Michael MacKenzie. Mac. Just so you know."

She almost didn't say back, "Gwen Badura. Gwen. Just so you know." But she did, and she turned her head ever so slightly to say it over her shoulder, and she saw enough of him to catch the sudden alarm on his face—

A wall hit her. A wall with a linebacker's touch and an expert grab at her bag and then she was slammed to the pavement, her fingers losing their grasp on the bag strap and her protest lost along with all the air in her lungs.

And Michael MacKenzie leaped in response, barreling past her to—

To double over with a cry of pain and frustration both, spilling down to the asphalt and already trying to claw his way back up. But it was Gwen who made it to her feet first—or at least, to her hands and knees. She crawled out of the cross street and over to Mac's side just in time to see a startling vulnerability of expression.

Not in time to figure out what it meant.

And there, beside him, was the weapon she'd been so sure of—the one she'd suspected but couldn't feel—and now the one she couldn't imagine he'd ever had at all, at least not concealed. It was too big for that, a huge clip-blade Bowie with nowhere to hide. And it gleamed in the night, reflecting an unnatural clear blue-steel light.

Michael MacKenzie's harsh, pained breathing faded into the background, becoming a thing that no longer tugged at her concern or her empathy.

The knife gleamed brighter.

It shone a beguiling thing of stunning beauty, full of danger and poison and power.

She watched as a hand reached for it—hovering, trembling…*wanting*—and realized it was her own.

Devin James slipped into the pickup and slammed the door. Not out of any particular pique, but simply because it was the only way the door would close at all.

"You know," Natalie said, sitting against the passenger door with her knees drawn up, "now that you've, like, inherited Sawyer Compton's entire estate, I bet you could afford a new truck."

He scowled. "I like *this* one. It's mine." And other than the comfortable old furniture he'd dragged to Atrisco del Sur from his little stucco home—former home—not far from here, it was the only thing left that was, indeed, fully his.

Even if the damned door *was* sticky.

He grumbled.

"Didn't go well?" Natalie asked. She had the detachment in her voice that meant she'd been doing exercises—the control grounding exercises they both did, were *learning* to do, to stave off the inevitable descent into depraved insanity that came with a demon blade.

He'd seen it on the face of the man who had jumped his brother in the night and died for it when Leo had wrenched away the blade; he'd seen it in Leo's life and then on Leo's face, as Leo had jumped Devin in the night...and Devin had ended up with the blade.

He didn't know if the man he'd just encountered now walked the wild road or not. He only knew...

He shook his head. "I have no idea."

"What does Anheriel say?"

"As little as possible," Devin told her, darkly enough. But he passed a hand over where the blade resided in his pocket, innocuous and cool. Humbled by the experience with Compton's blade, tamed by his new understanding of it, kept at bay by the new exercises...

Right. Who was he kidding? The thing was a bastard, a demon soul entangled with metal that wanted nothing more than redemption but actively sought only what its nature allowed—to corrupt those it bonded with.

He let go of a pent-up breath and took her hand, so casually proprietary, and pretended not to notice the little smile at the corner of her mouth—nothing that darkness could hide from him, not with the little perk of the night vision that came with the blade. "I don't know," he admitted. "Anheriel is pretending to be above it all at the moment. If I didn't know better, I'd say it was afraid. Baitlia?"

"Baitlia's not a primary blade," she reminded him. "I rarely get the same big picture sense of things that you do. It's more like a two-year-old. *I want this* and *I want that.*"

Devin snorted. "Right, if two-year-olds drink blood and crave killing."

"Still," she said. "What's *your* sense of it?"

He shook his head again. "Hard to pin down. I wouldn't say the guy was looking for trouble. I wouldn't say he was running away from it, either. He looked beat to hell. And the girl with him…shell-shocked. She has no idea." He gave Natalie a quick glance. "Did you feel…?"

"Something," she admitted. "Was that him?"

He had to shrug; it made him irritable. "It was *some*thing. Whether it happened to him or because of him or by him…I have no idea."

"Well, you've rattled his cage," Natalie said, rubbing a thumb over Devin's knuckles. "You've let him know you're here and what you want. It's his move now. Then we'll know."

Mac slapped his hand over the blade; it came to him, flaring bright enough to make Gwen wince away—and by the time she looked back, he'd palmed it back into a pocketknife.

Gwen blinked at the spot where the knife had been, no doubt still half-blind from the preternatural flash of its change. "Where—" she asked, and then, as if absorbing the impact of the past few moments all in one fell swoop, dismay crossed features that until now had been determined. "My purse! That rat bastard! He came out of nowhere!"

That he had. Out of nowhere on a dark night that so far held nothing but people striking out beyond all reason.

Mainly, people striking out at *him*.

No, not quite right. For once, they'd simply failed to fall back in the face of the threat he presented.

The tarry wave of hatred splashing through the night—now, that felt more personal.

"My *purse!*" Gwen said, her voice rising, and then she cursed a heartfelt word he doubted she ever said all that often at all. "My keys, my wallet! I'm not even checked in yet—"

Mac came to the conclusion that this would take a while. Wearier than he would have imagined only an hour earlier, he crawled to the curb and sat there, hands over his face. Assessing.

He was vulnerable now. Burning up with the blade's attempt to absorb the energies that had struck at them both, battered by the scuffles he should have skimmed through with ease. "I can't be here," he said out loud, no plan or thought behind it. Just knowing what he needed. Sleep. A safe place. Healing, before weakness overtook him altogether.

"No?" she said, fuming and with no particular insight to his unfathomable personal world. "Then go! I can deal with this. I just need to call the credit card people and I need to get the car towed to get new locks on it and—and—"

Her expression shifted to horror as she realized she was crying. She spun away from him, pressing her hands over her eyes. "No, no, *no!*"

"My room," he said. "King bed. Huge. You stay on your side. I'll stay on mine."

It had made sense in his head. From the look on her face as she spun back around, he wasn't sure it had made sense out loud.

"You must be kidding," she said. "Do I know you? Do I know anything about you?" She threw her hands up in the air. "Oh, right, I *do*. I know you carry an effing big knife that suddenly isn't anywhere to be seen! I know you dive into random street fights! I know you were bloody when I met you and you're bloodier now!" She gave the hotel a determined look, her mouth pressed tight in thought. "I bet they'd let me use the phone. I bet the cops would take me to a YMCA. Or something."

"Lice," he said, sighing. "Don't stay, then. But if you would help—"

"Right," she said skeptically. "*Now* you need help? Or now you just want to lure me up— Hey...*hey.* Are you fainting?"

The second time she'd said that, dammit. "Not *fainting*," he told her, watching the world go wavery and grey. *"Passing out."*

"Gah!" she said, making it there in time to keep his head from clunking on pavement—a distant, pleasant and living pillow. With excellent form. "Stop that! Okay! What's your room number?"

As impatient as her voice came to his ears, her hands stayed gentle at his shoulders, touching his face. "God, you really *are* hot. C'mon, then, big guy. Hotel, you, me. Let's go be a cliché."

# *Chapter 3*

*Think, Gwen Badura,* she told herself. *Think about what you're doing.*

Because here she was in front of the hotel room where the man named Michael MacKenzie, AKA Mac, slumped wearily against the wall. She routed through his pockets for the room key.

He didn't look like trouble.

He barely looked conscious.

It didn't mean he'd stay that way.

*First a police report...then how many hours till I sleep? At a shelter. With lice.*

Ugh.

"You're doing the right thing," she told herself. Out loud. Firmly. And then just shrugged when he gave her a bleary and questioning look, finally producing the card key. She took it from him, pushed it into the lock, and flicked the handle open.

Whew. The decorating theme du jour must have been *garish*.

But the bed was indeed huge. And there was a little fridge and an even smaller microwave, and the bathroom with its separate sink area didn't greet her with any smells, drips, or puddles of untoward water.

Mac headed straight for the fridge. She closed the door behind them, far too aware of the absence of things—not throwing her purse on the bed, her overnighter beside the closet. At least she had the cheapo toothbrush the hotel had given her on the way in.

*You're doing the right thing.*

And not just for her. She watched as he pulled a small plastic bottle from the fridge, broke the cap seal, and gulped it down. Some sort of protein drink, as best as she could read upside down.

Well, at least it wasn't blood. The way things had gone this evening, wouldn't it be just her luck to have hooked up with a vampire? And would it truly have been any less believable? "You don't drink blood, do you?"

He startled, spilling the last of the drink down his chin, and looked at her. For an instant she thought she might have seen guilt as he wiped the back of his hand over his chin, but then he said, his voice gone hoarse with fatigue, "Do you just say whatever comes into your head, then?"

"Gets it out of the way," Gwen said promptly. "Besides, the best defense is a good offense."

Right. And she'd learned it early. If she *was* going to poke her nose into the gut feelings that so often drove her, it was easier to prod the situation right out into the open. That way she could see just what she had to deal with. "You didn't say no, by the way. About drinking blood."

He tossed the bottle into the minuscule wastebasket beside the fridge, practically filling it with that single item. "*I* don't, no."

While she was pondering that unexpected response, he peeled his jacket off and dropped it over the straight-backed chair beside the ubiquitous token desk. "Bed," he said, gesturing at it. And then a nod at the closet. "Extra blanket, extra pillow. I'll hang out on top of the sheets, if you'd like."

Yeah, she'd like. She grabbed the items, then belatedly thought to say, "Hey, I should do that. I mean, I'll sleep on top."

She stopped herself, her back to him, feeling the warmth suffusing her face. "If you're a gentleman," she said, "you'll pretend I didn't say that."

The noise he made might have been amusement. "Relax," he said, albeit through a rustling noise. "Beautiful as you are, I have my own plans for the night."

She whirled on him, bedding in hand, mouth open on words already lost.

"Sometimes I say what I think, too," he told her. He regarded the bloodied shirt in his hand and tossed it toward the wastebasket.

"Um," she said, over the top of the pillow. And stood there as he took his newly stripped torso over to the

sink, not quite sure if she was stunned by the beauty
of said torso, muscle strapped over muscle and tightly
defining the form of him, or by the damage done to it.

*Okay, maybe you can have your way with me after
all.*

But thankfully, she didn't say it out loud this time.

And thankfully, it wasn't in her nature to mean it
if she did. No one-night stands on irresponsible road
trips with men picked up in a diner for her. No, sirree.

She did, however, drop her armload onto the bed,
and by then it was clear enough he intended to do
nothing more than rinse his mouth, splash water onto
his face and let the rest of him quietly finish bleeding on its own.

"Oh, no," she said. "You need to clean that…
*those*…" She waved in the general direction of the
bruises and abrasions and— "Is that… Did you get
*stabbed?*"

"Huh." He twisted to look at his ribs beneath his
arm. "Maybe. A little."

She found herself speechless. Pointing at the cut
and its oozing blood and the stains all over his skin,
gesturing at the sink and the water, unable to fathom
his reaction to the entire situation. Finally she grabbed
the desk chair and dragged it into the bathroom, pointing at *the wound*.

"You," she said. "You're delirious. That's what. Sit
there. I'm going to see what's what. If I had my purse
I'd have Band-Aids, but I don't suppose—"

"It'll be okay," he said, gently—surprisingly gentle
at that, in spite of his bleariness. Reassuring, as if she

had been the one who'd been hurt—beyond the sting of skinned palms that were truly hers to own. "Nothing here is that bad. I just need some sleep. *You* need some sleep. Things will look different tomorrow."

"My purse," she muttered, "will still be stolen." But she reached for the hotel washcloth—which would surely never be the same after this—and ran the hot water, ripping the teeny bar of soap free from its wrapping.

He hesitated another moment, just looking at her— enough so she stopped what she was doing to look back, finding herself rooted there. Just long enough to realize what the expression on his face meant—that he *did* find her beautiful, that he *did* want her, and that his hand, rising, was going to curl around the back of her head and twine through her hair and—

She blinked. He closed his eyes, clenched his fist; let it drop back to his side.

She remembered to breathe.

He didn't, thank God, mutter some lame apology that would draw even more attention to the moment. He grabbed the chair and flipped it around, sitting backward on it to rest his arms along the top.

Gwen stuck a hand under the water, found it blistering, and jerked away. How long had that moment lasted, anyway? She added cold, filled the sink, and soaked the washcloth.

And then she knew better than to pretend that it didn't affect her to touch him—not his beauty, not his pain. She started with the spots that didn't look too bad and moved carefully to the abrasions, washing off dried blood to reveal the truth of what lay beneath, discovering the strange little twist of a tattoo over his heart and keeping the washcloth as warm and soothing as possible. "Sorry," she murmured when he twitched, and "This is a bad one," and "Face, please."

He lifted it for her, the full light on the cuts and bruises, displaying remarkably little swelling aside from one puffy eye and the corner of his mouth.

Not that he made it easy. Oh, no. He watched her.

Her heart beat just a little faster, and she tipped a finger under his chin to examine her work. *Right.* Stormy grey-blue eyes, no longer hiding in shadow and no longer hiding weariness of the deepest kind— or even the expression that still smoldered from when he'd almost—*almost*—touched her. She eyed the cut of his mouth, unexpectedly sweet in repose and just begging for another gentle brush of the washcloth… or her thumb.

*What the hell is wrong with me?* She closed her eyes and turned away, her hand settling on her necklace and clenching it, if ever so briefly, tight in her fist. "You're right," she said. "Except for that, you know, *maybe a little* stab wound, nothing there is too bad. It's just that there's so much of it."

"It'll be okay," he said, but his voice had faded, and when she turned back she found the connection between them had faded, too, and his eyes were half-closed. He shook himself, reached for a hand towel, and pushed away from the chair. "I've got to sleep. Make yourself at home. You won't bother me."

He only staggered a little on the way to the bed.

There he put down the towel to protect the bedspread from his short but gaping cut and its trickling blood, flopped on top of it, flung a forearm over his eyes and, to all appearances, fell instantly asleep.

Gwen stood beside the bed, caught in the surrealism of it all.

A stranger's hotel room.

A beautiful stranger she could hardly stop herself from touching even as he stretched out asleep, completely unaware of her.

Apparently trusting her.

Or not having any choice in the matter, from the looks of him.

She held her hands out under the light of the sink area...his blood stained them; her own blood stained them. Not the smartest thing she could have done.

She cleaned up, replacing the chair, wringing out the stained washcloth and neatly hanging it, wiping down the sink counter. She pondered her hands; she pondered the shower, sending a glance at her erstwhile host.

He slept on. He hadn't moved so much as a muscle twitch. She approached him, her hand hovering over his shoulder. Strong, well-formed bones beneath working muscle and gleaming skin.

Heat radiated back at her.

She shook her head—and, glancing at the blanket she'd dumped, decided against spreading it over him just yet.

Instead she headed for the shower. Not without trepidation—she'd wash her underwear and hang it to dry, but it would leave her commando in her slacks.

And the hotel shampoo? No way was it going to do well by her hair. No comb, no leave-in conditioner…

She settled on a good sponge bath and felt much the better for it, the commando situation notwithstanding.

When she came out of the bathroom, he hadn't moved.

Slowly, she sank down by the side of the bed, resting her chin on the mattress, her arms folded in front of her. From here, she could watch him breathe.

She could make sure he was in fact doing it.

Absurd, the comfort that gave her.

Her hand crept to the pendant at her neck. He'd noticed it, she was sure. Inevitably, he'd ask about it. Everyone did. So obviously old, so obviously heavy with metal and meaning.

She knew that story by heart.

*I am nine years old, and something is wrong with my father. My daddy. My mommy is dead and has been for years. Daddy changed on the night she died. He always carries a knife; he won't let me see it. He acts like he knows how to use it, but my daddy is a briefcase man with a briefcase job.*

*He was. Now he is something else. Someone else.*

*He presses a pendant into my hand, cold and heavy, incised with symbols so worn I can't read them.*

*Not that I could anyway. I don't know this language. I don't think anyone does.*

*The pendant means nothing to me. I only want my daddy to be who he was: with his shaven cheeks, smelling of aftershave and giving warm hugs when he comes home from the office.*

*This man is scratchy-faced and smells of stale drink and something sharp and unfamiliar; this man has hard new muscles and keeps strange hours.*

*This man sometimes burns like the hottest fever, and sleeps like the dead.*

Gwen's hand tightened around the pendant. She straightened, and this time, when she reached out to Mac's shoulder, she let her fingers rest on the heat of that smooth, gleaming skin.

He slept like the dead.

Mac slept deep and hard and hot.

But the blade didn't sleep at all.

The blade *wanted*...and the blade feared.

It tugged at him, taking him to its own unfulfilled hunger, the need to taste, the need to drink. Blood and emotions both—and both denied to it this day, lost to the hatred and to the resounding, staggering weakness of its human partner.

So many blows absorbed. So much healing to do.

It healed with a vicious touch.

And beneath its needs ran a sweeter song, moments of connection, moments of near-connection—a soft touch not quite complete, an undercurrent of certainty.

Mac woke gasping in the darkness.

Except it was no longer darkness to him; there was no way to shut out the night, not any longer. And so he saw her, sitting beside the bed, glorious hair spilling around her shoulders, neat teeth biting her lower lip... concern in her eyes. "Hey," she said, her voice much more matter of fact than those eyes, if softer than usual.

He meant to respond, but a great wrenching shudder took him, ice twisting through his spine, heat washing over his skin. His teeth chattered; words stuck in his throat as a gravelly moan.

"Hey," she said again, reaching over to the bedside table and the ice bucket to pull out the soiled wash-cloth, wring it out, and draw it over his bare shoulder, his chest…along his collarbone and up his neck. Goose bumps sprang out over his skin as it tightened in response; fast on the heels of that, another twisting shudder pressed his head back into the pillow and sent his hands reaching for…reaching for…

Something.

One hand found hers, clamped down tight.

"I know," she said, and, one-handed, she refreshed the washcloth. "I'm sorry. But you've got to cool down. You were…" She hesitated. "Thrashing."

He could believe it. He could feel it. The grip of the blade, deeper than it had ever gone. Filling him with whispers of its want and need, feeding him tidbits that soaked into his consciousness without understanding. *The wild road. Take it. Use it. Crave it.*

"This will help," she said, less than certainly. "Not that I…I mean, there's no infection anywhere. You look…you look great."

Yes. Healing. Hot fiery brands of healing, marking the worst spots. The others, already fading beyond notice.

The next spasm took him, pushed out a groan from between clenched teeth and left him shivering and fractured; she gasped from the grip of his hand around hers. The washcloth felt like ice on his neck, along his side. *Was* ice. He tried to twist away but didn't have the coordination for it.

"I *know*," she said, and her voice held a note of pleading. "I'm sorry. But unless I call an ambulance—" His grunt of alarm, slicing through increasingly shattered thoughts, stopped her short. "I didn't think so. Then this is what we've got. My father—" She hesitated, then seemed to decide it wouldn't matter now. "It helped my father. Sometimes."

And left so many words unspoken, even as fire and ice twined together to rake along his bones.

She knew something. She *knew*. Here, the woman who'd found him in the midst of their random journeys, who'd piqued the interest of the blade, who'd roused feelings in him long overwhelmed by that same blade.

*Coincidence.*

He didn't trust coincidence.

And he—he who had a demon blade that amplified and fed him emotions, that had its own wants and desires—he looked at this woman whose very presence spoke to him, and he knew better than to believe in what wasn't real.

Even as the blade's cruel healing snatched him up and crashed him back down into darkness.

Gwen flicked the light on and winced at the sight of herself in the mirror. All the usual—mouth a little too wide, upper lip a little unbalanced in its fullness, cheekbones a little broad in that heart-shaped face, all the undertones of red hair and faint copper freckles. Hair desperately out of control and her hair sticks locked in the car. Chinos and stretchy lightweight shirt travel-wrinkled and slept in.

She gave the bruised swelling at the corner of her eye a tentative prod and winced.

Right. *Thrashing.*

It had been an interesting awakening. An interesting night. All in all, bringing back memories she'd submerged so far as to nearly have forgotten.

*I am eight years old, and my father comes home sick. There is blood. He won't let me see, but then he falls into a strange, hot sleep and I look anyway.*

*I wish I hadn't.*

*I am eight years old and I don't know what to do for him, but I remember my mother soothing my forehead with a cool cloth, and I try that.*

*It seems to help.*

It had helped this man, in the end. As difficult and miserable as it had been.

For both of them, thank you very much. Especially the not knowing, from moment to moment, if she was doing the right thing at all, or if she should call for help. Only those memories, as nonsensical as they were, had kept her from doing just that.

*I am eight years old, and my father forbids me to call for help. He grabs my wrist and he spits the words at me, and then he falls back on the couch, barely conscious.*

*My wrist hurts for a week.*

Not that she was afraid of Michael MacKenzie— not when she could have simply walked out, so unlike her young self. But that emphasis had made its mark nonetheless.

She finished poking at her face and gave it up. She had no makeup to cover the bruising, and it wasn't worth fretting about otherwise. She washed her face, wiped down her arms and legs and torso, and grabbed her now-dry underwear.

In the bed, her accidental patient slept. Deeply and undisturbed, a natural sleep and with a nearly normal body temperature as close as she could tell. Oh, now and then he got restless, and once he even shifted in that particular way that let her know he was aroused.

Man in the morning. Something reassuring about that little piece of *normal*.

She dropped her summer-weight jacket over the chair so he'd know she was coming back and lifted the room key from the bedside table, slipping out to grab more than her share of the continental breakfast offerings in the lobby, far too aware that the single twenty tucked in her back pocket constituted the entirety of her current funds.

But when she tuned in and overheard the universal topic of conversation among the other hotel guests, she lost her appetite.

*Phase of the moon...loonies were out last night... break-ins...muggings...something in the air...*

And the ultrahassled desk clerk, reassuring people that this was all highly unusual, that they prided themselves on running a safe establishment, that they'd do what they could to assist.

Her first thought came with odd relief. It hadn't been just her; it hadn't been just Michael MacKenzie.

The second came with sick certainty—that the mugging hadn't been the last of it for her, and she just hadn't known it.

She dropped her half-full coffee cup into the trash and the croissant along with it, and she didn't pretend she wasn't rushing when she dashed out the door and down the row of parking spaces, looking for her dark little VW Bug.

The door stood slightly ajar.

She stopped, not quite within reach. Not *wanting* to be within reach. Really, really not wanting to look. Because truly, who would want a battered old soft-sided suitcase with zippers that had cable ties instead of pulls and a fair amount of duct tape holding it together? Who would want her travel-worn shirts and bras and undies and *aurgh,* her sanitary supplies?

"Hair sticks," she moaned out loud. "Conditioner."

Another few hours without either, and she'd have to make do with a paper bag.

But there was no point in guessing, so she looked.

Gone.

The suitcase, the little netbook case, the phone charger. The glove box contents were strewn over the passenger seat and foot well, and—was that a *condom* draped over the steering wheel? Limp and used? In her *Volkswagen?* Good God, had someone been on a dare?

With a quiet, firm nudge she pushed the door closed. No point in locking it. The open door had run down the battery; the interior lights were out.

Besides, she didn't exactly have the keys anymore, did she?

She turned and left the car, ravaged as it was. She kept her steps firm and regular and her chin firm, too, if perhaps held a little too high. Convincing even herself. Through the lobby, past the elevator and to the stairs and up to the third-floor room she'd shared with a stranger.

A sick, raving stranger who had accidentally clocked her one during the night.

But there at the third-floor landing, she couldn't quite continue. She lowered herself to the top step, propped her elbows on her knees, and hid her face in her hands. She tried to think logically—what she'd do now, how she'd replace her cash and her credit cards and her keys and her toothbrush; how she'd get the Bug to a garage. And there was identity theft to consider, the credit running up on her thankfully minimalistic cards—

And what had she been doing here anyway? If she'd wanted to lose everything, couldn't she have gone to Vegas and had *fun* doing it? How the hell had she ended up in the stairwell outside the room of a guy she didn't even know but had nursed through the night, maybe making all the wrong decisions after all?

The hell with logical.

Gwen dropped her forehead to her knees and started to cry. Good, hard, earnest sobs. The pain of disturbed memories, the violation of not one but two robberies, the loss of her things, the suddenly surrealistic sensation that she didn't even know who she was any longer, never mind *where* she was.

The door slammed open behind her; she startled wildly, flattening up against the wall and smacking her head on the metal handrail. Michael MacKenzie stood in the doorway, looking both disoriented and fierce—until he saw her, at which point his expression flickered to the kind of man panic that meant, *Oh, God, she's crying. What do I do?*

She flapped her hand in a useless gesture, hunting for explanation—and instead burst into a sad wail: *"Hair sticks!"*

She wouldn't have blamed him if he'd turned and run in the opposite direction. But instead—barefoot, shirtless, tattooed, and sporting only half the injuries he'd displayed the evening before, he sat down beside her, tucked her in under his arm and pulled her close. And then he kissed the top of her head, and that was the end of that; she burst into tears all over again.

"You—you—*you*," she said, never getting further than that word.

"Yeah," he said. "I know."

So she cried a little more, and then she sniffled mightily, and she muttered, "I'd go get a tissue, but they've probably been *stolen*."

Wisely, he said nothing; just stroked her hair—her horrible hair—and squeezed her shoulder.

But she must have been thinking again, because she narrowed eyes that felt distinctly puffy, pulling back to aim that stare at him. "How did you find me? I was *quiet*."

Surprise crossed his face. "I—" He shook his head. "I must have heard you."

But she was sure she'd seen a flinch. Some truth he didn't want to face any more than she wanted hers. "No," she said. "You didn't." And eased away from him.

Gotta give it to him. He wasn't slow to turn the tables. "What about your father?"

She blinked. "I— What?"

"Last night. You said—"

Offense. Best defense. *Now.* "You mean, when you were thrashing?" She pointed at her face. "Thrashing."

He did his own double take, absorbing the implication of her new bruise. When he spoke, his voice sounded forced. "So it would seem. You said—"

No. That had been a mistake. A long day, a dark night, and words that had slipped out. "I don't want to talk about my father."

"Funny," he said. "Because I really do."

"Really? *I* want to talk about how everything was going *just fine* until I met you, and now suddenly I'm out my purse, everything that was in my car, and apparently every bit of good sense I ever possessed!"

He drew breath as though he'd come right back at her, but at the last moment he didn't—instead, frowning…trying to work out the meaning behind her words.

It maybe wasn't fair to use shorthand against a man who'd been so very sick so very recently and who, for all his absurd recovery, still looked very much battered.

In a heroic sort of—

*Oh, my God. Stop that.*

Coming to conclusions—and the right conclusions at that—he said, "Hair sticks?"

She nodded. "From my car. Which was broken into. Along with a whole lot of other people's, it seems, not to mention various muggings and a lot of disgruntlement overheard in the lobby over the free breakfast. You should get down there, by the way. It won't last forever."

He stood, on his feet faster than she'd ever expected of him—pacing away and back again on the limited landing area, moments during which she paid too much attention to the way his jeans settled over his hips.

*Note to self: ogling does not count as "stopping that."*

Shock. It was the emotional shock. Surely. Her hand closed over the pendant, as if she would possibly, after all these years, receive some sort of divine guidance from it. Some voice from her father's past, before he became what he became.

Michael MacKenzie held his hand out. "We can't talk about this here."

Right. Because it was so much safer in the room.

But she took his hand, and she stood and brushed herself off, and she dabbed the last bit of moisture from beneath her eyes, and then she followed him back to the room.

Where he stopped, a vulnerable chagrin coloring his expression—mingled with that same wry self-awareness. Barefooted, bare-chested, and staring at the door lock. "This," he said, "could be a bad moment."

Gwen's laugh was a little watery, but held a smile nonetheless. She held the key between two fingers, turning it back and forth in the hall light. His relief made her smile bigger, and he stood aside so she could unlock the door and lead the way.

But she didn't fail to notice the truth of it all. He'd heard her, he said.

He'd heard her, as impossible as it was, and he'd come to her—without regard to shoes, shirt, or even the key to get back in.

He'd just come.

*For her.*

# *Chapter 4*

Mac grabbed another protein drink. It wasn't nearly enough to fuel a body being force-healed from layers of assaults, but it would assuage the immediate gnawing in his belly. And then, while Gwen pressed a washcloth to her face as if she could hide the bright shine of lingering tears and the strong pink of high emotion, he grabbed a quick shower, brushing his teeth in the spray.

He came out to discover her doing the same at the sink and set himself to pacing the room—driven by the blade's restlessness, driven by the picture he was forming of the previous night and knowing that this surge of energy would be all too brief. The burning in his blood told him as much—told him the damage had gone deep, that the blade still worked on him.

That the toll had yet to be completely paid.

He had to get a handle on the situation before he lost these moments.

He found himself drawn to the window—pulling back the privacy drapes, letting the light wash over his face…letting his eyes adjust.

Plenty of chaos below. Broken glass in the parking lot. A police car—no, two of them—parked skewed across the lines, and people milling around. Gesturing. Upset.

Gwen was right. More right than she knew.

No coincidence at all.

But what it meant, he didn't yet understand. Only that he now had a very good idea why the blade had brought him here. The blade that thrived on high feeling and righteous death and other people's pain. The blade that used him to gain these things even as he used *it* to stop them.

But he didn't know why Gwen was here. And he didn't know why she was *here*. With him.

He did know what the blade thought of it. What the blade *wanted*.

*They aren't my feelings. Aren't who I am.*

Was it?

She came out of the bathroom and stood uncertainly in the middle of the room.

*Uncertainly.* Not like her.

*As if I'd know.*

But he did. The hesitation in her movement, the way she'd so briefly held her breath, her hands jammed into the pockets of that snug thin stretch thing passing for a jacket. She'd done what she could with her hair, coiling it in a knot and wrapping her hair band around it, but it was clearly out of control, gleaming subtly red in the morning light.

He said, "Your father."

Her lower lip—round and full—firmed. "No."

He stepped away from the window, taking advantage of the uncertainty while he had it—fighting the impulse to restore her confidence instead. "It's no coincidence. You know it. I know it. I need to know *why*."

"I need a lot of things," she told him. "I'm guessing I won't get them."

"It's not about *me*," he said, his temper taking an edge. The blade warmed happily in his pocket, sipping up both conflict and promise. "It's bigger than that."

Her eyes narrowed; he thrilled to the spirit behind it and just as quickly doubted himself as the knife hummed in response. *My feelings?*

She knew none of it; she said, "Think much of yourself?"

He crossed the room in three long strides; she held her ground, lifting her gaze to his even as he crowded close—rude, deliberate. He jabbed a finger toward the window. "I think *nothing* of myself," he told her, feeling the truth of that; feeling the burn as it rose in him. "But I can *see*. Can you?"

"Maybe more than you think," she muttered, and it was then that she looked away. "Look," she said. "I'm here. I'm following my nose. That's all. Okay?"

He gave her the darkest of looks. "It would be okay if I believed that was all there is to it."

She regained some asperity. "What there is to it,"

she said, "is that I've been robbed every which way but loose, and I have to go take care of that. If you don't mind."

Right. Yes. Of course.

Time to remember how people lived in the world when there wasn't a demon blade involved.

He rubbed a hand across the back of his neck, rolling his head. Releasing tension. "Listen," he said. "I need to finish sleeping this off." He didn't define *this;* he suspected that after the previous night, he didn't have to. "There's no telling how long it'll take to get your finances sorted out, and I could use a favor."

She crossed her arms, not hiding her suspicion, and waited.

"Food," he said. "More of those workout drinks. Something microwaveable." As her face cleared with understanding, he added, "Necessities for you in exchange."

"I—" she said, protest in that single syllable...until she closed her mouth and looked away, then back again. "I can pay my own way."

He suddenly felt unutterably weary. *Burning.* "Please. Just...please."

Her surprise showed. "Oh," she said, disarmed. "Oh. Okay then. I mean...you're all right?"

"I'm fine." But at her skeptical expression, he smiled wryly. "I *will* be fine." A day of rest—full, deep rest—and he could start tracking down what he'd felt in this place so far—the origins, the areas of deeper feeling, lingering traces. He'd sort out the undercurrents of this place; he'd figure out what was going on.

And he'd figure out how she was part of it.

* * *

Gwen found something disconcerting about filing reports—the car break-in, the mugging—with someone else's wallet tucked away in her jacket.

The good thing—could there possibly be a *good* thing?—about the situation was that on this day, she was just one of many. Resulting in perhaps the oddest thing of all: no one saw anything strange about the siege of incredibly bad and possibly not coincidental luck she'd apparently had painted on her back the evening before.

*Get out of Albuquerque. Just get out.*

She could have done it. A bus ticket home, just like that. She'd pay more for rekeying the damned car than it was probably worth anyway.

But she didn't go to the bus station, and she couldn't quite have said why she hadn't.

Maybe it was the way he'd said *please.* Maybe it had been the look on his face as he'd burst into the stairwell first thing that morning, ready to do battle when he could barely stand. Ready to lend a shoulder when battle hadn't been necessary.

Anyway. He'd asked her to bring back some food. She could do that much. She flexed her lightly skinned palms and went to work.

She stopped in an internet café and quickly searched up the contact information for her credit cards and her bank. The first thing she bought with Michael Mac-Kenzie's money—*Mac...you've got your fingers in his wallet, so call him Mac*—was a disposable cell. From that she called the credit card companies, already heading for the bus stop.

The closest store wasn't far from the hotel; she walked back from there, soaking up the Albuquerque valley heat on a crispy dry spring day in a marginal neighborhood of real-life people, the city's tall buildings and fancy business district looming off to the west. Colors, sun bright even through new sunglasses, a constant stream of traffic and people.

How long could a single day be?

Amazing to discover it was still barely noon as she dragged herself back to the hotel. Laden with the reusable cloth grocery bags she'd picked up along with the groceries—and basic toiletries, and underwear, and a few basic Ts and sport shorts—she hesitated in the lobby.

She could get her own room. On his card, sure, but it wasn't like she wouldn't pay him back, and—

The wallet felt heavy in the grocery bag where she'd dropped it.

His whole *wallet*. His whole identity. Entrusted to her, just like that.

And if anyone knew what it was like to lose that little bundle of selfhood…

No. She'd ask before charging her own room.

She adjusted her grip on her various burdens and headed for the elevator, bumping the call button with her knuckles. Getting the hotel key from her front pocket was an exercise in persistence and dexterity; getting the door unlocked, more of the same.

She took no more than a step into the room before

dropping the whole kit and kaboodle, exhaling a huge sigh of relief as she shook out her hands. She rescued the key card, pushed the door closed, and leaned back against it with a dramatic groan.

And that's when she noticed he hadn't so much as moved. Still in bed, still just as she'd left him, moments after he'd flopped down in the first place. One arm flung out over the center of the bed, the other over his eyes, angled so one leg bent over the side of the mattress, that foot still on the floor.

"Um," she said. "Mac?" And didn't expect the spurt of concern, nudging purchases out of the way to hurry over, putting a hand on his leg. "You okay?"

Unbelievable. She was watching his chest, battered and tattooed—waiting for the rise of it—and it seemed to take forever, dammit.

But there it was, slow and long and even. A man deeply asleep. Just as she'd left him.

She bet his arm was asleep, too, dead weight on his face.

Without much thinking about it, she perched on the small slice of mattress beside him. This muscle-strapped body had become familiar to her last night— but in the light of day, those hours now seemed a marginal reality. And she no longer had the right or the reason to touch him. Nothing more than what she did now, laying the back of her hand across the side of his face and then on his neck.

No longer so very hot. Now just warm, another human being going about the business of being alive— and not so very bruised anymore at that. He didn't stir at the transgression, but a brief spate of goose bumps rippled over his arms and shoulders.

She let her hands rest in her lap, considering him. Considering *this*. The situation…the moments that had led her here, and the stark understanding that she had no idea where to go. Not in the next moment, not in the next hour, not in the next day.

He'd wanted to know about her father.

He was going to ask her again. She'd seen that much in him. If she stayed. She looked at the tattoo. Here, in the daylight, hardly obscured by the faint pattern of hair across his chest. She looked, and her breath caught and—

*No wonder.*

No wonder she'd thought of her father. Just no freaking wonder.

*I am nine years old, and my father is dead.*

*No one will talk about him.*

*I live with my aunt. She won't talk about him, either. I learn through overheard whispers—car abandoned, body not found. Witnesses who say they saw a horrible fight, but neither the victor nor the victim are identified or located.*

*They wonder if he's coming back. But I don't.*

*I know.*

*I am nine years old, and my father is dead.*

She found her hand wrapped around the pendant, her eyes closed and her head tipped back. Curse and boon, that pendant. A reminder of the past—but not just the good of it. The awful of it, too. The way it clung to her…the way it sometimes seemed to call to her, something far away and just beneath the threshold of what she was able to hear.

Other times, other places, she had dismissed that sensation—wasn't her life strange enough, in the wake of what her father had done to her?

Here and now, it seemed all too real. As if the metal breathed with her, breathing *into* her.

As if she wasn't alone.

*I know you.*

She jerked, hand clenching, sucking in a surprised breath.

That trickle of thought hadn't been hers.

Not hers at all.

*I KNOW YOU.*

More than a trickle. She jerked from it, eyes flying open in time to see Mac jerk awake in sync with her, his body trembling, his blue-grey eyes dark and confused and downright feral—his voice, when he spoke, distant and hoarse. "I...know..."

And then he seemed to wrench himself out of whatever gripped him and he saw her, truly *saw* her. And as she opened her mouth to say she had no idea what, just that fast, he was up and pivoting over her on one knee, pushing her back flat.

And now she was the one to tremble. But there he stopped, hands on either side of her shoulders, his eyes closing briefly and his face twisting in something that seemed like pain. It left him breathing hard, but when he opened his eyes, they were clear and bright and looking directly at her. Seeing her, in truth.

Why she hadn't fought him off, she didn't know.

Why she hadn't kicked and screamed and shoved and scratched—

She didn't know.

"Mac," she said, barely more than a whisper. No more than that, and whether it was question or request, she didn't know that, either.

He lifted one hand to clear the hair from her face, to touch her cheek and brow. "I'm sorry," he said, and brought his mouth down on hers. Not the ferocity she'd expected, but a gentle, cherishing kiss. And in that, more—so much more—than any crushing demand.

When he straightened, she could only look at him, feeling the surprise still etched on her own face, her mouth still open—still feeling his touch.

He ran a thumb across the line of her lower lip, hesitated—muscles working in his jaw, nostrils flaring briefly—and then pushed himself away. "I'm sorry," he said again.

She didn't move. "Why?"

It seemed to surprise him. "Why?"

She propped herself up on her elbows. "Why are you sorry? Why did you do it? Why did you stop?"

"You're crying." It wasn't an answer to any of that. It didn't even seem like part of the apology. Just the next step in a disjointed conversation.

"I'm not," she said, and ran fingers across the corner of her eye, discovered it wet—discovered tears trickled down into her hair. "Am I?"

That wry grin of his, on the mouth that was made for it.

*Among other things.*

He said, "I think we need to talk."

Devin dropped the scant pages of the Albuquerque paper onto Natalie's desk.

She never took her eyes from the computer monitor before her. "I wondered what you'd think of that."

Devin snorted. "He didn't take my warning very seriously."

*Rash of thefts* indeed. The least of it. There had been fights, assaults, break-ins…a swath of violence across that lower right quarter of the city, with enough trickling into their southwest turf to keep them busy on the way home. Enough to shove aside the little hate fest demonstration by the local better-than-thou group currently targeting a diversity support group.

She laughed, looking at him over the precisely organized workspace. From there she followed her own passion for research into things that might help blade wielders cope, handling the unsavory interactions with the lawyer they seemed to have inherited along with this estate—a man who knew too much, while not truly knowing anything at all. "Devin," she said, "last night you said he looked beat to hell. And you know he wasn't in all these places last night."

"Maybe not." He headed for the huge, bright bank of windows across the outside wall.

The grounds outside the window showed him nothing. A huge expanse of aquecia-watered lawn, here in the elm and cottonwood-littered bosque of the Rio Grande; the guesthouse that had been Natalie's home when she worked for Sawyer Compton. But it wasn't the grounds that drew him.

It was the city beyond and the overreaching awareness of it. No, the newcomer couldn't have been in all those places the evening before. But— "Maybe he wasn't. But he's involved. *He's* the one Anheriel followed."

"That wasn't all we felt last night."

There, in the truck…the cold sensation that gripped both of them, leaving Devin aching for something to strike at and Natalie pushing focusing exercises on them both.

He shook his head, his gaze out the window, his feet restless. "He's involved," Devin repeated. "Damned if I know just how. I've half a mind to chase him down and—"

"Maybe he needs help," Natalie said.

"Maybe he's already heading for the wild road," Devin said darkly, knowing the truth of that even as he said it—feeling the tug from his blade, the suggestion that they should go take care of this interloper.

Or maybe just join him in madness.

Devin pushed it away—and saw understanding in Natalie's eyes. New to her blade, she'd never felt that beguiling touch of madness—and if her new techniques were as useful as she hoped they'd be, maybe she never would.

But the understanding wasn't just for him. "If that's true," she said, "then he does need us. But not as his enemy. He needs help. And if it doesn't come from us, then who?"

Natalie. Thoughtful, organized…and stubborn.

"We'll see," Devin said. "I want a better idea of what's going on out there." At Natalie's expression, he shook his head. "It's one thing to take him on. It's another to leave ourselves vulnerable to him." *You,* he meant. *I won't take chances with you.*

Maybe she heard that. She settled, returning her attention to the ancient text she was examining via Project Gutenberg. "I think we'll want to try to find a copy of this one," she said. "You have to read between the lines, but I'm pretty sure this author has gathered anecdotal incidents about wielders." She made a few notes, then pushed back from the desk. "I'll head to the library and see if I can find anything about what we felt last night." She added a rueful expression. "In English."

"I'm headed to the gym," said Devin. His best option for building boundaries against the blade. "I have the feeling I'm going to need it."

She nodded. "Good idea." And then her attention drifted to the window, too. "I only hope he's got his own gym. Or that he knows what he's doing."

Devin snorted. "From what I saw last night?" There in the man's eyes, in his face…in the very energy accompanying him. "I'm not counting on it."

# Chapter 5

The blade insinuated itself into Mac's thoughts—into his body, reacting so strongly to the woman before him. Reacting to her feelings, her sensations…her uncertain realization that she had them at all.

He turned away from her, moving blindly toward the window—not seeing it. Seeing only his mind's eye, with her wide eyes writ large, her expression surprised and yet, as he moved away, somehow wistful. Propped back on her elbows in that familiar snug shirt, those wrinkled trim slacks.

He'd never had to imagine the shape of her, modest curves and toned body and profoundly excellent ass. He just hadn't expected her to *feel* so…

He hadn't expected himself to *react* so…

He put one hand flat against the window, eyes closed. Seeking escape.

From himself.

From what he thought he was becoming.

Because surely this feeling wasn't truly about what he felt for a woman he'd only just met, no matter how they'd skirmished together or how she'd sat with him through the hardest of nights.

It was about the blade and what it did to him.

It had to be.

"I don't understand what's happening here," she said, her voice backed by its usual determination but without its equally usual blithe spirit. "I don't understand what's happening to *me*. And I don't like it."

The knife fed him a dozen trickles of feeling, tugged him a dozen different ways. Someone in despair, someone in fear, a quick bubble of exaltation...the blade sifted it all, hunting for something on which to take action. Forgetting, apparently, its fear and danger from the night before.

Mac fought his way out of those places. *They aren't mine. I have my own feelings.* He glanced back at Gwen—sitting up on the bed now and just watching him. Knowing that he had answers for her and wasn't telling her. Feeding the blade her trickle of desire, her healthy dose of wistfulness, and her frustration. *Not mine.*

But somehow those words didn't ring as true.

Gwen didn't wait long.

"Look," she said. "I'm going to take the shower I so richly deserve and put on the stylish and clean clothes I managed to buy. When I come out, I'd really like there to be some answers waiting."

Answers. Wouldn't that be a change? He'd had nothing but questions for years now. Questions and the sly trickles of information granted him by the blade—coming more often now, even as its influence grew stronger within him.

*The wild road.* Not his words, not his term. But he knew, in his gut, what it meant.

And he knew that to get Gwen to talk about her father, he'd have to talk first. He just didn't know how to do that.

Not with words.

As she showered, he nuked the meal she'd brought, gulped down another protein drink, and changed his clothes—from one set of jeans to another, with the addition of a short-sleeved henley in a dark, bloodstain-hiding maroon, the Red Wing work boots from the night before traded off for basic black cross-trainers.

When she emerged from the shower, her hair sleek with conditioner and twisted into a knot at the back of her head, she'd exchanged her worn outfit for a bright turquoise T-shirt that did amazing things for her complexion and sport shorts that did amazing things for her legs. He took a deep breath and said, "Come with me."

She hesitated, eyeing him—assessing the changes in him. "I'm not dressed for—"

"Walking," he said. "You're dressed fine for walking."

"Okay." And then she laughed at him as she grabbed her new sunglasses from the counter and propped them atop her head. "Did you think I'd be hard to convince? What have I got to do for the next twenty-four hours but wait?"

"For new credit cards," he guessed.

"Being overnighted to the hotel." She slanted a look at him, reaching for her sport sandals. "I've been try-ing to decide how to ask if I can borrow your credit card to get a room here tonight."

*No.* His response came instantly, deeply—and he kept it entirely to himself.

Or tried to, but she sent a little frown in his direction that made him think he hadn't been successful. "Okay, then," she said. "I guess that wasn't the way to do it."

He shook his head. "Whatever you want to do."

"Look," she said. "It's not that I don't appreciate… No, you must be kidding. I'm not going to be sorry because I'm not gung ho to share a room with a man I don't even know. No matter how much I appreciate the help so far."

"There's more than that going on and you know it," he said, more sharply than he'd meant to, and then pushed the heel of his hand against his brow. He al-ready knew her well enough to know that hadn't been the right thing to say, oh, no.

"Do I?" she snapped, proving that instinct. "As if I can't manage from here on out perfectly well on my own?"

"No." Focus, dammit. Find the right words. "As if you *shouldn't.* As if there's not—" He stopped, gave into frustration. "Come with me. Walk."

She snatched up the hotel key and led the way, full of dignity in her generic gym clothes.

He could only follow. And hope he was doing the right thing.

*Stupid man,* Gwen thought. He couldn't just *tell* her whatever it was he was keeping from her. No doubt because he still all-too-obviously wanted to grill her about her father.

As if her past mattered to what was happening here. As if it was any of his business anyway. Simply because she'd made a single allusion...

Except in her heart, she knew if it didn't matter, talking about it wouldn't feel so big.

In that heart, she felt a twinge of guilt at his kindness—pushing the hotel door open, waiting for her to plunk the sunglasses from her head to her nose, waiting for her to adjust to the heat beating against exposed skin.

But if she made him wait for her to adjust to what had just happened on that hotel room bed, they'd be here forever. She nodded, more curtly than she'd meant to. "All right." And marched off.

"Hey, hey!" He laid the words on a laugh, ran a step to catch up, and took her hand, instantly and comfortably twining his fingers between hers. "Not like that."

"I—" She stopped, confused. "Then like...?"

"Like this." He stopped, closed his eyes, lifted his head, tilting it just a little. His chest rose with a deep breath; his nostrils briefly flared, as if he was hunting scent. She stared, fascinated, as some faint reaction chased across his face; she moved a little closer without thinking about it, watching.

Just like that, his eyes opened—catching her there, closer than she'd meant to be, more engaged than she'd meant to be. He smiled, holding his ground...giving her tacit permission to stay right there in his space.

"Pfeh," she said, stepping back—not far, considering he still had her hand, but a distinct distancing. "We're not walking, you may have noticed."

He gestured with their clasped hands. "This way." And that grin of his, just an edge of *wry*...an invitation.

Dammit. She bit her lip on the smile that wanted to respond to him and said, "Okay. That way."

She let him keep her hand.

She even let herself relax, walking in the bright sunshine, absorbing all over again the unique touches of the city—the propensity for sculptures, the little hints of sporadic beauty along the roadsides and in the signage, the street names that spoke of the area's Spanish heritage.

What she didn't notice—not until his hand twitched subtly tighter around hers—was the growing tension in him. As they headed first toward the airport, and then west on a wide but lightly traveled feeder road and past a school and an imposingly severe Homeland Security building, he withdrew from the amiable version of himself he'd shown her at the hotel and back into the man she'd very first seen.

The hunter.

On the prowl.

"Where—" she started, somewhat warily, then cut

herself short when he hesitated at a corner, closing his eyes, lifting his face…

*Hunting.*

Her free hand crept up to her father's pendant, hidden as it was beneath the T-shirt. A comforting and familiar weight…somehow grown new and strange again as she realized what she'd done and how often she'd done it since meeting this man less than a day earlier.

He said, "This is getting bigger than I thought it would," and took his eyes off his inner hunt long enough to glance at her. "I need to know you'll listen to me, if necessary."

"Could you be any more cryptic? And what will you do if I say no? Turn around and go back to the hotel?"

Something flared in his eyes, across his face. For an instant, she felt fear. Not just fear, but that same overwhelming surrealistic sense that this wasn't *real*. It was too strange, too inexplicable altogether. But when he answered, it was merely to give her the truth she'd already sensed, the strain of it evident in his voice. "No," he said. "It's too late for that."

And she thought, *Don't be an ass, Gwen.* Just because she was disgruntled and out of sorts and wanted her world to make sense again didn't mean it was fair or even smart to make things harder than they had to be.

"Okay," she said quietly. "I'm really, really confused and I really wish I knew what was going on, but I'll try to do what makes sense."

A glimmer of humor crossed his face, if ever so briefly. "That's the best I'm going to get, I think."

"Take it and run," she advised dryly—and found herself surprised when he squeezed her hand and moved on. Just as if they'd known each other for years.

Her bemusement didn't last long. A park came into sight to the west of them, green and thriving. And in the background, the peculiar and specific kind of noise that Gwen associated with chanting...with protests.

"How?" she asked him, struck by the understanding of it. That he'd indeed been hunting. That, somehow, from the hotel where they could see or hear none of this, he'd led them to this place of disturbance.

Just as the night before, he'd run straight for trouble. And not for the first time that night, not to judge by his appearance.

"How?" she said again, and this time it was a demand as she set her heels to the cement and stopped him short.

Not that he couldn't have dragged her on. But she had a sense of him now. She didn't think he'd do that.

And he didn't.

But she could clearly see the conflict in him—the way something had crept inside to haunt him, tugging at him—creating a strain in his eyes, a tension in his jaw and neck and shoulders.

"It's what I do," he said, and the look he turned on her frightened her more than anything about the past twenty-four hours. Full of the hunter's intensity, full of words he didn't quite seem to be able to say. "It's why I don't have a home. It's what happened last night. *It's what you wanted to see.*"

She didn't notice the sunny day, or the warmth on

her exposed skin, or the pleasant sensation of muscles loosening up with the walk. She found herself whispering, "Be careful."

It struck him in a way she hadn't expected—but he shook it off, and he went on.

She expected him to slow as they got closer, to take in the situation…to figure it out. Maybe he already had it figured out. It made little sense to her—a motley gathering of drab figures, each of which held signs on sticks: propped against their legs, attached to their torsos. They spread out along the edge of the park entry corner to which Mac had brought them, shouting incoherent slogans in an uncoordinated fashion.

Inside the park sat a pleasant cluster of trees and a fountain, a statue of a child and a burro not far away amid a clever surround of native desert stone and plantings. There, another, smaller group of people appeared to ignore the protestors completely.

Between the two, a bored cop sat on his motorcycle.

And then she felt it. The instinct that had been part of her for so long that she never questioned it, never doubted it. The self-righteous little group, working off their frenzy of entitled superiority, their chanting grown louder, more discordant. And there—that man in the baggy brown trousers and faded zip-front shirt. *Intent.* "Mac," she said, uneasy—glancing at the bored cop, thinking surely this ragtag little band of negativity wouldn't start anything with such supervision.

Mac gave her a glance of surprise. "Zip-front guy?"

She nodded tightly. "What's going on here?"

"Near as I can tell," Mac said, squinting at the quiet

party in the park, "it's a pagan thing. And some other people protesting the pagan thing."

"How—"

But he gave her a ghost of that grin and nodded at the long, narrow parking lot that ran along what looked to her like a giant concrete ditch. They weren't far from it, or from the protesters, and he'd eased their pace. "Bumper sticker."

She smacked his arm. Just as if they'd been together for years. He only grinned bigger—even if the moment didn't last. His expression abruptly faded; she saw the reason immediately. One of the quiet party, dressed in earth-child-casual and sandals much like hers, breaking away from his group to approach the chanters. *Oh. That is so not a good idea.*

And maybe he knew it. But he came anyway, exchanging a few words with the cop—who seemed equally skeptical but who then just watched as the man went on. Ordinary man, a bit dumpy around the middle, a bit thin on top...

Full of courage.

"I'd like to invite you to join us," he said, raising his voice to be heard over the chanting. "This is a day when we've chosen to give back to the Earth, even modestly, by picking up trash along the perimeter of the park and feasting here. Surely your own beliefs teach you to honor—"

"Sinner!" cried a woman, shrill and sudden, as if she'd startled even herself. "Sinner!"

"You'll rot in hell!" shouted a man.

"You pervert our world!"

"Okay then," the man said, barely audible as Gwen strained for his words, aware that they weren't far away at all now, having turned to head along the concrete ditch—Mac's doing, leading the way with his shoulders set. She slowed, dragging subtly against him, her hand still captured by his and now attempting to do the capturing.

And then her instinctive warning system spiked and she gasped, knowing the zip-shirt guy had reached his tipping point. She startled, too, when Mac whirled on her—

No, not on her—on the crowd. And she saw in his eyes the exact moment they each realized it—that the other had *known,* had felt it—and then the protesters broke. They dropped their signs and flung their banners and transformed from motley dull curiosities to vicious sheep, led by the flashpoint in a zip-front shirt. Fists became weapons, sign sticks became bludgeons—

A woman from the pagan group screamed; the man who'd played envoy flung dignity aside and bolted for it. The cop shouted, suddenly no longer bored. And Mac pulled his hand free of Gwen's and gave her a verbal shove. "Stay here!"

Almost, she didn't, as he ran the short distance to intercept the group—a wicked sprint, moving faster than she'd ever imagined and never losing the fierce purpose of his stride. But even as she moved to follow, she checked herself. She'd promised.

He flowed into that crowd, leaving men on the ground in his wake. Not wounding them—none of them athletic, some of them aging—but taking them down all the same. A clever shove here, a shift of weight there, a yank-and-tangle over there—all smooth and clean and bewildering.

From nowhere, it struck. A hard slap of ugliness, a startling wash of all things cruel and mean.

*It struck.*

She cried out—heard herself, didn't even know why. She didn't even understand what she felt—only that it made her feel sick and dirty.

Mac dropped as though felled, there at the edge of those he'd left tangled on the ground.

Gwen instantly broke her promise and ran for him—a glance at the small remaining protesters and their amplified frenzy, a glance at the cop's face as he aimed his Taser, one hand at his shoulder mike as he shouted for backup. She flung herself down beside Mac, who knelt back against his heels, his hands at his head and his face set in pain. He turned on her, fierce and wild and lightning-fast, and even her wildest effort to wrench aside wasn't enough.

She did the only thing left to her and grabbed him back, getting up in his face. "Get a grip, Mac!" she shouted at him. "We have to get out of here!"

Something got through to him. He shoved himself off the ground, taking her with him. If the cop noticed or cared, he cut his losses, fully engaged with the protesters he'd stopped.

Mac and Gwen ran for it. Or staggered for it. Tripping, fumbling, until slowly Gwen realized she was no longer holding him steady—and noticed that she was the one keeping up with his long strides and not the other way around, even as they turned a corner and slowed.

The pleasantly baking sun suddenly seemed more than hot. She dragged him a few steps farther, to the shade of a tree in storefront landscaping. "Guess I'm glad for these shorts after all," she said, wiping her face with the hem of her shirt.

Mac only looked grim. As much as he sent her a flicker of appreciation, as much as he tried to straighten up and shrug it off. After a moment, he said, "I'm sorry."

"Look," Gwen said. "A gas station. Let's get something to drink. Something cold. Maybe even crushed ice. Do you want a bright red tongue from the cherry or blue from the raspberry?" And then, because he didn't take the cue, didn't shed his grimness, she asked, "Why sorry? Because you did it, or because you stopped?"

He snorted appreciation for that. "I wouldn't have done that if I'd thought—" He shook his head. "I don't know why that happened."

She hesitated, then asked it anyway, blotting her face against her shoulder a final time. "You felt it coming, didn't you? Knew that man would start it?"

Not that she truly had any question.

He only gave her a grim look. "Crushed ice it is then."

But oh, too late. There, heading for the gas station, two young men with heads shaved close, wifebeater shirts, baggy pants, crude tattoos. And again…

*Intent.*

Gwen didn't think about it; she reached for Mac's arm, holding tight.

And Mac apparently didn't think about it, either. "What the hell *is* it about this place?" he muttered, striking out for gas station at an angle of interception—but only a few steps before a quick, hard hesitation, looking at Gwen.

She held both hands up in quick acquiescence. Maybe even surrender.

And only then realized the relief she felt—that it wasn't her, running into trouble. Trying to warn the people in the gas station store, inevitably just ending up in the line of fire. She didn't have to make the decision.

He was already doing it. As if he'd always done it. Intercepting the two incipient troublemakers, planting himself before them. And yes, she'd indicated she'd stay back...but not so far she couldn't keep track of things. She found herself easing in on the edge of it all as Mac said, "This place is closed to you. Find your trouble somewhere else."

They pushed up close to him, sneering the predictable responses—the insults and the threats, all rolled up into one. One of them gave him a hard shove, unable to conceal surprise when Mac stayed rooted.

She saw the man's sudden move—hand pulling out a switchblade and flicking it open—and she drew sharp breath to cry a warning she never had the chance to voice. Instead she froze, startled as splintered light lanced out from between them to make the toughs squint and hesitate—but not for long.

By then Mac had lifted the knife he now held between them—that big clip-blade Bowie he couldn't possibly have been carrying all this time. Couldn't *possibly*—

He said, "I don't think you heard me. This place is closed to you. And by the time you cut me with that little knife of yours, I'll have you gutted." He smiled; it sent a shiver between Gwen's shoulder blades.

It wasn't a bluff.

And they knew it.

But it was written there on their faces—the awareness that the odds were against Mac, that they were losing face, losing fun. *Run,* whispered Gwen's instinct. *Oh, run!*

Instead, Mac moved a step closer. "And here's the really fun thing," he said. "Your faces and your knife are on the security camera. Mine," he added, smiling again, "aren't."

Gwen could lip-read the curses from where she stood, even if the snarling made them almost unintelligible. "You won't always be here," one of them said, stepping back stiffly, his blade snicking closed; the Bowie knife glimmered revealed and...*eager,* Gwen would have said. Since when did that make sense?

"Security camera," Mac said. "Your faces. Images set aside for the police, should anything happen to this place." He smiled again. Not nice. "And I mean anything."

"Hey," the second guy protested, his sneer sliding over to indignant protest. "We can't control what happens to this place! It's run by a buncha spic fags! Plenty of reason for people to—"

*"Anything,"* Mac said. The blade glimmered. "So maybe you don't want to be around here, huh?"

Maybe not. Seething, out-maneuvered, out-bladed, and for that matter without nearly the necessary mojo, they backed away—wary steps at first, and then pivoting out to a jog.

And Mac, standing there, still lost in dark thoughts…

Gwen checked her impulse to go to him, but instead pushed through the entrance to the station storefront. There she found a slight and neatly turned out Latino who might very well have triggered the hateful response of the young men outside—and he knew it, too, his face tight and worried. "Hey," she said. "They're gone. If that security camera works, save the tape. But I think Mac scared 'em off for good. He told them they'd be blamed for anything that happened here, thanks to this big *fail* of theirs."

Relief flooded his features. "They been working up to this," he said. "This city…there's something going on…" He shook his head. "Hey…soda or something? On the house?"

She brightened. "Oh! You know, I was really thinking about a cherry crushed ice—"

He held up a hand. "Please. And one for your friend?"

She glanced out at Mac. "I don't think he's a cherry crushed ice sort of guy. Who knows? We really just met."

The station attendant scoffed, filling a large cup with more crushed ice than she could ever finish off. "The way he is with you? *¡Si se puede!*"

Gwen laughed. "Points for best use of inspirational phrase. And thank you!" She took the proffered cup and straw. "But seriously…get that security tape, okay? Just in case. Those guys were ugly."

He pointed at the phone. "Owner is on his way. I'm sure he'd like to meet—"

But Gwen stopped listening, swallowing that first sweet slurp of crushed ice and flavor, suddenly too cold as it hit her stomach. She felt the trickle of uncertain feeling, the wash of it over her skin, crawling and repulsive. "Do you feel—?"

The man shook his head. "Just the way the swamp cooler always feels—"

But he'd known what she meant. And he stopped, just as uncertain as she.

And Mac no longer stood out in front of the store.

Mac, who'd been so vulnerable to this inexplicable wall of hatred.

"Gotta go," Gwen said. "Be careful!"

*"Y tu, chica,"* he said as she pushed out the door, his voice nearly lost in the jingle of the bells there. *"Y tu."*

She stood outside in the bright world again, the heat washing against her so strongly that it momentarily overwhelmed that subtle sensation of…*something.* Two cars at the pumps, everyone minding their own business, no one happy. She squelched an urge to call for him; wherever he was, he wouldn't want that.

*Like you know him so well.*

Well enough. And he couldn't have gone far. *Wouldn't* have, surely—

As if she was confident, she headed around the side

of the little station, where the lot grew weedy and untended, an adobe wall angling to cut it off nearly at the back corner of the station and not even enough room for a trash bin.

Mac stood, back to the wall, head tipped back, eyes closed—his face was tense, jaw tight, hands flat against the building.

"Mac!" She ran to him, dodging the stickery weed clumps and stuttering to a stop at the look on his face, the way he turned from her—understanding the message of it. *Don't come any closer.*

As if she had a choice. As if she could leave him like that.

As if she *would*.

# Chapter 6

*Run away, Gwen. Please run away.*

"Mac," she said, determination lacing her voice—penetrating even the darkness. "I feel it, too. Not like you do, but I can tell. Whatever it is, let me help." Her hand on his upper arm and he couldn't help it—it came on him like a lightning reflex, knocking her hand away, snatching her in his own grip—a cruel grip, fingers tight, eyes never even opening.

She cried out—nothing more than a sharp gasp, as offended as she was frightened—but she didn't even try to break away. She stepped up to him.

He lost track, then, as the blade pounded him.

"Dammit, Mac, I need some help here! Come *on!*"

Bright light flashed through his mind, reflected

through his body…slicing mirror-bright shards, bouncing and multiplying and the blade—

—*wail fury desperation kill you kill her no no no*—

The stucco wall of the gas station grated against his skin, lifted the back of his shirt as he slid, legs no longer holding him—but Gwen was right there keeping him from falling outright.

*Gone.*

It was gone.

The tarry darkness, the blade's fear, its fury. Light flickered within and became soothing dapples, and Mac gulped air—a gasp profound enough to be his very first breath. He found himself sitting on his heels, his back still to the stucco, an unexpected crouch.

And still he held Gwen's arm. She knelt before him, and her eyes sparked determination, a bold light blue in a freckled surround. One hand pressed up against his chest, there where the unbuttoned henley gapped to show skin; one hand clutched the pendant that fell just below the notch of her collarbones. "Mac," she said, and only then did he hear the fear lurking behind the determination.

*What did you do?* He meant to say it out loud, but his breath hitched on new realization.

The blade was gone.

Oh, still in his pocket. Still warm with fury.

But not in his mind.

Not feeding him trickles of feelings, of emotions that weren't his. Not ramping up what he might otherwise feel himself with what it wanted him to seek out and enhance.

Just him. Michael MacKenzie, free and clear.

And realizing, just as suddenly, how much he still wanted this woman. All on his own, without trickles of stolen feelings or ramped-up reactions. How he was still entranced by the spark of her, the *life* of her. Still beguiled by the heart-shaped face, the barely there cleft in her chin, the way her eyebrows lifted as she looked at him now.

Relief flooded in to replace the startled emptiness. The blade had screwed with his head, but it hadn't replaced what he was.

Not yet.

And for whatever reason, he had this moment. Freed, he found himself with no restraint at all. He pulled her between his knees with hands both gentled and intractable, watching her eyes widen as he guided her right up to meet his mouth, his hands sliding up her arms to cup her head, losing himself in the inexplicable luxury of just being himself.

Of being *them.*

Oh, hell *yes,* he kissed her.

Her hand crept to the back of his neck, fingers against damp skin, and oh, hell *yes,* she kissed him back.

Until her breathing quickened and she made the smallest of sounds deep in her throat, and he realized where he was and who he was and that he no longer trusted himself to know what was truly real and what wasn't—or that he'd know when he crossed the line.

And so he ran his thumbs along her jaw, there where the skin was so soft, and he managed to pull away from her. And then he would have said *I'm sorry,* but those words never made it to the surface, either.

Instead, he looked at eyes gone big and cheeks gone flushed and lips gone from striking to stunning, and he realized out loud, voice tinged with surprise, "You knew I was going to do that."

She laughed, as small and shaky as it was. "The look on your face?" She smiled, just a little one, self-aware and amused at them both. "I for sure knew you were going to do that." Then she tossed her head, a token motion. "Do you think," she said, "we could get back to the hotel without more of—" and she removed her hand from the back of his neck to wave it expansively around them *"—this?"*

He couldn't help the faint self-deprecating smile tugging at the corner of his mouth. "I don't know," he told her. "I'm used to looking for it, not running from it."

"It hardly seems necessary to *look.*" She eased back from him, her hand lingering at the open neck of his shirt, and glanced around—checking to see if they'd made a spectacle of themselves, he thought, though he'd sought this place for its relative privacy when the darkness had struck him. "Is it always like this for you?"

He shook his head and took the liberty of tucking a stray curl back behind her ear, the red of it glinting through. One knee lowered to the ground, stabilizing them both. "No. Not like this." He shook his head, closing his eyes to breathe deeply. Even the air felt clearer. "What did you *do?*"

She looked at the spot where her hand rested against his skin; her other hand crept back to the pendant. He'd seen that, he remembered...vaguely. But then she looked away. "You're just going to laugh."

"It doesn't seem the time." His hand slid under her elbow; he stood, lifting her along with him—and realized then how deliberately she did it. Kept her hand on his chest. "You—"

She nodded. "I don't understand. I don't think I *want* to. But I think..." She lifted the pendant, the faintest of gestures, and shrugged.

He looked at the pendant, there in her hand—a small hand, with freckles dusting the knuckles and pale pink, chipping polish on her nails—and his eyes narrowed. "We need to talk."

"So you said." Some of her normal asperity returned. "But we haven't, have we? And I don't think I'm going to make it very far walking like this." She glanced at their connection again.

"Sooner or later," he said, and before either of them could think about it, he stepped aside from her, cleanly breaking the contact.

*—fury indignation retribution strikestrikestrike!—*

The blade lashed out at him, striking hard—burning an incandescent punishment through the soul of him. He choked on it and stiffened, and his eyes rolled back and his jaw spasmed shut, teeth catching skin; his head jerked back. He clung to the strength of clarity and freedom, so long denied, and he forced his head back down and he forced his eyes open and he gritted out, *"Fuck you,"* through those clenched teeth.

And Gwen, watching him with worried eyes, expressive brows drawn, seemed to understand perfectly that he wasn't talking to her.

The blade sent a final spear of flame roiling along his bones and faded into a sulk.

Okay then.

Mac took a deep breath, settled himself into balance, and leaned away from Gwen to spit blood. "Dammit," he said, probing the cut with his tongue. "That really hurts."

Gwen laughed—just a little too freely, driven by evident relief. "Baby," she told him. "Men just can't deal with pain." And while he got stuck on that, bemused and trying to reconcile it with his life and especially with his life in the past twenty-four hours, she cast him a devilish look and caught him completely by surprise, whirling to sprint a few playful steps away—and disappointed when he just grinned instead of taking her up on it. "Poke," she said, in case he hadn't gotten it. "Now you try to poke me back. Maybe tickle me. At least try to put your hands on me."

He bent to scoop up her cup of crushed ice from where she'd placed it against the side of the building and waggled it at her. "Maybe I thought I could lure you back into range."

Her expression fell. "Oh, damn. Strategic error." She hesitated, hovering between options. "I really, really want that. I deserve it. I stopped that…that… whatever was happening."

He grinned and held the cup outstretched, a peace offering. "Yeah," he said. "You really, really deserve it. Let's see if we can make it back to the hotel before it's gone. I hear there's a good diner just up the block, and on a day like today…well, let's just say I need to get my hands on some food."

"I've heard about that diner, too," she said, dead-pan, and came back to get the cup. She was taken by surprise when he made a lightning-swift grab once it was in her hand, pulling her in close, holding her—just for a moment, just to do it and to feel her against him. To see the delighted surprise in her eyes.

To pretend, somehow, that the blade's little spill of emotions no longer trickled through his mind and body, but that he was still free.

Gwen took a long pull on the straw, letting cold cherry flavor slide down her throat and striding along the sidewalk with a guy she suddenly seemed to know. Someone with whom in the past twenty-four hours she'd shared a rumble, a mugging, a protest-turned-to-hate crime, and a hate crime turned to failure. Not to mention whatever strange and painful event had preceded quite a wonderful kiss.

"You're blushing," he said, not breaking stride.

"I am not!"

But of course she was. And smiling to herself, too.

Complete absurdity. Twenty-four hours, a little action, a little weirdly mystical woo-woo…that's what it took to make a girl happy? With wallet gone, car broken into, life askew?

Maybe so.

They took the long way around on the way back,

looping around the park in a route that avoided the pagans, protestors, and police. They cut away from the stark white concrete of the artificial arroyo, and through the luxury of the grassy park, and past the midday heat of the basketball courts. And then, in a cluster of trees, he stopped her, catching her with the straw in her mouth.

She let it slip away from between her lips as he turned her to face him, stepping up close and running his fingers gently over the sides of her head. Petting her. Watching her.

Damned sweet.

Couldn't have that.

"What makes you think you can just touch me as you please?" she demanded, one hand on her hip and her head cocked back.

"Mmm," he said, not considering his response for very long. "Because I want to."

She gave him a squinty look that should have made him think twice.

Instead, he said, quite seriously, "Because now I know what's real." And then he turned away from her, hands jammed into his back pockets.

Somewhere on that tightly muscled body, he'd hidden a Bowie knife.

*Right.*

He said, "Talk to me, Gwen. What is that thing? Where did you get it?"

The sudden chill down her back had nothing to do with the final slurp of crushed ice she'd just taken.

He looked back over his shoulder, an oblique and

mostly hidden gaze. "Because I think that's how we've ended up in this together. You and me and whatever's going on here."

She didn't answer; couldn't. Not just like that. She walked the stretch of open grass to the nearest trash container, tossed the cup away…and then just stood there.

*I am nine years old, and my daddy just tried to kill me.*

*He didn't mean it. It wasn't really him at all. Not with that wild look in his eye, the pure insanity etched across his face.*

*He wants the pendant. The one he gave me and told me to care for, always. But even as he wants it, he doesn't.*

*Or else, something in him doesn't.*

*I am locked in the bathroom, bleeding. I have never seen so much blood. I have never seen the tender skin of my stomach cut so deeply. I have never seen any-thing cut so deeply.*

*Even through the worst of it, I never thought my daddy would hurt me.*

*He slams against the door. "I'm sorry, baby!" he cries and sounds like he means it. "I'm so sorry! I thought I could do this!" And slams against the door again. "Run, baby, run! Please run!"*

*And I am small enough to slip through the window, blood and all. But I am old enough to tell the neighbors that my daddy isn't home, that I fell on glass.*

*And I am young enough to cry the whole time.*

*I never see my daddy again.*

"Gwen." Mac's voice, but he hadn't come any closer. He waited in the shade, giving her the option to return.

Still cold from the inside out, she did. Slowly. And returned to him—coming around front to face him square but lifting her chin to warn him off when he would have lightly touched her arm.

She didn't want to be touched just now.

"I probably can't even tell you what you want to know," she said. "But then, I'm not sure, am I? Just how what fits together with what? Because what have you told me?" One more defiant attempt to pretend it all didn't matter, that her past had nothing to do with this present. "Anyway, it could be coincidence, couldn't it? We both got restless feet, we both ended up here. Travelers stay at a hotel—that's what it's for. Is it such a mystery that we ran into each other?"

He only regarded her with a steady gaze. Not an unkind gaze…far from it. And *I wish I wasn't doing this, but I am. And I will.*

She heard it loud enough, unspoken or not, and blew out an impatient breath. "You know, I can tell when people are trouble. But it didn't work with you. I don't get that. If *anyone* has the potential to cause trouble—"

"But not to you," he said. "Never to you. Not like you mean."

She blinked. Damn, he was right. With anyone else, *everyone* else, she never knew. Could be chance, could be intent, could be collateral damage. But whatever he was up to, he'd made sure she was safe. Whatever his intent elsewhere, his intent toward her had been not only benign, but protective.

"Oh," she said, her voice coming out smaller than usual. "Well." She took a deep breath. "I don't know what the pendant is." She took it out from beneath her shirt, pulled the chain over her head, and held it out to him. Ancient metal, crude stamped design, indecipherable runelike markings.

He drew himself up, nearly stepped back—but visibly stopped himself. And then gave a rueful shake of his head. "Not right now."

"Like my father," she said, just a touch of bitterness. "You want it, but you can't stand it."

He looked as if he might say something but didn't quite. It left her room to continue. "My father gave me the pendant. He was strange about it, but at that point... he was strange about everything. He told me to protect it, to always keep it. He didn't tell me why. And then later he tried to kill me to get it back." She found her hand on her stomach, tracing the thin white line of the scar that slanted from just inside her hip bone up and over her neat little innie. On second thought, she pulled the new T-shirt up and the elastic waist of the sport shorts down—just enough to reveal the scar. She didn't miss the grim look on Mac's face. "Yeah," she said. "He tried to warn me, even as he did it. I didn't believe him. Lucky for me I was a slippery little thing, or that would have been the end of it."

After a moment, Mac cleared his throat. "That's all? He didn't tell you anything about it?"

She shook her head. "Keep it always. Protect it. I think..." And she did, pausing to consider those confusing days, the times her father tried to talk to her and seemed to get tangled in his thoughts—to struggle with himself, as if it was a fight to say the words at all. "I think he tried to. He was just too far gone." She shrugged. "I don't know why."

He wanted to reach for her—she saw it all too clearly. He wanted to hold her. But that wouldn't make it better or different, and now...

Now she needed to pretend she was past all that. "Anyway," she said, shrugging again, "after that night...after I got away and healed up and they found his car and no one ever saw him again—not completely in that order—things were different with me. I had this..." She looked at her hands, at the pendant; brought them in against her chest to close her eyes and think of the feel of it. The deep unease, the sharp stutter of warning that told her when someone was out for trouble. The schoolyard bully, the soccer team mean girls, the high school toughs. At first just when the trouble was aimed for her...but later, so fine-tuned that she could see it coming regardless.

She looked straight at him. "I'd had the pendant for...what, two years before that night? But it was after that night that I turned into a human trouble detector. And *boy*, did I get into trouble until I figured out how to deal with it." She wrinkled her nose at him, commentary on days gone by. "It is just *so* not a good idea to go pointing fingers at people before they've even done anything. Suddenly you're the one who's causing trouble, so the good guys blame you for that—and then the bad guys blame you for spoiling their fun."

He grinned, that mouth that was made for it, a sudden thing that surprised her with its genuine nature. "No wonder you've got that fast-talking mouth," he said, but there was understanding behind it. Understanding and...affection.

She gave him a narrow-eyed stare. "That's not fair. Do you know how long it took me to figure out where that came from?"

The smile turned somewhat rueful. "Let's just say I've had reason to think about it."

"Yeah," she said, not letting up on the glare. "Let's just."

But it didn't inspire him to any grand revelations, so she gave up and dropped it, throwing her hands up in a loose gesture of finality. "So that's it. I'm a freak of nature trouble-detector, and I don't have any answers about the pendant. What happened back there..." She struggled with saying it and pushed through in a rush. "What happened is that I've worn that thing so long and my dad gave it to me and I was so frightened for you that I just grabbed it like a little kid and *wished* on it." A little girl wishing for her father, more like it. The one she had once known, and not what he'd become. "So there. All is confessed. In a pretty one-sided way, I might add."

He winced a little at that, but didn't look away. "Yeah," he said. "I know. I just..." He blew out air, jammed his hands into his back pockets again. "I have to think." Then he gave her a sidelong glance, a deliberate thing from beneath a half-turned brow. "And eat. I have to eat. Man cannot live on crushed ice alone."

She snorted. "The only crushed ice you had," she

said, with as much asperity as she could muster, "was the cool taste of it on my lips."

That did it. He looked at her as though briefly stunned, stuck there—his eyes so clearly on her mouth. And then he said, with some visible effort, "You did that on purpose."

She tossed her head ever so slightly. Just enough to shorthand that she'd done it. "You looked like you could use a reminder." She headed for the sidewalk, and she knew what her legs looked like in the shorts and what her ass looked like in retreat. She glanced over her shoulder at him. "Not just fast-talking. *Smart*."

"I…" He took a deep and audible breath, if only to finish his response in a mutter. "I consider myself reminded."

## Chapter 7

*I have to think.*

That's what he'd told her. Cowardly in its way, but true enough.

There was too much new, too much different.

And though Mac thought he'd learned to deal with this blade, to compensate for it…

He was no longer so sure.

Either the balance had changed, or it simply wasn't working any longer.

Understanding how Gwen's pendant—how her father, how *she*—fit together with the blade, or how any of them fit with what was happening here in Albuquerque…

He definitely needed to think.

Even if he pretty much already knew what had

driven Gwen's father. And even if he wished it didn't give him some clues about what was happening with him.

*The hell with that.*

"Fierce," Gwen said. They sat at a table in the diner, and the waitress served them with a knowing smile. When he glanced at her with question on his face, she said, "Your expression. Fierce."

"Good," he said as she forked a piece of his burger right off his plate. He feigned offense. "You sure make yourself right at home."

"You betcha," she said. "Your hotel room, your food. Can't imagine what's next." And then bit her lip, clearly hearing how the words sounded outside her own head, eyes wide...until she went for the head toss. Perfection, that toss—so understated, so perfectly paired with the gleam in her eye.

"No," he said, deadpan. "It boggles the mind."

Deliberately, she took a baby carrot out of his salad, crunching hard to bite it in half, and then pointed the remainder at him. "Your turn."

Yeah. It was.

But he thought it would be nice to have just a few more moments of *this*. Normal meal, normal diner, even though he ate around a gash inside his mouth and she mooched entirely off his vastly overloaded plate.

"That's better," she said—softly now, and he realized he'd smiled. "For being the inscrutable hero type, you're awfully easy to read."

He snorted. "The *what?*"

"You heard me." She sat back, cocked her head.

"Of course you wouldn't know it. That's just all the more perfect."

He only stared at her, just a little narrow-eyed, just a little thoughtful.

She asked, abruptly, "Do you have family?"

It startled him. "Do I—"

She acknowledged the suddenness of the question with a lift of one shoulder. "For some reason, I'm thinking of my father. It's where my mind went. I wonder what my father would have thought of me—of how I turned out, thanks to what he did. Of what's happening here today. And I wonder what makes a man like you."

He smiled, shook his head. "Nothing exciting there. Two parents, an older brother and younger sister, all in the family printing business. All back in Washington state, still wondering why I ever left it to work my way around the country." At the question in her eyes, he added, "For the sake of seeing it."

She briefly pursed her lips. "I don't actually get the impression that's what you're doing now. Seems to me the emphasis isn't quite right."

"Seems to *me*," he said, brow raised, "that you see too much." But he was still looking at her mouth as she said it, drawn by the curve of the lower lip and the full, wide nature of the upper.

"And know far too little." She said it with her own pointed look and went for one of his steak fries.

"Actually," he told her, "I think you know a lot." But of course that only made her frown. He tipped his head at the door…a question. Because this wasn't something he intended to talk about here.

"Oh, look," she said brightly. "Here comes some-one with a big take-out box. I can't imagine how she anticipated you would need it."

He looked at the pile of food before him, more than half of it ordered with the intent of takeout and an eve-ning snack—for he was still fueling up in the wake of the healing, and in the more recent wake of the day's events.

"I intend to be hungry this evening," he told her—leaving her pondering, narrow-eyed, if she'd just been handed a warning or a promise, or if he was talking about food after all.

But when they walked back out into the late after-noon heat, she with the food and one hand wrapped lightly around the inside of his arm, he with the sense of equilibrium restored, everything changed. As if a shadow had dropped out of the sky to encompass them, with the blade crying warning, Gwen stiffen-ing in alarm, every nerve and muscle shouting for him to act while every instinct called out for him to wait until he knew—

There.

Behind them. The corner of the diner.

*It's a video game. A never-ending round of hate and violence.* And he and Gwen had become so tan-gled in it—

Her grip on his arm tightened. The knife sliced through his thoughts—a snarl of displeasure and warn-ing, letting him know that these men weren't angry, weren't despairing, weren't any of the things it loved to drink.

These men were doing a job.

"He said you'd find us." A faint cockney accent behind those words, the voice itself without concern. "And that you'd know we're ready for you."

Gwen's grip squeezed even more tightly, if only for an instant. Confirming it. They had weapons, and no doubt the weapons were discreetly already trained on them.

"No guns, he said," the man continued. "But mate, I'm telling you—these Tazers pack a hell of a punch."

Mac didn't have to turn around to know it. They were out of range. He could throw—deadly accuracy, that throw—but he wouldn't get the blade back in time for number two.

And number two might yet be silent, but he was there.

"Look, now, he only wants a chat." So reasonable.

The blade spat its sour resentment at their calm— at the way they gave it nothing to work with. No fear, no hatred, no resentment, no frenzied high. It floundered, unable to muster its deadly song.

He could still use it—*would,* if he got the chance— but not at peak. Not with the avaricious hunger that made it so very deadly.

"Mac," Gwen whispered, close enough to read every line of his body—including his hesitation.

"Come on, then," the second man said, joining the conversation with a deep and lazy voice. Even less invested than his partner, and well chosen for this chore.

By someone who knew what the blade needed? How the hell—

Only one way to find out.

"She's not part of this," Mac said with little hope, but determined all the same. "She stays."

They laughed.

Big empty plots of land and dirty industry followed the Rio Grande, isolated from the bosque by the levee, open community land, and their own back lots. Alfalfa fields interspersed with industry right through the southern half of the city. Warehouses clustered by the railroad track spur off the north-south Rail Runner line.

Mac got only a glimpse of it all as the men opened the back doors of the closed van in which they'd crammed him after they'd cuffed him. The warehouse beside them was smaller than most and had an abandoned air; it gave him no clues. The men pulled Gwen out ahead of him—a clear hostage for his good behavior—released his cuffs, and hauled him out for a rude escort to the warehouse.

But they didn't try to take the blade. And they didn't touch Gwen so much as they herded her, leaving the threat an implied one. *Giving him no reason. Giving the blade no reason, no excitement.* Nor did they say anything else—simply put them through a door into the dimly cavernous space of that building, with only dim light from a dirty window set high.

The first thing he did was find Gwen. He put his arms around her and drew her close. To outside eyes he might have been murmuring words of comfort, but what he really said was, "I can see in the dark. Trust me if it comes to that."

"You can *what?*" She didn't keep her voice down at all. But she didn't give anything away, either, and he thought that both were deliberate. A show of mettle, tempered by discretion.

"See," he said, "In. The. Dark." And then went sardonic. "Secrets. Told you we'd get around to them."

She wasn't impressed, apparently. "Nice timing." But she took a deep breath and added, her voice just as low, "There's something lurking here. But I don't get the sense that we're in direct danger."

He wasn't betting on it. He just wasn't sure if the danger would come from an obvious direction.

A voice came from the catwalk on the far side of the space, high against the wall opposite them. Even Mac's eyes couldn't penetrate that corner of darkness. "I'd say I'm glad you could come, but of course you didn't have any choice."

Their bad guy. Their own personal kidnapper. The man who had ordered them dragged off in broad daylight in a city under siege.

Under *his* siege? And if so, to what purpose?

Gwen lifted her head. "Do you have delusions of supervillainy or *what*—He Who Must Not Be Named, lurking in the shadows?"

Mac winced, but the man's voice stayed mild. Nothing of the sort to put chills down anyone's back. "Close enough, for now."

Gwen drew breath—Mac felt the suddenness of it,

and closed a hand around her arm to stop her words. They were *supposed* to ask questions, make demands... that was their role here.

He was not inclined to fill it.

She subsided, and he turned the hold into one of reassurance.

After a few moments, he heard a disgruntled noise.

For damned sure an object came hurtling out of the darkness. Mac jerked Gwen aside, and her leap of fear funneled in through the blade, slicing along nerves that felt too much of its pleasure.

Far too much.

*It didn't used to be that way.*

The object slammed to the pocked concrete beside them, and even as Mac recognized it as a suitcase, the man—disdainful, somewhat amused—said, "You should dress your girlfriend."

He felt Gwen's frown as surely as he'd felt her fear, but this time she kept her voice low. "What—"

"A suitcase. Your suitcase."

"Wow," she said, and this time she didn't mutter it. "That *is* impressive. Supervillain-wise, I mean. Stealing suitcases."

Mac couldn't help a smile at that. So damned bold.

"I didn't," the man said. "But I did take it from the one who did. His fear was delicious."

*His fear was delicious.*

Mac stepped away from Gwen, unconscious of it— took another step, all the while staring up at that dark corner. *This man knew...*

"I thought that might get your attention," the man said.

*"Who are you?"*

Now he was playing by the man's rules. Now the voice held satisfaction. "The proper question is, who are *you?* I had my reasons for coming here…you were not among them. Yet here you are." A considering pause. "Perhaps drawn, much as I. Perhaps chance. Or perhaps it simply doesn't matter. However, I have found you now."

"And you think that's a good thing?" Mac asked. "For you, I mean?"

"I expect it to be." The dry voice could have been a warning.

Probably was. The blade spoke to him then— whispering a sudden song of terror and despair and confusion, infusing it with glee.

"Mac," Gwen whispered, and he recognized it for the warning it was—her own instincts, crying out. He found his hand in his pocket, the knife settling instantly into his palm.

Never a good sign.

It flared blue-white light through the darkness, startling Gwen into a cry. A blade mutable, reshaping from stout pocketknife to arcing saber, the guard a graceful sweep enclosing his hand. A deadly beauty, gleaming in the darkness. Ready. *Eager.*

Overhead lights flickered on—one by one. Not quite slowly enough to keep Mac from wincing, but with more consideration than he would have expected. Until he realized it wasn't for him.

It was because the other man, too, needed to take such care. *This man knew...*

A glance at that corner showed exactly why Mac hadn't been able to penetrate those shadows—a thin fabric screen separated them. Thin enough so the man could see out but offering Mac little more than a hazy shadow as he spoke. "Pardon the dramatics," he said. "I'm not ready to be seen, but blindfolding you wouldn't serve my purpose."

Mac asked what he was supposed to ask, even if he did it with a growl. "And that would be?"

"Getting your attention." The voice held no menace—simply a confidence. An expectation that he would get from Mac what he wanted from Mac.

It set a growl in Mac's throat, not quite voiced.

The two men from earlier marched into the vast room, paying no attention at all to its occupants. One removed the suitcase; the other simply *was*. When the first returned, they approached. Gwen made no protest at all when Mac put himself between them and moved to stay that way.

"'Ere now, she comes with us," the cockney said, and the blade picked up on Gwen's fear, too—a more familiar and poignant connection than the unknown surges in which it had already been basking. *Not my feelings.*

One of the men reached for Gwen.

"No," Mac said, flatly standing ground—pushing back at the blade, even as he churned with the strength of what it threw at him, so much more intense than only a few days earlier. "She doesn't."

"Wasn't a question," the other man said. It was the first Mac had seen of his face, with skin so dark it seemed to hint of blue, features broad. His deep and lazy voice had grown impatient.

*Grown stupid.*

The man reached for Gwen, as if the mere presence of his boss in the shadows guaranteed his safety.

It didn't.

The blade flashed.

It wanted him all. It fought to take him all, gulping in his first startled flash of reaction and grasping for the rest. Wanting the life-and-death struggle, wanting to feed on shock and terror and then flesh and blood itself. Mac fought it back—not wanting that needless death and not willing to leave Gwen vulnerable.

A stark frozen instant of time, that's all it took. Then the man stumbled back, staring agape at his forearm—at the sight of bone peeking through the gash laid from the inside of his elbow to his wrist, the blood spurting.

The second man didn't hesitate, leaving his comrade to flounder while he leaped back, hand darting for the gun in the cross-draw holster at his belt.

"Hold!" The command came in an inexorable shout, and as the man froze, as Mac regained his ready stance before Gwen, the puppet master from above took an audible breath, slow and deep. "Did I not tell you to treat them with care? See to Maitho. It will be to our new friend's regret that the woman stays, but he has made his decision."

Mac barely heard him; he took his cue from the other two men. Their change of body language, the emotions rippling through the blade—*resentment shock pain frustration fear acceptance*. And still the blade resisted, wanting to lay in—to *bathe* in—the destruction it could wrought. It took a grunt of effort, a step back...

Right into Gwen, who was probably pretty damned sorry she'd been crowding him at all.

"Further gone than I thought," the man above said; the other two had found their exit, leaving the room bare again. "I don't imagine the past twenty-four hours have been easy on you. Let me get right to the point, then."

*"Please,"* Gwen said, but her bravado had a tremor in it.

"You have something I can use. You *are* something I can use. And you are unexpectedly ripe—pushed, perhaps, to a maturation that might have taken several months more. The wild road."

Mac couldn't help it. He jerked back into sudden focus, aiming glare and demand up at that screened corner. *The wild road.* His hand clenched so tightly around the saber hilt that his forearm shook with the tension of it. "What do you know of it?"

"Everything." The man's voice deepened further. "I have struck a bargain the likes of which would astonish you and the likes of which you will never quite see—there can only be one of us. But I can nonetheless guide you to fruition. I would find you useful, thus."

"I find myself perfectly useful as I am," Mac snapped back, as Gwen made a little vibrating noise in her throat. Warning, perhaps. Just plain creeped out, definitely.

But the improved lighting had finally given Mac what he needed—the way out. Just a glimpse of it, a plain old push door in the corner, half-hidden behind a sheltering entry wall. He nudged Gwen in that direction, waited for the glimmer of bright hope that would tell him she'd seen it.

Their host seemed undisturbed. "I'm fully prepared to demonstrate what I can offer you." He took a deep breath; when he spoke again there was a smile behind his words. "And how deeply impossible it will be to resist."

"Now you're just getting cocky," Mac muttered, more to see Gwen rise to it than through any impulse to mouth off. And still the unidentified terror, bundled in with the bizarre nature of this man…his minions… the emotions battering at him…

Time to go.

He looked straight up at the screen. "I'd say I appreciate the effort, but I don't. I'd say no offense, but I don't give a damn. We're leaving. You know that I could have taken your guys out anytime I wanted between here and there, right?"

"In fact, I do." That rich voice sounded—inexplicably—amused.

"They won't be as lucky another time. You know that, too, right?"

That voice gave nothing away. "Circumstances vary."

"Is that a door?" Gwen squinted at it, finally understanding. "Hell, yes. Let's get outta here!"

"That's your option," the man said. "But I believe your companion will choose to stay."

Mac snorted. "The hell I—"

—*fresh terror, pure spurting pain*—

A scream, short and harsh.

Mac stiffened, assaulted from within, the blade going sharp and hard and past all his defenses. *Wanting.*

"Mac," Gwen said, desperation in her tone as she tugged at him to no effect, "he's playing you. You *know* he's playing you."

"It's real," he said, his voice gone raspy, the *want* of the blade so deep and fierce he could barely think. "Whatever they're doing is *real.*"

"She is," the man said modestly, "entirely for you."

That jerked him back to himself—against the pull of the blade, propelling him toward a future he didn't want. Going beyond what had always satisfied it: the moments of revenge, the vigilante justice that kept it fed while keeping everyone else safe. "No," he said. *"No."*

"You still think you have a choice?"

"Mac?" Gwen said, and doubt crept into her voice.

The man laughed. "Your decision to trust him was premature, my dear."

And Gwen didn't spit at him for saying *my dear,* which—in some hazy corner of Mac's even hazier thoughts—was how he knew just how far gone he was.

*The wild road.*

# Chapter 8

Gwen sent a desperate glance at the door. *Freedom.* So close. The two men were gone, and the third did nothing but stand up there behind his screen and gloat and posture.

And Mac stood, still rooted to the ground like a tree. Mesmerized—or locked in some deep struggle.

One she was no longer sure he would win. If he was even still sane. And he had a sword in his hand. A big, gently curved, gleaming sharp, *glowing sword.*

*Step back, Gwen.* Just one step. Then two. Then, the door.

But she didn't move. And that damned gut instinct of hers, born of blood and loss…it shouted of intent, but it spoke nothing of her.

A door beneath that man's catwalk opened—a brief

slash of light in the dimness through which Mac saw so well. Mac took three swift steps and froze again, trembling. She had no idea why.

*I am nine years old, and I don't understand what's going on.*

Nothing ever changed, it seemed.

A woman stumbled into the middle of the warehouse—hunched over herself, cradling her hand to her stout body. She wore mom jeans over ample hips, a basic purse clutched tightly over her shoulder, her dark hair caught in a careless clip in the back. Her complexion spoke of mixed blood and her faintly plumping jowls spoke of her age.

An average woman, plucked out of her errands and dropped into this nightmare.

She saw Gwen and her eyes lit with hope. "Please," the woman said, holding out her hands in entreaty—one slashed wide-open and dripping blood. "Help me."

Mac made a low sound, like a man inexplicably stretched too far.

Gwen glared up at the screened corner. "I don't know the rules to this sick game," she said, "but we're leaving."

"You should have done that very thing when I gave you the chance." There was little regret in that voice. "Now you're part of *'this sick game,'* which I have been playing for longer than you can even imagine. You may or may not survive."

Gwen said something very, very rude indeed, tossed her head, and marched up to grab the woman's arm—

ignoring her questions and fears and heading to march right out the door.

Until Mac growled.

Like an animal.

*Growled.*

Gwen froze. Slowly, she turned—just her head, looking over her shoulder.

This man, she didn't know. Wouldn't have kissed. Wouldn't have spoken to. Wouldn't have ever gotten that close.

Not with that made-for-a-grin mouth twisted in a snarl and that dangerous stance and the sword flowing out from his hand like an extension of his arm and the shadows gathered darkly around him like close companions.

"Mac," she said, trying not to let the uncertainty out.

The woman tugged Gwen's arm, little whimpering sounds in her throat, and Gwen turned on her. "Stop it!" she snapped, her words as much of a command as she could make them—thinking about the high emotions of the park, of the gas station. That's when Mac had been so staggered before. Then, and those times when the ugly, viscous wash of feeling had crept over her. "Stop it! You'll make things worse!"

"Clever woman," the man told her, both approving and unmoved.

The woman clutched at her, unable to comprehend, little sounds stuck in her throat where she might have been trying for words.

Mac's inhuman growling had ceased; his breath came hard and fast through clenched jaws.

Gwen doubted it was an improvement. She cast a desperate glance at him. The sword shone even brighter, she thought, as impossible as it was to be there at all.

"Pretend," she told the woman, not taking her eyes off Mac. "*Pretend*. You're not frightened. We're going to walk out of here. Think about it—us walking out of here." And then she held the woman back as she took a single step, certain that any greater movement would push Mac over the edge of whatever line he walked. "*In your head*. Imagine it. We're walking out of here. There's nothing to stop us, is there? We can leave when we're ready." The whimpering had stopped; Gwen gave the woman's arm an encouraging squeeze. "That's right. Calm. Breathe deeply. Think kittens and unicorns and double rainbows."

But she didn't look away from Mac. Not anymore. Not as she calmed the woman—breathing deeply, murmuring reassurance…feeling some of the uncontrollable hysteria ease. Seeing the reflection of it in Mac—the slow return of sanity to his expression.

"You," the man said, now more annoyed than approving, "have been a mistake all along." A pause, too meaningful to amount to anything good, and then he added, "Or did you think I was too stupid to have a gun?"

Gwen's carefully even breathing stuttered to a stop, leaving her lungs instantly aching. The woman beside her exploded back into fear, from silence to a gasping cry, and Gwen—

Gwen just plain couldn't blame her. In some part of her mind, Gwen was gasping right along with her. But she never took her eyes off Mac, not even as she tightened her hold on the woman, giving her a little shake—

Mac threw a hand in front of his face, staggering back at the emotional onslaught. The sword flared a frightening quicksilver glow, coloring everything around it with hot silver-blue light. He cried out—pain or denial, Gwen couldn't tell—and his face twisted until he raised the sword, so full of intent that the sudden surety of imminent danger slammed into her.

The woman cowered, tearing away from Gwen to fling her hands out in a protective gesture, warding away the looming blows, her hand streaming blood and her knees grinding into the concrete.

*"No!"* Gwen screamed at Mac, a fierce cry into the echoing room. She flung herself toward him, up within his easy reach, leaving herself completely open. Not going for the weapon that loomed so large in the open room, but reaching for Mac himself. Finding his tortured gaze and looking straight at him and pouring out all the caring and understanding she could muster.

He closed his eyes, a noise of agony in his throat, and wrenched around—staggering, going down, and flinging the sword away.

She wanted to go to him. To wrap him up from behind and make it okay. All of it.

But she knew better. It wasn't okay. And that damned awareness of hers…the one that said she was a target…

Still shrieking as loudly as the woman behind her.

She snatched up the sword. Not sure what she was thinking, only that now she had a weapon and she still hadn't seen any damned gun and *let's get the hell out of here!*

"We're going," she told the woman without turning around—and told Mac, too.

She hadn't taken more than a step before the sword twitched in her hand, its unaccustomed weight startling her. She held it away from herself, eyes going wide.

*It changed.* The guard shrunk away, the hilt writhed in her grip—and before she could do so much as thrust it away from her, it jerked again and slid coldly along the palm of her hand, slicing deep.

She dropped it with a cry, as much repulsed as startled, watching with horror as it was, suddenly, nothing more than a pocketknife, a sullen and retreating glow.

"You really didn't think it would be that easy?" The man stepped out from behind the screen, arrogant—and entirely correct—in his assumption that unlike Mac, she couldn't see him in the darkness.

And Mac was down, wrapped in his own little world of shock and misery. The knife—but she'd only barely glanced away!—was gone.

Gwen glared up at the catwalk. "We," she said, all but spitting the words one by one, "are leaving now."

To her disbelief, the man nodded. "You may go," he said. "That I would turn him in one day wasn't to be expected. That he is so very close… It's enough. Return to your hotel, if you will. I will be pleased to have a talk with that blade once he takes the road."

"Not," Gwen said. "Gonna. Happen." Bold words. Full of complete crap, as she clutched her bleeding hand to her chest, cradling it. But only for an instant, as she turned her back on the man—oh, God, her skin crawled at that—and grabbed Mac's shoulders, giving him a little shake. "Come on," she said. "Come *on,* we're going—" A tug, a jerk. He moved with rigid uncertainty and a blank, dazed expression.

It was good enough. They made progress. Gwen hesitated beside the woman and tapped her on the shoulder. "C'mon," she said, plucking at the woman's sleeve, raising her from her protective hunch. "Outta here."

She barely heard the slice of sharp metal through air.

She didn't recognize the deep hollow thunk that followed.

She didn't understand why the woman suddenly stiffened, her eyes wide and her mouth dropping open.

Not until the man said coldly, "You presume. She was always mine."

And the woman slumped again, a heavy throwing knife deeply embedded in her back and her eyes already gone vague.

Gwen turned on him, awkward and tangled as Mac lurched against her. "You—"

"Go," he suggested, just as coldly. "While you still can. You're interfering with my feast."

Gwen didn't quite remember making it to the door. Or how she'd managed Mac, who bore his own weight but didn't seem to know what to do with it. Or how long, exactly, she stood blinking in the bright sunshine, trying to orient herself, once they were outside.

She found her injured hand wrapped around the pendant through the T-shirt, her mind gone to that habitual place of *oh, please let me get through this.*

She spat a noise of self-disgust. She wasn't Daddy's little girl any longer. She hadn't been for a long time. She just hadn't wanted to let it go.

Besides, who needed help? The van sat right where it had been left, and if memory served, the driver had simply dumped the keys in the cup holder. It was probably pretty damned safe to assume no one would steal from his employer.

Well, no one but Gwen.

"Borrow," she muttered, hauling Mac along—all muscles, no working brain—and jerking the driver's door open to discover *yes!*, the keys were there, right next to the handcuffs—and *yes!*, the van's side door slid right open. She managed it all, pushed Mac in through the side door with efficient haste, and then— out of the corner of her eye—caught sight of her suitcase sitting just outside the building.

*So is the van a trap?*

Or maybe they'd just expected her to walk out that door when she'd had the first chance, leaving Mac behind.

Scrambling, she grabbed the case, shoving it in beside Mac. She flipped his legs inside and slid the door closed with a resounding slam.

She didn't bother to readjust the driver's seat; she

perched on the edge, reaching for the pedals, and got the thing started, pulling away with an inadvertent squeal of tire as nerves overcame control and her foot jerked down. Out of the parking lot, along the feeder lane that ran parallel to the stockyard spur of the railroad line, and out onto—

Onto...

"What do *I* know about Albuquerque streets?"

This one didn't seem highly traveled, and the light traffic was exactly what she wanted. She shot out onto the road, turning left toward a distant cross street, and then fought a battle with her foot—getting their speed down enough so they wouldn't be a cop magnet.

How could she explain the blood to anyone? Hers and the woman's, all over her shirt. How could she explain Mac? Stunned but not drugged and still looking dangerous. And what the hell would she do if he roared out of his little daze in full dark warrior mode?

More than that...what would she do if he didn't?

She managed to slow the van. A glance in the rearview mirror revealed no pursuit. By the time she reached the cross street and recognized the I-25 onramp not far to the east of the intersection, her hands, wound and all, were nearly steady on the steering wheel.

The suitcase shifted as she took the turn; resolutely, she refused to check back. Either it was rolling around or it wasn't. Either Mac was rolling around or he wasn't.

"Shoulda woulda coulda been in Vegas," she muttered, shifting lanes to reach the highway entrance ramp.

And then, there they were. Merging with traffic, heading for the airport. Imagine that. Evil didn't just live in Albuquerque—it lived right in the middle of it.

"I am twenty-nine years old," she said, "and I have found evil."

It didn't even sound pretentious.

It just sounded true.

## Chapter 9

*Worst hangover in the world.*

Mac tried to think past the pounding in his head. The blade didn't help, lurking in sullen retreat. The awkward stretch of his arms to the side, the hard floor beneath him...those things didn't help, either. The metal biting into his wrists—

"What?" he said. *What the fu—*

"Dammit." Gwen's voice bit off in frustration—not far, but muffled all the same. "Ow!"

Frustration. Not fear. Pained, but not hurt.

The blade told him nothing. Sulking. Sulking, why, again?

He opened his eyes and found the hotel carpet an inch away. Wow. That sure as hell was dirtier than he'd thought it would be.

    —*hunger*—

He had no doubt. As much as the blade had indulged
its sickening obsession, slopping tortured emotions
through Mac with abandon, it hadn't truly engaged
anyone for days. Nearly a week. No blood, no flesh,
no sustenance. That its hunger plucked at him now...

No, no great surprise.

The handcuffs. Now, those were a surprise.

Gwen muttered another expletive.

"Maybe I can help," he suggested, wincing at the
very sound in his head but his voice no less dry for it.

"Mac!" Her footsteps vibrated lightly on the floor;
her bare feet came into view. "You're back!"

Had her voice always been that loud? He winced
again, making no manly effort to hide it. "I'm—"

    —*resentment anger feastfeastfeast BLAME*—

He found a growl in his throat, his wrists battering against metal cuffs looped around the leg of the
bed, his body burning with the blade and the sudden
exhaustion of the effort he'd apparently made to free
himself.

"And that," Gwen said, plunking down in a chair
she'd pulled up where he could see her, "is why you're
cuffed in the first place."

For the first time, he saw her shirt—stained with
blood both smeared and soaked in. "I don't—" He
couldn't quite finish past the dread in his throat. "God,
Gwen, tell me I didn't—"

    —*hurt her hurt hunger wantwantWANT*—

He burst through the other side of it with wrists
throbbing and head shattering and stomach *this close*

to retching, breathing fast through jaws grinding hard enough to ache.

The blade had him. After all this time—

"Tell me," he said, barely more than a whisper, and his eyes closed against the painful light of the room, "I didn't do that."

"I— What?" She must have realized, looking at herself. "It's not all mine. And what's mine is thanks to that…that…knife-sword-thing of yours." She said it defiantly, as though he might laugh at her for thinking she'd seen what she'd seen.

But he had no doubt. Whatever had happened during those missing moments in the warehouse— a woman, the high emotion boiling straight through the blade to his soul, the man above so very certain of Mac's nature—so very close to being right—the blade had obviously revealed itself to her.

"Please," he said, forcing himself to audible speech. "Tell me I didn't kill that woman."

"Not you," she said, fast enough. "But she's dead. And we're only here because that man thinks he can turn you. I'd ask what that means but I kinda maybe know. Even if I don't actually have any idea." She came down off the chair, creeping just close enough to touch his leg. Hesitant, but not for herself—more afraid she'd somehow hurt him. Her hand was wrapped in duct tape.

*—resentment hunger—*

"Back off!" he snarled, and then was so very sorry, groaning as his head split into shards of thought and being. Slowly eased, as he remembered to breathe again. Not yet. It didn't have him yet.

Dimly, he heard her say, "I think it's mad at me. I dared to touch it, you know. And I took you away from there. I...I think I stopped it, when it would have taken you. For good, I mean. Don't ask me how."

He forced his eyes open. He had a good view of her now, on her knees on the dirty carpet, one hand on his leg, her hair carelessly twisted back and her light blue eyes gone dark with concern.

Her T-shirt, smeared and blotted with blood, except for the clean wrinkled circle just beneath the notch of her collarbones. *The pendant.* The thing that stood as no coincidence between them. Her father. The way nothing seemed to work quite as expected for either of them when they were together—and at the same time exceeded all expectations.

*Don't ask me how,* she'd said, kneeling beside him with concern on her face and a clean, clear, bloodless spot where she had a habit of touching that pendant. He looked at her, then, full of darkness and light both— dread and hope—and he said, "I think I know."

But she still wouldn't unlock the cuffs.

She sat cross-legged beside him, she rested her hand on his thigh, she ached for his struggle and she found her heart pounding in overdrive every single time she thought of what they'd just been through, but she wouldn't unlock the cuffs.

And he didn't ask her to. That alone told her too much.

So did the tension beneath her hand, the flex and

play of muscle that sometimes trembled with an internal effort she couldn't even begin to measure.

"I'd stopped for gas," Mac said. Finally telling her. He couldn't be comfortable, his arms twisted to the side like that. The pillow she'd just tucked under his head seemed like a small thing. He didn't even seem to notice it, eyes focused on some point on the wall. "Indiana, I think. I'm not sure. Things got confusing—" Under her hand, muscle went rock-hard; his eyes went dark and his jaw tight and his whole body arched ever so slightly.

He forced his next words, fighting through it— fighting whatever had tried and come so close to possessing him. "It was late…one of those pitch-black nights. And there was this little bar next door, had food." He shook his head. "I didn't even see it coming. Two guys in a scuffle, one of them had a knife and this…*meanness*…"

He looked directly at her then and shrugged, as best he could. "I thought the other guy needed some help."

"Uh-huh," she said. "Because that's what you do, right?"

The words didn't quite seem to strike home for him; he frowned but let it go. "The guy with the knife knew how to use it. But he was…sick. Or high. Or something."

She wondered if he was thinking the same thing that crossed her mind. *Or possessed.* She only said, "Or something."

"He cut me before I even knew how far gone he was. And I—" Mac frowned, lost in that memory…

searching it. "I must have gotten the knife away from him. I'm not sure. Just…suddenly it was three days later, and I wasn't even in the same state. I didn't have any of those cuts, and there was this…*blade*." He took a deep breath. "I know more about it now. It's…in my head. I didn't know it thinks of itself as a demon blade, but now I do. I think…maybe it has a name, but it won't tell me. I learned pretty damned fast that it would patch me up when things went bad. There's a price for that, of course. And I learned what it wants."

She spoke softly, as if she might somehow avoid disturbing that blade. "That's how you find the trouble spots. It tells you."

He nodded, finding her gaze again. "It feeds. It wants the glory the bullies feel and the horror from the victims. For a while, I thought it was me—wanting those things, feeding on those things. I thought I'd gone mad. For a while, I…" Maybe, he wanted to look away from her. His gaze flickered, then solidified. "I didn't try very hard to survive the encounters it drew me to."

"Which," she said, forcing her voice to remain steady in her throat and her hand to remain steady on his leg, "is how you know all about the price it exacts for patching you up." She shook her head. "That explains what I found last night when I cleaned you up." She said it so casually—and then suddenly realized the implications of that moment, the liberties she'd taken to touch and care. A flash of memory, *gleaming flesh and small tattoo, the exact pattern of hair across chest and down defined muscle, denim waistband resting loosely over hip and—*

She flushed and made herself continue. "How some of the bruises were both new and old."

He was watching her. Closely. *Really* closely.

"Oh, my God," she said. "Did that blade just tattle on me?" And then she couldn't believe it when her heart beat a little faster because there in the middle of this story of his, he gave her that little half-lift grin at the corner of that mouth made for it.

It didn't last. Maybe that damned evil-possessed impossibility of a knife felt his distraction. Maybe it knew more than she ever expected. But it got him, all the same. He gave a sharp, sudden grunt, twisting against it—jerking his wrists mercilessly in the hand-cuffs, his expression turning dark and wild—and this time the blade didn't let him go.

Gwen instantly pushed herself away to safety, out of reach but not untouched. Not to see his wrists stream blood, not to see his mind and body so ill-used.

Her hand throbbed; she looked down to realize she'd again taken hold of the pendant. And looked back again at Mac, still raging against captivity, still less than sane.

*I think I know,* he'd said to her. How she'd brought him back at the warehouse. And he'd been looking at her chest, which she'd taken to mean he was looking at her *chest,* but now she glanced down and saw for the first time what he'd seen.

The clean spot.

And she remembered gripping the thing outside the warehouse, and she remembered her father's reaction to it—how he'd coveted it, how he'd feared it…how he'd given it to her. Not as a gift, but because he didn't have the strength to hold it—and he didn't have the strength to use it.

Amazing thing, adult hindsight. And hurtful. The thing she'd found comfort in all these years, and he had only just been using her, after all. Right before he'd tried to kill her.

Her father, with a knife. Her father, a changed man. Her father, dead in mysterious circumstances.

*Demon blade.*

She wondered when Mac had figured it out.

She pulled the pendant over her head, staring at the heavy, blunt metal features, trying to understand—

He made an animal noise, one that spoke of rage and revenge and death and no respect at all for the human body breaking under the strain—chest heaving, sweat glimmering at his temples, face gone pale... blood soaking into the carpet.

Gwen muttered self-imprecation. Who needed understanding? *Just do it.*

She hesitated a moment, on the edge of it.

And then, when what drove Mac allowed a lull in the fury, a chance for the body to breathe and recover, she threw herself at him. *On* him. The pendant in one hand, the other yanking open the unbuttoned placket of his shirt—thrusting the pendant upon him and hoping so very damned hard that it was the right thing to do and then not able to think much about anything at all as his face blazed fury and his body bucked wildly beneath her.

He collapsed, trapping one foot under his thigh and

throwing her completely off balance over him. Chest heaving, eyes closed, face turned from hers. She wasn't even sure he was still conscious—not until she saw the moisture at the corner of his eye. Not sweat, but the involuntary tears of a body driven beyond what it could endure.

She still had one hand free. She thumbed the dampness away. "There," she said. "Shh. We'll figure this out." But sudden fear gripped her when he didn't respond. Had she been too slow, too late? "Hey," she said, and the uncertainty trickled in. "We will. We have to. I'm part of this now, I can see that—"

His eyes flickered open, lashes dark and wet. Fully sane. Fully clear. "Gwen," he said, his voice abused and ragged. "It's not… It just…" He shook his head. "It's *clear*. My head is *clear*. It's just *me*. Whatever you're doing…"

"The pendant," she murmured, certain of it.

"I'm *free*, do you get that? My feelings are just…" That was wonder in his eyes, she was sure of it. "They're just *mine*." He lifted one hand, a foreshortened motion—one that had, she was also suddenly certain, been intended for a caress.

She felt the heat of him beneath her then—damp with sweat, soaking his own shirt, radiating through his jeans. And realized, too, the intimacy of how they twined together, her leg still trapped and her hands on his body. The awareness of it flushed through her, and then she winced, realizing he'd know that—

Except he didn't seem to. Still caught up in the wonder of freedom, still catching his breath. She said, "You didn't feel that, did you?"

Puzzlement crossed his features, as much of a question as anything.

"Me," she said.

"Oh," he said. "I feel you, all right."

She made an impatient gesture with her free hand, indicating the tangle of their bodies; the other still pressed the pendant to his skin. "Not *this*. That voice inside. Tattling."

He shook his head. "No tattling. Unless you want to tattle on yourself."

She looked down at them, at their intersecting bodies, and then back to him. "I'll just let you guess."

He laughed, a mere sharp huff of air. "*Guessing*. Now there's a concept." But his movement had jostled the cuffs, and a wince flickered over his face.

Gwen could have slapped herself. She pried her foot free—no matter that it had been very pleasantly cradled just where his thigh met his butt—and pushed herself up, pressing the pendant down in emphasis before she gingerly lifted her hand. "Okay? That do you?"

She hadn't expected his reaction to be moderately cross. "Hell. Now *every*thing sounds like an innuendo."

"Take it how you like," she said, realizing suddenly that she meant it. So much emotional intimacy in this past day, beyond what any two strangers could expect of one another and twining with the fleeting moments of mutual want and response and no little amount of aching.

No coincidence that they were here together, this place, this time. No doubt what they'd so suddenly come to mean to one another—or the trust they'd each earned. The only question was how long it would all last.

Gwen found herself not caring.

*What happens in Vegas, stays in Vegas.*

And she shoulda been in Vegas.

"Stay there," she said. "I'll get a washcloth for us, and we'll see what we can figure out about those cuffs. I happen to have the key."

# Chapter 10

"I told you to *stay there*."

Gwen's voice came insistent in his ear, sounding both irritated and worried. Her hands worked gently at his arm—patting, wrapping. The sound of ripping tape. The snatch of something at the hair on his forearm.

"Sorry," she murmured. "But *that's* not going to happen again."

He remembered it then. The blade, whispering so subtly in his mind, barely filtering through the effect of the pendant. Urging him, nudging him...pushing him to remove the pendant.

"Ow," he said, not opening his eyes.

"Baby," she told him. "You fainted."

*"Passed. Out."* An important distinction there.

A featherlight tight brushed across his brow; he

belatedly recognized lips and wished for them back when they'd gone. "Go to sleep," she said. "It won't happen again."

He did, for the moment, believe her.

Gwen's voice came tired in his ear—something reassuring, which was all that mattered for the moment. Her hands moved gently over his skin—damp cloth, healing touch. His arms throbbed; his body ached.

"Just patching you up again," she said. "Please excuse me if I don't even try to resist enjoying it. The touching part, anyway. Not the bandaging part."

"Ow," he said.

"Baby," she told him. "You had already fainted."

*"Sleeping."* Definitely a distinction to make.

Her fingers trailed down his side, unexpectedly proprietary. "Go back to sleep," she said, as if she was actually the boss of him. "You're safe for now."

He did, for the moment, believe her.

Something snored in Mac's ear.

A quiet, girly snore, there and gone again.

Mac opened his eyes. Saw, to his relief, not the filthy carpet in the nighttime darkness, but instead the more distant ceiling.

In the dark. The almost complete darkness, obscuring every fine detail—just as it should but as he barely remembered it ever doing. *Before the blade.*

The pieces fell into place. He was on the floor of their hotel room, on his back—one hand still cuffed to the bed, his head on a pillow, his shirt gone, a blanket soft against his skin.

His free arm, pretty much asleep, curved around Gwen as she used his shoulder for a pillow and tickled the side of his face with her magnificent hair. She draped over him, her leg resting over his, her arm heavy on his chest, her hand resting directly over the faintly raised tattoo over his heart.

Her breath tickled his skin.

His arms still throbbed; his body still ached. The blade hadn't worked on it, not any of it. A glance at his cuffed arm showed him the pendant, duct-taped to his lower arm above the bandaging there. Hot pink even in the darkness. *Yay?*

Slow as he was, he could put it together. She'd gone out, gotten supplies, cleaned him up again—proprietary hands—and trusted him just enough to uncuff one arm. Leaving him to heal the old-fashioned way—slowly. Without interference. Without any price to pay.

*I'll pay it sooner or later.*

Of that much he was sure. As soon as he lost contact with the pendant—or it failed on its own—the blade would come roaring back, exacting its price for these moments of freedom.

Freedom.

His mind, his own. His thoughts, his own. His feelings…

His own.

His body…

That, he thought, currently belonged to Gwen.

"Mmm," she said, barely waking, rubbing her cheek against his bare skin.

Oh, hell yeah. All Gwen's.

He found himself grinning.

She lifted her head; he thought he discerned a frown. A reach, a stretch, a soft grunt, all during which she managed to push herself quite firmly against him, and a light clicked on. Mac made a sound of protest, squinting away, but figured it out quickly enough— the inadequate little dresser lamp, relocated here to the floor.

She said, "Was that a *grin?*"

He said, "Come here," and trapped her leg beneath his own.

"Me?" she asked, waking fast, brow lifted—some sarcasm there. Challenging him.

He thought back over it—the moment in front of the hotel, the night of battle and illness, the day crammed with such intensities of vulnerability and trust that might not come in a decade of partnership. "Let me," he said, pulling her close with that one numbed arm, abruptly enough so she lost all her breath in a short laugh, "be perfectly clear."

She let herself fall on top of him—hesitating there for a moment, pressing against him from top to bottom and tangled along the way. When her smile came again, it was slow. "Yeah," she said, moving subtly against him—not so subtle that it didn't inspire an instant catch of his breath, a tremble of return thrust. "This was pretty much there from the start, wasn't it?"

Probably he was supposed to say words. He didn't

have them. She took his face in her hands—thumbs stroking the stubble of the past day, mouth coming down on his, hair tumbling free to surround them. Her leg twined between his thighs, her shirt crept up to give him soft skin, her breasts pressed against his chest with nipples sprung hard. One hand left his face to creep down his chest, lying flat against his stomach and reaching lower.

And all of it, *all* of it, was his to feel. His…and hers. The swell of sensation, the rush of heat. The groan in his throat born of wanting, the wicked hard thump of his heart pounding in his chest and ears. Gwen's hand reached his belt buckle. He sucked his stomach away, making it easy.

She froze, however briefly, and then tipped her head back and laughed.

"Ha ha?" he said, breathless and bemused.

"Ha," she said. "Do you see us? Rolling around on the floor a day after we first saw each other, one of us handcuffed to the bed and the other of us about to go down his pants?"

"It works for me," he said and then cursed softly as her hand slipped in under the belt. "It…totally…uh…"

"Yeah," she said. "It works for me, too."

And a moment later, he managed to say, more or less, "Cuffs?"

She left his zipper alone to push back her hair and regard him with regrettably serious eyes. "Ditch the knife-sword thing?"

Two syllables. He could do it. "Pocket."

"Oh!" she said. "Pocket diving!" And went for it.

He cursed, and crushed her close, and forgot he was supposed to be kissing her—straining against the cuff, straining against her hand, straining against sanity in the very best kind of way.

"Yeah," she said. "That *is* an impressive...sword."

"Cuffs, dammit!"

"Must be the other pocket."

It was, in fact. By the time she found the blade, working it free and withdrawing it with two very cautious fingers, he'd used his one free arm to roll her on top of him and start in on her neck—tender, silky skin, warm beneath her hair, smelling of her shampoo, tasting faintly of salt and ahh, there, that little earlobe with its three little gold hoops—

She stiffened, making a soft noise in her throat.

"Uh-huh," he murmured, right into her ear, and nibbled. His hand worked its way down her back, found her waistband, slipped under to cup soft, warm flesh.

"Oh," she breathed and shifted to offer better access, trembling against him just as he'd been straining moments earlier.

He jerked her a little closer. *"Cuffs."*

"Cuffs," she repeated blankly. "Oh! Cuffs!" And sat up, straddling him, tossing the blade across the room with vigor and moving against him so perfectly that his eyes rolled back and his hips lifted. She froze right where she was, hands at his chest, her gasp the only sound in the room. *"Oh,"* she said again on the next breath. "You— I—"

Not that he could truly hear her. Not with the blood pounding through every part of him and his body straining and the heat gathering, perfectly normal just-between-two-people heat.

*"You!"* She pulled off her shirt in one swift motion. No wonder those breasts had felt so perfect in every way, because there they were in that dim light and they so obviously were completely unfettered by a bra. She stood long enough to jerk off her shorts and that dim light shone golden on pale and lightly freckled skin. By then all he could do was whisper, quite hoarsely indeed, "Cuffs…"

She'd already gotten the belt; she bent to his pants, pulling them over his hips with quick efficiency, all the quicker when he lifted to make it easier but only as far as the shoes he still wore. She was more careful with the underwear, cupping him until he growled, reaching for her—

Underwear, gone. Gwen, coming down around him in damp, ready warmth, both of them crying out, clutching—gone mindless with what gathered between them. He grabbed her hip; she clung to his arm, bracing herself against his chest as they fell into one another, their cries building and mingling and panting through the air. They spiraled right through intensity and right past sanity. Gwen stiffened, head falling back; Mac strained, lifting her, every muscle corded tight and reaching—

And she wailed and he cried out, and the whole of it went spilling through him—through all the open places she'd made for him, the purity of what it was to simply be. Giving him back himself…giving him *her*.

And then they lay collapsed and panting together,

boneless unto absurdity, sweat quickly chilling. Mac finally gathered enough wit and enough breath to say, hoarsely and somewhat pathetically, "Cuffs? Now?"

And dammit, sprawled there on his chest, Gwen simply and helplessly began to laugh.

"I'm sorry," she said, but then couldn't help another giggle.

"Convincing." He looked as disgruntled as a man could look after mind-blowing sex, inspecting her first aid work. If anything, his expression grew more disgruntled yet—not that she didn't expect it. "Pink," he said. "Hot pink."

"You wear it well?" she offered. And then laughed.

Because, yeah. Mind-blowing sex. Decision made, chances taken.

Not physically. She'd seen the healing in action... believed the truth of that, and its effect throughout his body. Safe sex, if her body had been the only thing involved.

Chances with her heart...of that she was less certain. This man and his blade, his history—his life spiraling toward what her father's had been...and how it had ended. She hadn't meant to give him quite so much of herself.

But it was only what he had given her.

So maybe she'd pay for it. But she wouldn't regret it.

She touched the bright pink bandaging, smoothing one of the self-sticking edges. "Honestly," she said. "It was all they had. That time of night, driving that twitchy Jeep of yours on unfamiliar city streets...I was just glad to stumble onto a big box store that had something besides duct tape."

His glance was wistful; clearly the duct tape would have worked for him.

"Confident men can wear pink," she said firmly. She stroked a thumb along the inside of his elbow, there above where she'd secured the pendant—indeed, with duct tape—snugly against his skin. She purred inwardly when his breath caught.

"Trying," he said, "to think."

"I'm not sure why." She ran her nails lightly up his arm to his shoulder; he exhaled in a gust and gave up, tipping his head back against the bed to absorb the touch.

They still sat on the floor, up against the bed, using the bedspread for their picnic blanket. Gwen had folded a corner of the bedspread over her shoulder, not yet interested in searching for her clothes. Mac had divested himself of his shoes and pants, kicking away his briefs—not much of those to begin with, and she almost wished he'd don them just so she could take them off all over again. Now he leaned against the bed, one leg propped up.

Okay, that worked for her. A body like this? Maybe it never needed to be covered.

He touched his arm, frowned. Nothing to do with the pink. "How bad is it?"

That took her mind from the briefs or lack thereof, all right, and she winced. "How bad does it feel?"

He sent her a sharp glance, and she lifted a shoulder. "It's probably about that bad. That blade has no care for you."

"No," he murmured. "For a while...we worked together, as strange as it seems. But now it's...broken through. I don't know how much longer I can control it."

"That man at that warehouse seems to think not very much longer." Gwen scowled, a look meant for *that man*. "He talked about the wild road."

"Right," Mac said. "When I give over to the blade to become a monster among men." He shook his head. "You know, I was just your average slacker guy, following work down the road and happy enough to do it. Figuring that one day I'd head back to the family business, but until then, just making my own way."

Right. The guy who'd stepped into the middle of a scuffle outside a bar because the other fellow looked like he needed help. The guy who'd spent this day following trouble around simply so he could stop it— doing his best to bend the blade's hedonistic inclinations to good.

"I doubt," Gwen said, her voice suddenly tight around the world's biggest lump in her throat, "that you were ever an average slacker guy."

His grin was slow and maybe just a little bit delicious. He curved one hand around the back of her head and pulled her over for a kiss that sent a great big wave of heat and longing straight from her toes to her mouth. Her hands crept around his chest, sliding down tight skin, quite greedy. She could have done that possibly forever had he not tipped his head away. For that moment, his eyes had gone serious again. "You know...I can't wear this thing forever."

*I am twenty-nine years old, and I have been wearing this pendant forever.*

"You could," she said. "Whatever it is. It's yours. Maybe this is what it's been waiting for."

The smile was bittersweet this time. "It would take only a slip. When we weren't expecting it. When we weren't ready for the consequences. No, I think this blade is something I have to face. One way or the other."

"Not yet," she whispered.

"No," he said. "Not yet." And just like that, he rolled up to his knees, tucked his arms beneath her, and lifted her onto the bed, coming right down on top of her. She thought to reach for him—to play her hands over all the favorite places she'd already found in him, the ones she already knew would make him forget how to think.

She thought wrong. He slid his hands up her arms, clasping fingers through hers, pressing them back into the pillow. Where, she suddenly realized, she was as good as cuffed. *Turnabout.* And where she both giggled and squirmed as he traced the line of her throat with his tongue—hesitating only long enough to both nip and soothe and murmur, "Okay?"

"Shut up," she said. "I'm busy." And not completely without recourse, because he hadn't quite pinned her legs, had he? And she was perfectly capable of wrapping them around him, shifting around until she found what she wanted.

Definitely one of the favorite places.

"We're not—" he reminded her, and the ragged nature of his voice was nearly as gratifying as the sweet, fiery insanity that had apparently replaced all the blood in her body.

"We're not—" He tried again, and the concern came through this time.

Oh. That. "I am," she said, arching her neck to offer him better access. "On the Pill. Which I knew the first time. And you said you were safe—"

"Healthy," he corrected her, fingers tightening through hers as she dug her heels into the back of his thighs and shifted her hips. "I haven't been *safe* for a very long time now. And oh, *please,* do that again."

She did.

And for a moment she thought she had him. No brains, all body—oh, glorious body—all groan and fierce hazy need into the night.

Right up until the moment he slipped both her hands into the grip of his one and turned his other hand loose on her body.

It turned out that he was a fast learner, too.

Gwen woke an hour later and eased from the bed to leave him there. Sleeping—the normal way. Healing—the normal way. Exhausted and worshipped and sated.

And then she dressed and went out to the hotel's back lot to cry while sitting on a curb beside desultory bushes that a thousand dogs had no doubt used for a toilet and pretending it was private.

"Do you cry for him or for yourself?"

So much for privacy.

But no sense of *intent*. No warning. Just the hard-to-define trickle that she often felt around Mac, when it came to that—a thing independent of the pendant. So, no panic, either.

Gwen lifted her head to look through tears at the new intruder, not much helped by the glaring streetlight. "Having a moment, here," she said, squinting at a tidy and petite woman with a wash of natural blond highlights and a face of striking if not beautiful features, angled Slavic cheeks on a narrow face and eyes to match. "Having a freaking *day*."

"I can see that."

Gwen squinted harder, bringing that tidiness into focus. *All* of it—clothes, hair, even posture. Slender and curvy and tastefully dressed to show it. And Gwen—too moderate in all ways to be lush and curvy or beguilingly petite, dressed again in horrible wrinkled sports shorts and a bloody T-shirt—scowled. "Go to hell."

The woman smiled. "Trying really hard to avoid that."

She experienced that hard-to-define trickle that she often felt around Mac. Gwen's head came up all the way. Fear washed down her spine. "You have a blade."

And so had that man.

The woman opened her hand, displaying a small knife with a stunted, curved blade, just big enough to fill her palm. No mistaking the eerie play of light on metal, no matter how subtle. "Baitlia," she said. "Just showing off now. So very eclectic." She tipped it to the light. "Yes, Baitlia, we see. Spanish skinning blade.

Very nice. Now behave." At Gwen's trepidation, she added, "We're in a truce."

Yeah, right. She had the feeling that man would have said he had a truce with his blade, too. A truce of *evil,* that's what.

"They're not very subtle," Gwen said. "Glowing like that. Are we supposed to not notice?"

That, of all things, took the woman back some; she closed her hand over the blade, extinguishing its faint gleam, and didn't exactly answer. She tipped her head at the hotel. "He's on the edge, isn't he?"

Gwen only frowned, her gaze darting to where the van had been and not at all surprised to find it missing. That man knew where to find them if he really wanted them—he'd made that perfectly clear. That he'd give Mac some time to *turn* on his own...that, too, had been clear.

But she knew nothing about this woman. "What are you doing here? Were you *following* us? Did you—"

*Did you know we were kidnapped this afternoon? Were you part of that? Or did you see it and not help?*

But the woman shook her head. "My name is Natalie," she said. "And I've been waiting. We figured you were staying here. Hoped it, anyway." She hesitated, taking a step closer and then holding off when Gwen raised her chin in warning. "He is, isn't he? On the edge. You need to know...we can help."

She should have caught it the first time. "*We?* You and that very friendly man who threatened us last night?"

Natalie whoever-she-was bit her lip. "Warned, not threatened. And not you. Your friend."

Gwen was startled at her own scowl—at her instant reaction. Same thing.

It must have told Natalie something; understanding crossed her face. "That's why you're out here. You're crying for *him*."

"For both of us," Gwen snapped, but it sounded more ragged than she wanted.

"We can help."

Gwen just stared at her. So self-possessed, so neatly self-contained. Unlike Gwen and her fast-moving mouth, her ability to skim the surface of life without really living it.

Until, she realized, this past day. In which she'd laughed more, lived more, *loved* more...

"You shouldn't be going through this on your own," Natalie said, trying again. "You have no idea what's going on—"

"And you do?" Gwen tipped her head. "I'm guessing not. Because if you had, you'd have been going after *the right man* last night. And today. You know, the one who tortures and kills people and likes it? Unless, of course, you're on his side. So you see? You're either no good at this, or you're on the wrong side."

This time Natalie did come closer, and Gwen scrambled to her feet, putting the distance back between them. Knives could be thrown, and she couldn't do anything about that. But she wasn't putting herself within sword-length of anyone who held a blade that glowed.

Natalie got the message. She threw her hands up in brief frustration. "Ah, *Devin*. I told you—" And then stopped herself. "I'm going to leave a card on the curb. Phone, address, the usual. In case you change your mind. But you need to know—there's a way for him to fight this. Devin has been there. He's done it."

Gwen thought of the pendant taped to Mac's arm. Of the relief it gave him, the price the knife exacted when it returned. The fierce freedom in his lovemaking, in his care for her—and the knowledge of exactly how much they'd lose when the pendant gave way, or lost its contact, or Mac just plain took it off, ready to face a battle he was already so clearly losing. She said with bitter certainty, "You don't know anything."

Another woman might have backed away, faced with such emotion from a stranger. This one stood her ground. "I know that Baitlia and I will never reach that point. I make my own decisions, keep my own control."

*Baitlia.* The name Natalie had used before. *It has a name.*

Did Mac's blade have a name? Did he know it?

Natalie didn't give her any room to think about it. "You should know—your friend should know—that it works. That it *can* work. The blades yearn for redemption…and they can't help but sabotage it in any way possible. Read about the scorpion and the frog."

She didn't have to. Orphaned daughter of an insane blade wielder, she might be. Foster daughter of an aunt who had cared for her without nurturing her, she might be…an indifferent scholar, she might be.

But in spite of it all—*because of it all*—she knew that cautionary tale about the scorpion and the frog.

Natalie crossed her arms. "There's something big and bad going on in this city. We know it, and we know your friend is involved. You can help him, or you can watch while events overtake him. Events, by the way, *will* include us."

Scorpion, riding across the river on frog's back. Killing them both halfway across, unable to stop himself from stinging frog. True to his nature in spite of himself.

Natalie asked, "What's your name?"

*Am I scorpion, too?* So deeply, so suddenly tangled with a man who carried death in his pocket and clung to his own persistently heroic nature with nothing more than thinning tenacity? She'd seen it coming. She'd seen what there was to fear. And she'd given herself to him anyway. "Gwen," she said, seeing little harm in it against all that.

"And your friend?"

But Gwen shook her head, offering only a knowing smile. "Not my name to give you."

Natalie smiled back—a genuine one at that. "I didn't think so. I'll leave the card. We're at Compton Sawyer's old estate when you're ready." She made a face. "Devin is going to be really mad I told you that."

And then, as quiet as Mac—full of that same confidence of movement and yet something else again, something more contained and balanced—she left.

Gwen picked up the card.

\* \* \*

Gwen let herself back into the hotel room, latching and chaining the door as quietly as possible.

Not that it made a difference. When that man wanted them again, he'd come for them. And after him, nothing else really seemed frightening enough to chain the door against.

Still, she did it, and turned to the mess they'd made of the room. The air conditioner blasted out cold air as best it could, still working against the retained heat of the day.

Mac slept like a boy. Not in body—not with those shoulders, that lean, strapping form, those long legs. But in the vulnerable intensity of it, the sheet pulled up just barely high enough to cover his hips and one leg sticking out. One arm hung over the edge of the bed; the other over his eyes. The habitual tension on his face had smoothed, leaving his mouth fascinating for the curve of it in repose.

Gwen put the business card on the bedside table, stripped off her clothes and crawled into bed with him. She pressed a kiss to that mouth, watched it stir in the faintest of sleeping smiles, and snuggled up close, pulling the sheet up to cover them both.

She watched him sleep.

On this night, Devin James found the view from the estate's immense office window to be not nearly immense enough.

He paced the grounds instead.

Not that she'd be pleased to find him fretting at

her solo foray into the city. *How fair is that?* she'd point out. It wasn't as though he didn't go out on his own more often than not, following Anheriel's call—finding trouble and stopping it.

It wasn't as though he hadn't done as much this very night, and now bore the elusive scars to prove it.

Nasty out there tonight.

Really nasty.

She'd point out that she had a blade, too, and that it had a vested interest in keeping her alive. It was too young, too new with her to even start playing games—and with the grounding and balancing techniques she was now also teaching him, it would likely never get that foothold.

All true.

*But, dammit, you only just started!* She was toned and fit; she ran and did tai chi. But she didn't know the subtleties of living with the blade. And unlike Devin, she hadn't spent the first years of her life in a tough neighborhood, slipping into a kickboxing routine at Enrique's gym. She hadn't watched her brother absorb the blade into his life, or stuck by his side during the learning phase…during the changes as they'd happened.

He'd seen what she hadn't—a man without understanding, on the verge of taking the wild road. He could well recognize it again.

So he had no intention of cutting their intruder any slack, and he damned well didn't want her anywhere near him.

And he damned well suspected that's exactly where she was.

The faint burn of healing washed through his blood; he ignored it. Nothing but bruises, maybe something going on with his forearm. It wouldn't get bad. He could sleep it off later.

He didn't hear the Prius slip into the secluded driveway. Never did. But even an electric motor couldn't change the distinctive sound of a quietly closed car door; by the time she reached the long covered front porch of the blocky old Southwest mansion, he was waiting for her.

No blood. No bruises. She looked as put together as always, and Baitlia, tucked away in its pocket, roused no more than a sneer of greeting from Anheriel.

Natalie stopped short to take him in, dismay on her face. "One of us," she said, "looks better than the other of us." And she stepped forward to take his chin and tip his face aside for a better look, complete with a *tsk* noise.

His manly pride stung. "Hey," he said. "There were a lot of them. And they were bigger than me. And I was trying not to kill them."

"Uh-huh," she said, smudging a thumb along his cheek. "Was it like last night?"

"More of the same," he agreed. "Lots of little spontaneous flares by people who aren't really any good at it."

She gave him a pointed look, up and down; he returned it with a growl, reaching out to yank her closer. Very much closer, at which point he put his arms around her and—*ow!*—swore resoundingly.

"Point made," Natalie said. "I thought that arm looked wrong."

"You never mind," he told her. "I have caramel popcorn inside, and *True Grit* in the player. And I unmade the bed. I say we race for it."

She rested a cheek against his shoulder, but she sighed. "There's something scary going on in this city, Devin. I was listening to the radio news…"

He sighed right along with her. Business first, even as he tucked her up close and breathed in the scent of her, letting it ease the humming burn of the blade. "The cops are riled—they're traveling in groups. Watching their backs. They see it, too."

"It's all about the hate," she said. "People hating other people because of their skin or their religion or their preferences or their politics—"

"Or their first language." He'd stopped a beat-down on a young immigrant during the evening. It had taken only a glance to communicate with the young man across the language barrier, but the hate group couldn't hear a word he'd said.

"Hating," Natalie said. "Little eruptions of it from people who have been nurturing it inside."

"Hating," he agreed.

"And you think the new wielder is doing it?"

That took him by surprise. "I… What? That guy?" He thought back to what he'd seen, what he'd felt. Unsettled, unfocused…a guy who'd been into something and had let it get the best of him. One who'd been in the nexus of the evening's incidents.

One who'd needed to be warned.

"He's involved," Devin told her.

"Mmm."

*Mmm* was never good.

"You disagree?"

She didn't answer right away. She held him; she breathed with him. Long enough so he started to consider the way they fit together, and that was never good—not if he had thinking to do.

Finally, she said, "You didn't say she loved him."

"What?" So much for the thinking.

"The woman who was with him. She loves him." She tipped her head back to look up at him. "She has some understanding of what's happening, but not enough. She sees the blades—even when Baitlia was silent, she saw it for what it was. Having her with him...this could change things."

She ran her hand down his back, and her expression grew more thoughtful. "He needs help, there's no doubt. But, dammit, Devin, they've labeled us enemies. They think we're in league with whatever's going on here—and something *is*. Someone messed with them today. I think someone was killed, too, but if there was a blade involved—"

Right. Body and blood devoured. Just a missing persons report waiting to happen.

Okay. So they had a trust problem when it would have been convenient to start on neutral ground with this intruder. He sighed, annoyed at the situation in general. Worried about it, too. He could walk this city all night, but he couldn't be everywhere. "It seemed like the thing to do at the time. The guy's a walking trouble magnet, and he's about to go over."

She nodded. "I think he probably is. But we have to fix this. If what's happening out there isn't about him—if he's just gotten caught up in the middle—then there's something else going on. And I think it's big."

"Yeah," he murmured, kissing the top of her head. "It's big."

# Chapter 11

$M$ac woke to tangled sheets and tangled limbs and tangled thoughts.

Tangled, but all his own.

His arms still throbbed beneath their pink wrappings; the pendant pressed into his skin beneath a stiff layer of duct tape. Pink cyborg warrior. No burn, no blade-given healing.

The tangle of limbs was mostly Gwen, delightful soft skin pressed against his in every possible way.

"Healthy," he murmured into her ear, "but not *safe*." And loved her awake to prove it, watching sleepy confusion warm to a languid sensuality, her hands reaching and then clutching—that particular surprised and husky noise he'd learned to wring from her. Once, and then he buried himself in her and did it all over again, greedy with the scent of her, the sound of her, the gift of her.

While it lasted.

He left her catching her breath and made the shower quick and careful. Even then the water in the wake of the night's activities shifted the duct tape—shifted the pendant—enough so a warning slice of retribution doubled him over beneath the pounding water.

*Oh, yeah.* He straightened, slow to pull himself back together. Much better to choose his own time and place.

He opened the bathroom door wearing nothing more than a pair of briefs, and ran right into Gwen. She burst into laughter as she pushed past him to close the door on his heels, trailing the sheet she wore.

"Laughter," he told the door, "is not the appropriate response to seeing me naked."

"Not naked enough," she told him, muffled by the door. "Go away. I'm busy."

Fair enough. He pulled a protein drink from the fridge, a fresh pair of jeans from his giant duffel, and downed one while climbing into the other. The knife found its way into his front pocket, and he pulled a plain heather T-shirt over his head, careful of his arms. He left his wrists to the open air—bruised, swollen and weeping—and his duct-tape arm torque peeking out from beneath his sleeve.

As he sat on the end of the bed to pull on a pair of socks, he eyed the discarded handcuffs—lying there, right next to the key—and inevitably, he scooped them up.

He didn't know who he'd be when the blade came back. That was the hard truth of it.

Gwen popped out of the bathroom long enough to grab her newly acquired toiletries and disappear again. By the time she came out for good, still draped in the sheet and heading for her suitcase, Mac had a pretty good idea what they'd be doing next.

Not what they wanted to be doing, he was sure.

"We need to go back to that warehouse," he told her.

That stopped her short, clothes gathered in her hand, sheet slipping and blue eyes narrowing. "I think some words just mistakenly came out of your mouth."

He grinned. "Nice try. You don't have to come if you don't want to."

Spark showed in those eyes, faint freckles on pale gleaming skin and the red in her hair glinting with its dampness. "Damned right I don't want to. But I don't want you to, either. We need to figure out what's going on, but *surely* there are other options."

He lifted a shoulder. "Wander the city and follow the hate? We already know it's out there and where it's coming from. I need to know more about the warehouse guy. I need to know if he's working with other blades." Such as the man who'd accosted them near the hotel, his words blunt: *This is my turf.*

"That's it?" she asked. "Not interested in who that woman was, or why he took her, or why he *killed* her?"

"She was no one," Mac said harshly. "She was everyone. It doesn't matter to him. He took her for the same reason he offered her to me—for his blade to feed on. And if I'm going to stop him, I've got to know more about him."

She narrowed her eyes at him. "And you think he'll have left some honkin' big clue for us to find? As opposed to, say…a *guard* of some sort?"

"I think he underestimates us." Mac looked right at her. "I think he underestimates *you*. We wouldn't be here now if he hadn't."

"Bullshit," she said, but her flush looked pleased. "If I hadn't been there, you wouldn't have hung around talking to him. You who can see in the dark, you with your ill-mannered blade. You'd have taken out those guys and gone for him. Or you wouldn't have left the diner parking lot in the first place."

There was something to that.

"Doesn't change anything," Mac said. "You got us out of what it was." He touched the duct tape on his arm, pushing cold, lumpy metal beneath it against his skin. "I don't think he knows about this, either. Maybe he gets some sense of it—I did—or maybe not. But if he'd truly known, then he wouldn't have let us go."

"He might not let us go a second time." She'd scrambled into her clothes, a pale green summer top of some filmy material with cap sleeves and a neckline of which he approved, and white capri pants that turned out to be perfectly snug across her bottom and loose below the knee. "Are you listening to me, or are you looking at my ass?"

"Looking at your ass," he said promptly. "And I don't think he'll be hanging around at the warehouse. It's too exposed."

She plunked her hands on her hips, pointedly turning her bottom in another direction as she picked up her sport sandals. "And what if he is?"

He shrugged. "We'll knock." And then, at her impatience, he added, "I need to know. I don't think he'll have left any easy clues, but maybe the blade can pick up on something."

Alarm replaced her impatience. "But that means—"

"That's the other thing," he said gently. "It's a big place. You'll be safe."

"When you let the blade back in." Her voice was flat with disbelief. "You *can't*—"

"I have to!" he snapped, up on his feet and stalking in close, ignoring her widened eyes. "You don't get it, Gwen. This pendant isn't a magic pill. I'm free, but the blade is *there*—it's trying to get in. *Always.* And if it does that, in a place and time not of my own choosing? If it does that while we're in public? What if it happens while I'm around someone's kid? Someone's mother? While I'm with *you*?" One more step, taking her upper arms with a ferocity he hadn't expected to pour out so unfettered. "Because that's what I want, Gwen. *You.* I don't know you, but dammit, I *do.* Call it one of the blade's few gifts."

She reached across his chest with one encumbered arm, touching the duct tape. "And this," she whispered, more sadly than not. "So fast…"

"Sometimes," he said, easing his grip on her to rub his hands more gently up and down soft bare skin, "it's like that. Even without such things."

"It's why I came to Albuquerque," she said simply,

meeting his gaze without qualm. Big, pale blue, full
of life—and then suddenly narrowing. "Not that you
should think I'm a pushover. I still have a brain, you
know. I can do what's best for me."

A smile tugged the corner of his mouth. "Noted."
But then he had to do it—to take a deep breath and
push. "But this warehouse thing…it has to be done."

She turned away from him with a grumble; he let
her go. "Check it out," she said, so obviously changing the subject as she pointed to her suitcase. "My
purse was in there, too. Along with the credit cards
I've already replaced—those should get here today."
She picked it up, pawed briefly through the contents,
plucked out a small ID wallet and slipped it into her
back pocket. It hardly made a ripple against her magnificent—

She cast him a look, brow raised, and he rearranged
his visual focus. "Grab something quick to eat," he
suggested. "I think the sooner we do this, the better."

"I'm not convinced of that," she told him, not missing a beat. But she found a yogurt drink in the little
fridge and sat down at the edge of the bed, where she
picked up a business card, turning it over in her hand.
She glanced at him, tucking the card away with the ID
wallet. "But I have to admit…you're the only one who
really knows. The only one inside your head."

"Not exactly," he said. "That's the damned problem." But he held out his hand, and she took it as she
rose from the bed, casting a glance out the window behind her. For all they'd loved hard during the night—
for all he'd fought through—they'd slept hard, too,

and beyond the quiescent window air conditioner, the shadows were still strung out long with the early hour.

"Come," he said gently, and she raised her chin, swiped the room key off the table, and tugged him on toward the door, out toward the stairs. At his Jeep, he handed her the keys, fending off her sharp look. "I'm good," he said—and he had been, since that moment in the shower. "But I'm not taking any chances."

She made a little face. "No guarantees on the driving. This shift—"

"Has personality." He bent to clear the passenger seat, gathering up the garbage from the trip into the city.

She glanced at her VW Bug and its dead battery and made another little face—this one of acquiescence— and opened the Jeep door.

He looked out over the hotel access road. "You know, I don't have any idea how we got back here."

"The warehouse is off I-25," she told him, settling into the driver's seat. "It's not actually that far." She gave him a glance as she inserted the keys and added, "Oh, you mean *how*. I stole their van. Where do you think I got the handcuffs? I figured they'd know where to find it, and I guess they did. Of course, I *did* leave the keys in it, so maybe someone else found it first. That would be their bad luck, I'm thinking."

"We should relocate," he said, sliding into the Jeep and buckling in—and would have kicked himself for not thinking of it sooner, except when exactly had he had time to think at all?

"He could have had us at the warehouse if he'd

really wanted us." She backed out of their spot with
the care of someone who didn't quite know the vehicle. "He quite specifically *didn't* want us. He wants
you on his side, and he's pretty sure he's going to get
you. No need to come after us when he thinks you're
going to come to him."

"He's right about that," Mac said under his breath.
It just wouldn't be how he expected.

"Besides, you broke some of his people."

Mac snorted. "I'm sure he has more." He found
himself scowling out the window. "I just wish I knew
what he really wants."

She gave him a startled glance, missing a chance
to pull out into traffic. "Don't you know?" she asked.
"Didn't you see it?" She bit her lip, marshaling her
thoughts as she found an opportunity and got them
moving, no mean hand on the cranky shift after all.
"Maybe you don't remember, given…the way things
were. He's just like your blade—what you told me of
it. When he brought that woman out yesterday…I think
it was all he could do to offer her to you."

*"Not to me,"* Mac said, and his words came so hard
and sudden that they startled him nearly as much as
they'd startled her. He took a deep breath. "Sorry. I
mean… Yeah. Sorry. Touchy. Just—"

"I get it." But her voice was quiet, and she pondered
her next words with obvious care. "I think he's doing
more than glorying in whatever's going on in this city."
She didn't have to explain that; they'd both been in
the middle of it. "I think he's making it happen. And
I think he's really, really good at it."

The words hit home with the starkness of truth. Truth…but they still knew nothing. Not really. "All the more reason to do this." Mac closed a hand over his pocket…resolute.

And yet some part of him already regretted the decision to bring Gwen into this at all. *I should have turned around when I saw her at that diner.* If this turned out to be bigger than he was…

"Did you say something?"

He shook his head, watching the highway exits, watching their route. "Just…be careful. Don't…" He took a breath. "Don't fight me. If this thing goes… If they find us there—" He turned to look at her then. "I need to know, going in, that you'll run like hell. This is a last chance for me—it's something I have to do. You don't. I need to know—"

"Stop it," she said, sharply at that. "Trying to drive, here. That's hard to do when I can't decide between smacking you silly or climbing into your lap."

He ducked his head, hiding the bittersweet grin.

They were silent until they reached the exit, Gwen gearing down for the city streets and then quickly turning north on a less traveled road. Over a spur of tracks, a quick left, and—

"Yeah," he said. "This looks familiar." A bright wash of morning light, a perfectly ordinary building, a smattering of activity all around it and truck backup beepers piercing the air.

Gwen pulled up near the door—where the van had been the day before—and then, with an obvious second thought, reoriented the Jeep to point in a getaway direction, leaving the keys in the ignition. There she sat for a moment, looking at him—frank and open and worried. "You doing okay?"

"Still," he said. "I'll let you know."

"I doubt that," she said smartly. She got out of the car, leaving him there to laugh, however briefly.

He walked into the warehouse as if he owned it. Quietly, eyes not nearly as sensitive to the dim light as if the blade hadn't been blocked out...controlled by the baffling pendant that Gwen had long treasured as the last vestige of a father who had tried to kill her with his own blade.

There was, he thought suddenly, so very much more to this demon blade than he'd ever guessed. He *should* have. But he'd been too complacent, too willing to trust his ability to keep the walls between them. Too willing to let it ride.

Gwen breathed lightly at his shoulder—spooked and wary, and he knew it without any intervention from the blade at all. He took her hand, and they stood in silence. Assessing. Listening.

Finally, Gwen murmured, "If they were gonna come for us, I think it would have happened by now."

"Or they're playing with us." Maybe he shouldn't have said it, the way her hand tightened around his. But if the man was here, and if he did indeed have a demon blade that acted as Mac's did, then Gwen's trepidation would be a fine and savory appetizer to what awaited them.

She needed to know. To think that way.

Together, they walked the interior of this main

room, full of the usual warehouse detritus—pallets stacked over here, a few empty plastic barrels over there, the catwalk lining three walls and an oddball projection of structures for various smaller rooms or offices. The door through which they'd dragged the woman led to a warren of stumpy halls.

Mac backed out again, peering up at the catwalk.

"That's what you really want," Gwen murmured, pretty much reading his mind. "To see where that man was. Right where he stood."

"Right where he stood," Mac agreed. He loosened his grip on her hand—giving her an obvious choice—but she stayed with him as he followed his nose through those back halls. When he found the narrow wooden stairs, her hand slipped away—but she still rested her fingers at the small of his back. Just a small connection.

The stairway spilled out onto the catwalk. Plenty sturdy, good railings…the perfect vantage point from which to oversee the contents of a warehouse.

Or a killing field.

But the man had left nothing of himself here.

The blade slipped into his mind, into his body—lightning-fast, shredding nerves. The vast warehouse space wheeled around him.

"Mac?"

Because there he was, grappling with the handrail as if it was the only thing that kept him anchored to this world at all. "Still here," he said hoarsely. "Probably not for much longer."

And this time she said nothing. As if she'd seen

enough to believe he was right. She lingered back by the door, watching him.

Back to the task at hand. His thumb slipped over rough wood. He glanced down—and then looked twice. The deep mark exposed pale new wood at the edges...a fresh wound. A single, plunging strike, gone deeper and cleaner than any ordinary blade.

"Yeah," he said out loud.

"What?" She pushed close to see and squinted down at the mark. "How— No, never mind. We know how, don't we? But why? Showing off?"

"Something like that." Mac looked out over the empty space, tried to imagine himself in the man's shoes—watching himself and Gwen...watching as he struggled with the blade, both winning and losing.

Satisfaction. Power. This view had given him everything—as well as the perfect vantage point from which to wield the blade he'd eventually thrown.

"Showing off," he repeated. "And leaving me a message."

"Leaving *us* a message," Gwen told him. "He just doesn't know it yet." She rubbed her arms, looking around the space. "This place gives me the creeps."

"Something would be wrong if it didn't." Just a little too abruptly, he turned away from the railing, heading back down the stairs. No obvious clues here, but then...that would have been too easy.

A man with hate in his heart and the ability to wield it as he wielded his blade. Where had he come from? What did he truly want?

And how far would he go to get it?

Gwen was the one to nail the important question as she descended the stairs on his heels. "How are we gonna find out more about this guy? It's not like we can search for him on LinkedIn."

"Should've gotten the van's license plate," Mac said.

Gwen laughed, dark humor in the face of it all. "And done what with it?"

"Okay," he said, acknowledging the flaw in that with his own dark humor. "Good point." He stopped suddenly, turning around on the stairs; one step behind, she was now nearly of a height with him. "What we do," he said, "is follow the hate. I let the blade back in, and I follow the hate. Right to the source."

She scowled. Opened her mouth. Closed it. Looked away, a flush settling on her cheeks and her eyes bright in the dim light. So clearly wanting to argue it all— the part about letting the blade back in, the part about getting any closer at all to that hate. But without the blade, he couldn't trace the hate—or feel it coming. And without the hate, he couldn't figure out what was happening here...or how to protect them from it.

Finally, her voice no more than a strained whisper, she said, "One thing at a time."

"Okay." He passed a gentle thumb over her cheek, and when she leaned into it, ever so slightly, he let his hand travel around and under her bound hair, sweeping past her ear and behind her nape. "One thing at a time."

He would have hesitated, a chance for her to say *not here, not now*—but she didn't hesitate at all. She kissed him hard, full of unspoken words.

But only until an anguished, animal cry rang through

the back warren of halls and rooms. They jerked apart and turned to it as one. "Stay here!" he told her, with little to no hope that she actually would.

She didn't. She was right on his heels as he followed the sound, a series of hopeless wails that led him past closed doors and pretty much straight to the source, plunging into enemy territory without care or preparation.

That one door was open. Maybe it had been a lunch room. An unfinished counter and sink arrangement ran the length of one wall, complete with an empty cutout of refrigerator-width. Cheap, filthy industrial tiles covered the floor, and a stench filled the air.

"Ugh!" Gwen said as it hit her, coming up behind him and still unable to see the room. He blocked her way—wanting to warn her, wanting to make it less horrible.

Because he'd already seen the dog. Chained to the wall, both front feet crushed in leg-hold traps, and both of those nailed straight into the floor to keep it stretched out. The stench came from its own filth...its blood, its fear. It stopped wailing when it saw them, whining under its breath instead.

But Mac couldn't fill the whole doorway. She ducked under his arm, her hand resting on his stomach—and then froze there. When she caught her breath, she swore resoundingly. "What is *this* supposed to prove?"

"It's a message," Mac said, barely able to say it around the cold sick feeling in his throat. "A gift. A last straw. He knew I'd be back."

"But he doesn't know you have the pendant," Gwen realized. "He thought this would tip you over... Oh!" This last as the dog looked at her and wagged the very tip of its tail, hopeful beyond hope. Big, brawny black Labrador-type, no collar, no tags. In the wrong place at the wrong time. "Oh," Gwen said again. "We have to—" And she looked at Mac, beyond determined.

Mac couldn't muster the same determination...only grim reality. "It would be kinder to put him down. Right here."

Gwen recoiled. "No!"

She didn't see it. Not all of it. Not yet. What he would be, if he lost this fight. What he would do. "Gwen, I've got to get rid of this pendant. And once I do—"

She looked from him to the dog and back again. "Oh, my God," she said. "You think you'll do it."

"I think," he said, gritting the words out, "that I'm not going to be myself for a while. I think it'll be hours before we can get him to help—or you, if it comes to that. I think circumstances could keep either of us from helping him at all."

She shoved past him. "I think I'm going to be true to myself right up until something prevents it," she said, walking right up to the dog. "How about you?"

He looked away from her for what seemed like a very long time. When he could talk again, he said, "I think you're right."

# Chapter 12

Gwen washed her hands in the nasty sink and tried to pretend she couldn't see them shaking.

She wasn't very successful.

It hadn't been hard to release the dog. He was chained so closely to the wall that they were in no danger, and Mac's strong hands pushed down the trap springs with brutal efficiency to free the animal.

Gwen had pretended she wasn't crying, but that only lasted until the dog tried desperately to lick her even though she was out of reach.

And then she'd left him, and washed her hands, and said to Mac, "Let's get this over with."

It was a surprise when he reached into his back pocket and pulled out the handcuffs. Surprise enough that she just blinked at him, her hands dripping over the sink.

"Here," he said, a gruff tone in his voice. Embarrassed, she might have said. She gave her hands a hasty swipe along her shirt and took the cuffs, if only to spare him the moment.

Except she then gave his horribly battered wrists a pointed look. "But…"

He lifted one shoulder in a shrug. "If I get through this, it won't matter. The blade will deal with it. If I don't get through this…it won't matter."

Okay then. "Where—"

"Anywhere," he said, closing his eyes—closing her out, or maybe closing himself in.

The visible ripple of pain through his body answered that one. *Running out of time.* "Find a support. Something that can't be broken. Put me in one of these rooms, if possible—it's not as exposed."

Which is how Gwen found herself prowling around the stark, worn little rooms, kicking aside an empty box here or there, wrinkling her nose at the filth of it all. One room startled her with gleaming new office furniture, a couch, and a flat-screen television and wet bar.

The minion hangout. Nothing so prosaic for the man who owned them.

No, she knew his room when she saw it—when she found Mac in the doorway staring at it. A quiet, starkly clean Zen space of a single sleek-shaped metal chair, a large cushion on the floor. A huge U-bolt set into the corner.

"He doesn't want any distractions," Mac said quietly.

She didn't ask him how he would know. She just asked, "This is the place?"

"There's an irony to it," Mac said, with that lift at the corner of his mouth.

Gwen muttered a distinct suggestion about what irony could do to itself and handed the cuffs back to him. "I'm here," she said, "but I think this is something you need to do."

Without a word, he took the cuffs—and her hands with them. Just when she thought he'd ravage her with a kiss to end all kisses, he wrapped his arms around her, so desperately tight it almost surpassed comfort, and buried his face in her neck and hair, breathing raggedly in her ear.

"Shh," she found herself saying. "I'll be here."

Eventually he released her, pulling back just enough to offer her that kiss—tender and sweet and grieving. "Yeah," he said, a strained voice. "I know. That's who *you* are." But when he stepped away from her, he'd turned brusque. All business. "If this goes bad, Gwen, you run. Run and don't stop running. You hear me?"

"If this goes bad," Gwen said, lifting her chin, "I know exactly what I'll do."

And she did.

Gwen stood in silence as Mac crouched at the corner, securing himself to the U-bolt. She didn't need any signal to know when he was ready; she saw his deep breath, saw him settle into himself.

He'd left the blade on the floor in its folded antique pocketknife form; she reached for it.

She thought better of it, of course. Feeling more foolish than she could remember, she said sternly to it, "Keep your sharp edges to yourself—I'm going to give him back to you. If you mess with me, it'll only delay things."

And then, matter-of-fact, she picked it up, pulled open the biggest blade of the two and slipped it under the duct tape.

The tough material parted like finest silk. The pendant fell into her hand, and Mac stiffened, sending her one last panicked and desperate look, and half a word with it. "Gwe—"

The blade took him.

He threw himself against the cuffs with such abrupt viciousness that Gwen fell back, scrambling away— cursing a frantic streak of words even as she bumped into the chair, clawed her way to her feet and got her bearings. Mac's arms bled freely; he snarled at her, threats and curses and vicious mindlessness.

And already, the drywall around the U-bolt cracked.

Mac, blood at his mouth, eyes streaming and sweat at his brow, grabbed the bolt and held on—not to yank it, but grounding himself. He grasped on to that thin control just long enough to look at her from desperate dark eyes and grate a single word. "Run."

Gwen did just that.

* * *

She fled to the hallway, chased by the renewed sounds of his battle. She fled to the Jeep, leaving both man and dog.

She couldn't go any farther.

Looking over her shoulder, endlessly listening for sounds that meant Mac had actually freed himself, she dug the business card out of her back pocket and grabbed Mac's neglected cell phone from the cup holder between the front seats, and dialed.

"Fifteen minutes," said the woman named Natalie upon hearing her voice, her cry for help. "It'll take me fifteen minutes."

"Alone," Gwen told her, and then made sure the Jeep was ready to go. Ready to run on all counts, and knowing that she'd find Mac again if she had to. That she could.

But Natalie came alone.

Or as alone as she ever got, with a blade in her hand.

And she came on time. Her Prius swooped silently down the vaguely defined drive to the warehouse and braked to a stop. She exited the car with a folder in her hand.

"Did you tell him?" Gwen's suspicion poked out everywhere.

"Devin?" Natalie shook her head, the sun-streaked glints of blond bright in daylight. "He knows I'm doing something I'm distinctly not telling him. I'll pay my own price for that. Now, what am I doing here?"

"The blade," Gwen blurted out, and then stopped herself. More controlled, she said, "He's fighting it.

In there. I don't know if he'll win. I need to be able to help him, and I don't know how. You said you could help. Also there's a dog and he's hurt, so we need a vet. And this place might not be safe."

Natalie absorbed it all without any visible shock. Her blue-grey eyes, a shade darker than Gwen's, widened only slightly, glancing quickly to the warehouse and back. She said, "A dog."

"We found him here," Gwen said, not with any patience. "He's hurt."

"So you said." As aware as she seemed of Gwen's turmoil, as meaningful as her glance to the warehouse had been, Natalie stood fast. "And you both came to this place—that might not be safe—why?"

Gwen wanted to stomp her foot like a little girl. "He didn't want to be in public for this." But she didn't mention how they'd first come to find this place, or any of the other details they'd discovered here.

Not yet.

Trust only went so far.

Natalie gave her an even look. Gwen had the sudden impression that she wasn't fooling anyone—and suddenly she had no more patience for waiting. She stabbed a finger at the warehouse. "He's in there! And he needs help!"

"He's in there," Natalie agreed, her gaze distant as if she could perceive something that Gwen couldn't. "And he's in agony. But he hasn't lost yet."

Gwen couldn't stand it. She turned on her heel, heading for the warehouse—only to find herself restrained, a single slim hand on her arm.

Damn, the woman was fast.

Calling her might not have been such a good idea after all.

Natalie stepped back. "Did he send you away?"

Slowly, Gwen nodded.

"Then that's what you can do for him right now." She touched the pocket of her tailored slacks. Gwen suddenly thought to notice that for all the sleek lines of Natalie's clothing, the cut gave her room to move. "Baitlia would tell me if he had lost his battle."

"Would it?" Gwen wanted to know. "Why?"

Natalie's expression was somber in the bright sunshine. "Because then he becomes a danger to us all. Including Baitlia."

Gwen looked away. "Translated—because then you will try to kill him."

In lieu of an answer, Natalie put the folder in Gwen's hands. "Take a look."

Gwen was surprised by how steadily she glanced at it, how casually she opened it. Like someone else's hands, going about their own business. Finding, inside, a sketch of her pendant. Her gaze snapped up to Natalie's; she touched the pendant, back at her throat. "How—"

"I told you I have resources." Natalie responded quickly, but she'd taken a step toward the warehouse, her head lifted slightly. Her hand flexed, then slowly released—and then she was suddenly completely *there* again—with Gwen, outside the building. "Sorry," she said, not pretending it hadn't happened. "He has heart. I hope he stays with us."

Then Gwen's hands shook. She swiped an errant tear off the paper and held it out to Natalie. "Suppose you just tell me what this is all about. Because I never showed this to you."

"I saw it," Natalie said. "Baitlia saw it, too. Do you know what it is that you carry around?"

Gwen felt the stubbornness of her own chin. "My father gave it to me."

"Did he?" Natalie studied her. "I don't imagine he's alive, then." She held up a hand to fend off Gwen's response. "Never mind. I won't play this game with you. The information is yours to keep and study if you'd like, but this is what I know—the pendant is *Demardel*. Don't ask me what that means—the language isn't one I'm familiar with, and for the moment I'm cribbing off of other people's notes. What I've gathered is this— that pendant started out as a medallion, and the medallion was made with power as much as it was with smelting—long enough ago that it should be copper or bronze or just some lump of star metal, because no one had the technology for *that*." She nodded at the pendant, still hidden as it was. "There's no indication that it binds a demon as the blades do, but there are hints of…well…something."

Gwen resisted the urge to pull the pendant free and study it. She'd do that later…running her fingers over it, seeing it with new eyes…

If she had the chance.

Instead she said, "Just like that. You know so much." And then made a face and waved away the rejoinder. "I know, I know. You have resources. I don't suppose the resources know what this thing is all about, then. The *why* of it."

"In fact," Natalie said, "my *resources* are divided over whether it's even real. But they agree on what it's supposed to do." She made a little bit of a face herself, then—skepticism escaping. "The bond between blade and wielder is lifelong. You learn to live with it, or you die. And then generally you die early anyway—although I hasten to add that I have no such intent. But that pendant of yours is supposed to provide an alternative."

Gwen forgot to breathe for a moment—knowing what the pendant had done for Mac, even with their fumbling ignorance. Knowing that her connection with it had strengthened these past few days.

Natalie didn't fail to notice. "Ahh," she said. "More true than not, after all."

Gwen nodded. "Maybe. Keep talking."

Natalie shrugged. "That's pretty much it. There's a procedure, but I don't know it."

"No, I mean—" Gwen gestured impatience. "Is it for good? Can it be permanent?"

Natalie returned a blank look. "That's the whole point. It severs the bond. It frees the wielder without allowing the blade to control the circumstances or transfer to a new wielder."

Hell, yes. She *could* help Mac. She could give him just what he needed.

Had her father known what it was when he'd given it to her? When he'd let himself go too long, slipped so close to the wild road and then over? Had he simply miscalculated, trying to hang on to the blade long enough to…

*To what?*

What could possibly even have been so important? When he could have saved himself, saved her childhood, saved her world?

It hit her hard enough to hurt. To twist her heart and clamp down in her throat and take her breath away all over again.

Her mother had been killed, and her father had never been the same.

Right. It had been his version of Mac's night outside the bar. He'd been unable to save her mother but he'd ended up with the blade…and then he'd spent his time seeking retribution. A personal crusade that had somehow become more important than anything else. *Anyone* else.

Including his daughter.

*Wrong choice, Daddy.*

"Gwen?"

Gwen sent her such a fierce and sudden look that Natalie took a step back. "Can you figure it out?" she asked. "What needs to be done?"

From her new distance, Natalie said, "You look like you already know."

Gwen frowned. "Don't get coy with me now. I've seen some…effects. They weren't permanent. I need to do better."

"It's awake, you know," Natalie told her, glancing at the slight ripple in Gwen's shirt where the pendant fell. "Last night it wasn't. What have you done?"

Gwen laughed, more loudly than she'd meant to. "What *haven't* I done?" she said. She held out her hand, now bandaged in what was left of the stretchy pink first aid wrap. "I fed it blood, apparently. And I fed it—"

She couldn't quite say it. But it seemed she didn't need to.

"Ah," Natalie said again. And then, thoughtfully, added, "Baitlia is aware of it in a way that it wasn't before. And really doesn't want me anywhere near it."

"You can tell Baitlia that Demardel and I are no threat. I have no idea what I'm doing." *But I will.*

Natalie lifted her head again. "There," she said, and if she breathed a sigh of relief, her face had none-theless found an expression that seemed bittersweet. "He's made it, your unnamed one. For now. And he's probably got a bit of a lull period to work with." She glanced at Gwen. "The blades tend to lick their wounds quietly."

Gwen jammed the folder in through the open Jeep window. "I still have questions—"

"As do I."

"But they'll have to wait. I've said what I'm going to say for now. Can you take the dog to the vet?"

"About that—"

"Yeah," Gwen said, already heading for the door. "Questions. They have to wait. I still have your card. I'll call you. The dog is this way."

Natalie came right on her heels. "He won't want me to see him—"

"Different room," Gwen said, running now across that open space.

And of course then Natalie wanted to know what had happened to the dog and, upon seeing him, who the hell had done this thing. Of course she remembered what Gwen had said the evening before, the single throwaway line, the probe in the dark—kidnapping and torture and killing.

Gwen said only, "I'll call you." She held the door to the room open so Natalie could carry the dog out—his tail wagging nervously, his tongue looking for something to lick—handling his awkward weight with more ease than Gwen would have expected.

And Natalie turned back to say, "We need to know, Gwen. We need to be part of this."

"Yada yada," Gwen said, snapping the words. *"Later."*

To her surprise, Natalie let it go. "Later," she said. "Go be with him."

# Chapter 13

Mac sat on his knees, bent over cuffed hands, and felt the sullen retreat of the blade pounding through his body with every beat of his heart—a strong and wild pattern, settling to merely galloping. To mere trickles of feeling—concern and determination of an unfamiliar flavor, and turmoil with the taste of Gwen attached.

*Not my turmoil. Not my concern.*

And this time, it worked. As exhausted as he found himself, as much as the feelings danced around the edges, for now, the core of his soul was intact. All his.

The blade, he knew, would be back. And meanwhile it did what it had to in order to protect itself... it healed him. The burn of it spread through his body, dull and bearable and familiar. His wrists—small bones cracked, skin abraded raw—had already stopped bleeding.

The door cracked open, shifting the patterns of light in the room.

"Mac?" Gwen murmured it—not as if they might be overheard, but as if she suspected his head might pound just exactly as much as it did right now.

He looked up at her. "Hey," he said, weary enough. And then, "Told you to run."

She slipped inside. "I did run," she said, with a distinctly haughty toss of her head—a deliberate gesture, and he felt the next line coming. "You didn't say how far."

He laughed, short and pained. "I think I probably walked right into that."

"Mmm," she agreed, coming over to crouch before him, swiping hair from above his eyes and rubbing some probably invisible smudge off his cheek; her hand lingered. "We need to go, huh? I bet that man felt every bit of what's gone on here, from finding the dog to— Oh, my God, you broke the wall."

He shrugged, lifting the cuffs up before her. "I broke the wall," he agreed. Behind him, the U-bolt lay on the floor, the drywall in chunks and, beneath it, wood in splinters. "It's why I had to win this one."

Her eyes widened slightly. "You knew I was still here."

"Every minute," he said. "I couldn't *not* know it." The blade had made it clear—suffering dog, anguished Gwen…each a special kind of delight. "Didn't leave me any choice, did it?"

"Well, there," she said and gave him a satisfied look. "I did the right thing."

He shook his head. "Gwen...it could have gone so wrong..."

"Didn't," she told him, firm and confident and not taking into account that her internal tremors of fear slipped right through the blade to him, a pathway grown polished in these past two days.

*Not Gwen,* he wanted to tell it. *Leave her alone. Leave her private.*

She lifted his hands, gentle with them, and ever so carefully inserted the handcuff key—first one wrist, then the other. She made no remark about the state of his wrists—or the fact that there, at the edges, they had already so obviously started to heal. But her vehemence when she threw the cuffs across the room was startling.

"We might need those," Mac said.

"No," she told him. "We won't."

And she meant it. The flat determination behind those words—he could have read it without the blade at all.

"What—" he started.

"We have to go," she told him. "Away from here."

"The dog—"

"Took care of it." She drew him to his feet.

"How—"

*"We have to go."*

And she was right. He pulled himself together beyond the burning, the pounding, the fatigue, and aimed himself for the door, presenting his words with careful dignity. "You drive."

She laughed, and he hid a grin, and for that briefest of moments, everything seemed just fine.

The blade was back, all right. Gwen could see the effects of it, bold and brash in the late morning light. The horrors of the damage already healing, the edges of the raw skin now merely pink and the swelling visibly diminished. Mac sat in the Jeep with his eyes closed, breathing deeply and regularly—but not, she thought, asleep.

All the same, she didn't consult him when she reached the hotel...and kept on driving. Not far. It was time to ask for help, *real* help. And from someone who didn't have an acquisitional interest in them—not in Mac's unnamed blade or a pendant called Demardel.

A pendant that had increasingly made its presence known. Nothing overt or demanding, just...awareness. She knew of Mac's blade. She even felt the petulant and defeated mood of it. She felt, too, the faint awareness of something behind them, to the south. *Natalie.* And probably the man named Devin.

But most unsettling, she could feel the malevolence crawling over the city, settling into the nooks and crannies of the place. Not active at the moment, but laying down connections in a conquering layer. A broadcast system of control and hate.

That man didn't just drink it in. He *made* it. And the things he'd said—about his immense age, about the nature of his bargain...

She knew enough about Mac's blade to guess. A wild guess, maybe, but one that felt right to her. That this blade had overcome its human partner. That together, the man and his bloodthirsty blade had met in a mutual quest for vicarious pain that they'd functioned so symbiotically, so perfectly…enough to create a creature of heinous power and destruction.

She hoped they wouldn't find out that she was right.

A block past the hotel, she turned into the diner parking lot, glancing inside to see, with some relief, that the same waitress worked the early lunch crowd as had served them twice before. She did a quick clothes check and found herself dusty but otherwise presentable. Then she put her quick-talking mouth into gear and pushed through the door.

"Are you in trouble?" the woman asked, her wary gaze flicking through the plate-glass window to check the Jeep, as if she could see trouble smeared across the windshield.

"No," Gwen said. "I mean, maybe. I mean, we're trying to stay out of it."

*Oh. Wow. Way to go, fast-talking mouth.*

She took a deep breath, moved to the far end of the counter where the customers would have to work harder to overhear and started again. She had, after all, only requested advice about the nearest place to hang out, to rest. A nice secluded park, a quiet church…she wasn't picky, although she didn't know if the blade might be. But the waitress had taken one look at her and jumped to conclusions.

It was only dust. Or so she'd thought. She made
a little self-deprecating face and said, "I must look
bad, huh?"

"You've been crying," the woman said. "And there's
blood on your face."

Gwen's expression shot straight to exasperation. "I
should have checked in the rearview mirror. Dammit."

Oddly enough, this little piece of honesty seemed
to relax the woman. Gwen barged ahead while she
thought she had a chance. "Look, you've seen the news,
right? All the stupid mean stuff going on out there
right now?"

Anger crossed her face. "My son's arm is broken."

To judge by the warning now easing in through
Demardel, it wasn't the only trouble this woman would
see. "Okay, the thing is, my friend and I—you know,
the one who was here with me yesterday?" Gwen
waited for the slight nod of recognition as the woman
peered out through sun- and dust-glazed glass and then
through the windshield, where Mac sat with his eyes
closed and his head tipped back. "We've run into some
of it, too. And we think someone might be, you know,
deliberately pushing it, and we're trying to figure that
out." That was one way to look at it. "And we've had
a really bad day, and my friend needs...well, he needs
rest. And we can't go back to the hotel right now, so
I'm just looking for a park or something—a quiet place
with shade. I thought maybe you might know—" She
stopped talking, seeing the look on the woman's face
and unable to read it. Either she was about to—

*Intent. Utensil turned weapon. Temper rising.*

Gwen spun around to the small dining area, found the man immediately—beefy, lots of neck, bullet-headed…black T-shirt in size enormous, long and baggy black shorts. And glaring with dark-eyed intensity at the oblivious tech-infested teen sitting across from him with some sort of unpleasantly beeping game gadget. Not just glaring, but clutching a fork in his meaty hand like a weapon and halfway out of his seat.

"Hey!" she snapped, not even thinking about it. "My brother the cop is meeting me here for lunch, so if you want to start something, do it somewhere else!"

Startled, he glanced at her—and then gave her the finger. His girlfriend—sturdy, dressed in tight clothes that would have been snug on Gwen's smaller frame—stood up and turned around. "Bitch," she said. "Did I hear you talking to my boyfriend?"

"Dammit," Gwen muttered, and the woman behind the counter met her glance with alarmed understanding. Right here, right now. Someone was deliberately pushing it, all right. The feel of it washed through her, as dull as it had ever been for her, and yet somehow not touching her.

*Demardel.*

She faced the girlfriend squarely. She might have lifted her chin, but it wasn't deliberate—or, probably, smart. "Brother," she said evenly. "Cop."

The girlfriend looked around the diner. "Don't see no brother."

By now the teen had lifted his head from the game, realized what he'd gotten in the middle of, and froze. The beefy guy slapped the game from his hand to clat-

ter across the tile floor, and that's when Gwen realized her mistake.

Too late.

These two had already been brimming with anger
and resentment. Like the church group in the park, the
young tough at the gas station…these two had been
cruising for a target, and the hatred had found them
willing hosts.

"Not in this diner!" the woman behind the counter
ordered them, but her voice had gone thin behind its
determination. "I have an alarm button back here and
if you don't leave, I'll hit it!"

"Plenty of time before the cops get here," the girlfriend said, and her fleshy features took a briefly inhuman cast—pure meanness incarnate.

With quiet and economical motion, the waitress
placed a baseball bat on the counter. It sat there for only
a single meaningful moment before Gwen grabbed it
up—finding it short, stout and weighted at the end.

The girl brought out a switchblade. The guy looked
plenty comfortable with his fork and his muscles.

And that gut instinct of hers cried *danger*. The teen
slid quietly under the table, an impressively Dali-esque
move.

"Dammit," Gwen said again. "I didn't know they
even made switchblades that big."

The couple marinated in the waves of hatred even
as they stayed outside of her—a surge of everything
cruel and mean and frightening, and a thing that had
twice taken Mac down already. She didn't dare glance
for the Jeep as she retreated a step. Didn't dare hope

the woman had meant it about that alarm button. And she wondered if she turned tail and ran, just how far she'd get.

Because she didn't think this was coincidence. She thought that man—*that man*—had realized his failure. Mac had come back, battled the fight he was expected to lose, and walked away in control. She thought that man had lost his patience, and she thought he meant to flush them out and take them down.

Or just plain take them down.

"Brother!" she said, and heard her own desperation. "Cop!"

But they came for her anyway, and she took a better grip on the bat—thinking of the absurdities that came with batting advice. *Stay loose. Hit beyond the ball.*

Adding one of her own: *Make the first one count.*

She'd go for the guy, not the switchblade. He could kill her with or without the knife. Yep, that was the plan, and because he was beefy and top-heavy, she'd go for the knee—because he didn't have to be out, he only had to be on the floor and— *Oh, my God what am I even thinking?*

They stopped, pure surprise on twin expressions.

Gwen felt it, then—the odd trill of acknowledgment from Demardel, the sensation of space in use behind. "That had better be you," she said, and wasn't at all surprised when her voice came out shaky.

"He's no cop." The girlfriend managed to make that sound mean, too.

"I'm not her brother, either."

But oh, he sounded dangerous—that confidence

coupled with the certainty of what he could and would do. *Had done.* The waitress saw it, reacting to him as she had not before, as he moved up beside Gwen.

Narrow diner, bottleneck at the counter—the troublemakers were trapped, though they didn't seem to know it.

Mac knew it. Gwen saw it on his face—worn in comparison to the night she'd met him, but honed by it. Lean and tight and fit, muscled in a way that showed through the fit of his shirt and the power of his stance. The healing abrasions on his arms, the lingering bruises on his face—they were the injuries of a man who had been where these two now only thought about going.

But in control. Who *he* was, and not who the blade was.

For now.

And if he still needed rest, if he needed recovery— he damned well didn't show it.

"Put your toys away," he told them. "Leave this place while you can. Don't forget to leave a tip."

The man pointed at Mac's empty hands with a jutting chin. "You got nothing."

"He doesn't need to have anything!" the waitress said, her voice both angry and shaking. "I want you to leave! For years you've gotten good food here, and now you think you can do this? You are no longer welcome!"

Gwen sucked in a breath with a new onslaught of warning, a jangle of nerves and anger swirling together with the flow of imposed feeling. Her ears warned her; her eyes warned her. Cocky male voices, careless steps—and there they were in the doorway, crowding it—taking the space, and taking in the situation. The rest of the local bullies had arrived—and just that fast, had taken sides.

The girlfriend smiled at Gwen, a smile reeking of nastiness and satisfaction that made words unnecessary.

Mac moved. He snagged Gwen by the waist and hoisted her up to the counter, shoving aside a napkin holder and industrial sugar shaker. She released the bat to him and swung over to the other side of the counter, where there was a red alarm button attached to…

Nothing.

The woman caught her eye, shook her head… shrugged.

Not that the cops weren't already a hundred percent occupied on this day in this town.

Or that Mac needed them.

The bat in one hand, the blade in the other—suddenly it turned saber, fast enough so Gwen had missed it and the assembled young toughs didn't at first understand. Not the usual thing, a sword. And they'd been busy, pulling out stout switchblades…pulling out a gun.

The waitress ducked behind the counter and tried to drag Gwen down with her—but Gwen clawed her way back up, looking around for a weapon, *any* weapon.

Mac said, "You leave now, or someone dies."

They snorted. Riding their overload of confidence and driven by somebody else's goals without even knowing it. Someone else's keen lust for violence and hatred. "Yeah," one of them said. *"You."*

Gwen couldn't help it; the words burst out. "You don't even know what this is about!"

"Don't have to." Only one of them said it, but they all meant it. And then one of them pointed at Mac, eyes narrowed in an exaggerated expression. "You," he said. "I know you. You got in our way the other night."

"I did more than that," Mac said, and Gwen had no idea how his voice kept that even tone, matter-of-fact while at the same time so full of meaning. Of promise. "You know damned well I can do it again."

"Naw," said the guy who spoke for them all, the one with the gun. "You can't swing that thing in here. You're goin' down."

The blade must have agreed. A glimmering runnel of light and the Bowie knife replaced the sword, but Mac struck out with the short bat first—lightning fast, a one-handed sweep, crowding them and making it clear that the tight space worked against them as much as him.

"This is crazy," Gwen muttered, disbelief overflowing. "This is crazy!"

Not that anyone heard her. With the girlfriend crying shrill encouragement, the guys piled on. Tried to pile on. One staggered back retching; another flung himself out of the way of the Bowie and tangled with a chair. On the bat's backswing, Mac slapped out the shin of the top-heavy guy who'd started it all and someone's knife went flying. Blood splashed and bodies collided and Mac stood in the center of it all, back to the counter, his movement swift and precise and economical, too fast to follow.

"Shoot him!" the girlfriend shrieked, crouched beside her felled boyfriend, whose olive complexion had gone stark-white. "Shoot him!"

Gwen saw it too well—that the guy with the gun suddenly remembered he had it, and at the same time realized that he and his friends would not win this fight. She saw his glance at the weapon—his gangsta-style hold as he brought it to bear. She scrambled back up onto the counter—on her knees, snatching up the heavy sugar shaker. The guy didn't even see it coming—a glancing blow off his shoulder, enough to jerk his body and his aim, his finger closing down on the trigger so the gun discharged.

The waitress screamed; Gwen ducked, so stupid and futile when the bullet was already buried in the wall behind her.

The cook, she thought, was long gone—fled, and smart to go.

It bought moments only—the guy cursed at her, dodged another of his friends as he came staggering back, and aimed the gun—

Gwen flung the napkin holder, a flimsy metal contraption that flew apart in midair and rained cheap white squares down on them all.

Mac's blade sliced through the air, cleaving paper in two without disturbing its passage…leaving blood in its wake. Nothing more than surface wounds so far, nothing uncontrolled. Nothing fatal. *Controlled.*

And now the gun pointed at Gwen.

"Gwen!" Mac shouted—ducking one set of reaching arms but missing the next as the boyfriend lurched up from the floor, latching around Mac in a beefy human noose, clamping his arms to his side; the bat fell away.

Gwen threw herself flat on the counter as the gun went off again, and she met Mac's eyes in the doing of it—met his despair.

He was going to have to kill someone. Not just wound, not just discourage, but kill. Gwen rolled aside just enough to grab the ketchup bottle and fling it at the guy with the gun. As he ducked, she grabbed the pendant.

"Do something!" she told it, not caring how crazy that was or that she had no idea what the thing really did or how to do it in the first place. Only knowing that as before, she wanted it. Wanted these men cut off from the hatred and the driving force that man had imposed on them all.

Mac gave her a startled glance. She had no idea what she'd done—she could barely feel the swamping effect in the first place—but done it she had. He quite suddenly broke free, and the boyfriend's equally sudden bafflement turned to green and horrified pain as Mac instantly jammed an elbow in the guy's gut and followed it through with a hammer strike to the groin using the butt end of the Bowie.

Just that fast, he scooped up the bat and backed up against the counter, his breathing coming fast now and with a faint tremor in his shoulders that might have been weakness or might have been a struggle for control.

The guy with the gun looked down at it and then at his friends—a couple of them on the floor, the others bleeding from shallow wounds and staggering, trying to pretend they weren't.

And then he took a step away.

Not, Gwen thought, that he wasn't perfectly willing to follow through on such intent as he'd had. Only that it needed to be his own intent, and now it suddenly wasn't.

The waitress stood, her face paled, her lips thinned. "This was neutral ground," she told them. "For years, you were all welcome here." She pointed at the door—her hand shaking but resolute. "Not any longer."

The guy with the gun regarded her with a chastised expression that Gwen wouldn't have expected. "You calling the cops?"

She drew herself up, looking around her place—a snowstorm of napkins, a teenager still in petrified hiding, blood splattered everywhere and young men shuffling themselves back together. "Not if you go. Now."

He looked as though he wanted to say something but couldn't find the words. Gwen didn't blame him. What did he know about *that man* and his machinations? In the end he jerked his chin at the door, and the guys headed for it.

"Wait," Gwen heard herself say. The waitress shot her an incredulous look; the guy with the gun did much the same. "You should know. There's something out there…and it's using you. It had a hand in this." She didn't have to hear him to understand the *what the effing kind of crazy lady are you* in his expression.

"I know, I know," she said. "But look back over the things you've done these past few days. Ask yourself if they were *your* things to do. And if not, then make the decision not to get pushed around by the thing we're fighting."

"You crazy, bitch," he said—but the scowl he wore wasn't for her; it was for the truth in her words.

Gwen released a pent-up breath. Yeah. Crazy. Maybe so.

But not so crazy she was just going to lie here on this counter now that they'd gone. She pushed back up to her knees. "Mac?" she asked, looking at his back and unable to tell what his silence meant. "Are you all—"

That was all she got out before he threw the bat away and turned on her, the blade slamming flat-handed to the counter as his hands clamped around her waist and shook her ever so slightly. "What..." he said, looking up at her with grey-blue eyes gone stormy and undefinable anguish on his face. "*What* did you think—" a little shake there "—you were doing?"

Her face went hot, looking at that accusation and pain. "Saving your ass!" she cried. "And I did a good job, too!"

But she was startled past words when he jerked her in close, wrapped his arms around her, and held her tight—his head against her chest, his breathing jerky... and the heat of his body telling her all that she had to know about his remaining need to heal and rest. He'd faked his way through that scene. All of it.

After a speechless moment, she rested her hands on

his shoulders and kissed the top of his head. "Okay," she said. "Okay." And stayed that way a moment.

When he pulled back, he lifted her off the counter as if that had been his intent all along, setting her gently on her feet. She looked at the waitress and said, "I'll help clean this place up. But we really do need a place to lie low a few hours." *A place that our warehouse friend doesn't already know about.* "A church or a community center…it doesn't have to be private, as long as it's public enough so we're lost in it."

"You saved that boy," the woman said. At Gwen's surprise, she shook her head. "No, no, I know that boy, and he would have mouthed off to Amado, and Amado had the look of a killer just then." She raised her voice slightly. "Isn't that right, Hector?"

"Yes, ma'am." The teen slunk into view, a skinny kid all elbows and tennis shoes.

"Go home now," she said. "And you stay home until something gets better out there, you hear me?"

"Yes, ma'am!" The kid ran for it, skirting fallen chairs, stools, and blood-smeared tile.

"And you," the woman said, looking at Gwen—and then, for a long time, at Mac.

The blade, Gwen noticed, was gone.

"You," the woman repeated. "There's a room in the back. You stay there until he looks better. Then, whatever you're after…you had better find it."

"I—" Gwen started—wanting to protest, feeling the guilt of what they'd wrought here in this pleasant little neighborhood diner. Feeling the worry of what their presence might do.

But that man didn't know where they were. He'd no doubt broadcast his hatred widely, causing fights all along the way. She doubted he cared about collateral damage. Or if he did, it wasn't in the same way she did.

And they needed the time. The space.

The woman must have seen it on her face. "Now flip that Closed sign and help me get a start on this."

Gwen said, "Yes, ma'am."

# Chapter 14

Devin James stood balanced in the estate workout room, barefoot on the mat with isochronic meditation tones sounding in the background, thinking of nothing.

Most deliberately thinking of nothing. Just *being*. There, where the blade couldn't reach him. A technique he hadn't known a year ago, barely a season ago—but one of the many that now offered him peace from Anheriel, and a way to control its effects on him.

Even on a day like today.

The door burst open. He didn't need to open his eyes to know it was Natalie, or that she was flustered.

"Oh," she said, dismay coming through. "I'm sorry—I thought you were running on the treadmill."

"Was," he said, bouncing on his toes a few times

before opening his eyes and reaching over to turn off the stereo. "Not a good day for it."

"Anheriel," she said. "As if I had to guess. I've been shut away in research and I can still feel it—the whole mess of it out there—through Baitlia." She lowered the sheaf of papers she'd brought in with her—their disorder alone testified to her flustered nature—and came to him, both confident in her welcome and careful of her approach. Nothing too sudden, nothing other than serene.

Because Anheriel was in that dangerous, riled place, and even though she trusted Devin utterly with her safety, she forbore to put him in the position where he'd have to fight for it. And once up close, she gave him what she'd always given him…the focus of her intimate touch. The sensations that overrode even Anheriel.

And when he lifted his head from that deeply involving kiss, he grinned big. "Just what the doctor ordered." Then he nodded down at her hand and her papers. "What's up?"

"Oh!" she said, the dismay completely replaced by excitement. "What I found— There are only partial translations, although we might begin to have enough to set an expert on it, if we could find someone we trust. I think Compton was gleaning most of his information through his blade, frankly, but that's one advantage to the wild road we can do without." She turned to the weight bench, spreading the papers out as best she could. "Okay, so here's Demardel."

"That dog doing okay at the vet's?" It was a sudden question, one he'd been careful about asking. Because earlier that day she'd gone to the warehouse not only without him, but without telling him.

Granted, he'd been quelling a little neighborhood set-to at the time, a fence-line argument gone bad between normally amiable people. But she'd obscured her contacts with the intruding blade wielder from the start.

No. *Be fair.* With the woman who now loved the intruding blade wielder. Or so Natalie had seen. Devin would pass his own judgments.

*Exactly why she left you out of it.*

And so his question about the dog was an apology of sorts.

She knew it, too. A hint of a smile tugged at her mouth. "He'll be there a day or two, just to make sure there's no infection—those wounds were dirty. He might limp when all is said and done. But he's got a good chance."

Devin cleared his throat, rocking on the balls of his feet. "Good thing you were there, then."

"You do realize that if I kiss you again, we won't get to this stuff at all?"

He eyed her mouth; he eyed the padded floor of the workout room and the lockable door. Ah, well. "Okay," he said. "Demardel. The mystery medallion."

She turned away from him, her movement resolute, and she, too, cleared her throat. "Right," she said. "It's not just a simple tool. Like the blades, it needs a wielder to act. So your average Joe Bladewielder can't just stumble over it and put it to use. It takes the participation of that second person—and that person has to be awake to it. Because unlike the blades, it has no agenda of its own. It'll sleep for centuries, if no one calls on it."

"So for however long your friend Gwen has had the thing, wherever she got it...she may not have any idea."

"She certainly knows now. She knows more than she's saying, too. I practically watched her put the pieces together right in front of me, even when she wasn't talking. And she's bonded to it, too—she was fresh off it when I talked to her yesterday evening at the hotel. Bonded with blood and probably—well...call it emotion." Right. Devin could read between those lines. She and her Joe Bladewielder had done the deed. Natalie eyed him, reading his expression and not giving him any space to comment. "She may have no idea how to use it, but she knows what she's got, and she knows it on a deep level."

Devin reached out to the sketch of it, propped haphazardly at the top of the bench's weight stack. "And we don't know how to use it, either."

"Not yet." She looked at the drawing, pensive around the eyes and mouth. "Our blades are about redemption, Devin. Demonic essence trapped in metal, searching for redemption. This..." She took a deep breath. "This medallion is about sacrifice. Whoever made it gave their life to it. Whoever uses it..." She flicked her gaze to his. "There's a price."

He got it. Right away, he got it. "She has no idea. Even if she figures out how to use it, she doesn't know there are consequences."

"And we don't know what they are. Perhaps to one

trained, they're nominal—just like we're figuring out how to balance the blades. But to someone who has no idea—"

Frustration settled over him. "You were right all along. I should have handled him differently. We'd be together on this if I had. Dammit, now we're ten kinds of screwed up here."

She didn't offer him platitudes. "Maybe twenty." At his sharp glance, she teased another of the papers free from the spread. A glance told him little—a copy of notes in several languages, old pen-and-ink sketches of a blade in several phases. Scimitar, khanjar, jambiya... everything a flavor of the Middle East. "This is a blade with enough of a reputation to gain its own documentation."

When he looked surprised, she added, "I'm beginning to think they're all documented, somewhere—I just haven't found it yet. But there are enough allusions..." She shook her head. "Anyway, this one's apparently made a name for itself, going through wielders one after the other—even supposedly destroying one of the other blades. And then it fell off the scene, to the tune of a lot of speculation."

"And you think it's back."

"What I think," she said, straightening to stare down at the sketches, "is that it never left. So do some other people, but I suppose that's beside the point. What I wonder—" She looked at him with some hesitation, the words not quite forming.

"Just say it," he advised her.

She made a face, closing and then flexing her hands.

Natalie, bringing herself to bear. "I'm reading between the lines of these notes, but…I think it found a wielder that matched its nature. I think they're in on it together, creating the circumstances that feed them. And I think they've been doing it for a very long time."

He looked at the sketches; he looked at her. "Define," he said, *"very long time."*

She met his gaze. "Lifetimes."

Mac prowled the tiny room inside the diner—fighting the blade's restlessness, far too aware of the exit that wasn't here. Just a confined little space with a watercooler, the tiniest of tables with a battered metal chair, and a cot crammed up against the wall.

Gwen pointed at it. "There," she said. "You."

"We can't stay here." The restlessness pushed those words out, the blade hungering for more action, for a better taste of blood—for that which their enigmatic captor had offered him.

But not hungering hard—at least not for now. For now, it understood that Mac would do as he needed to maintain control. For now, it offered a grudging—*very* grudging—respect.

"Right," Gwen said, hands on her hips and a smear of ketchup on her shirt. "Sure, then, let's go. Because hey, I don't need the chance to talk to you, or to reassure myself that you're okay, or to make clever plans, or even to be smart about where we go next. And you clearly don't need a chance to sleep off the whole demon blade hangover thing."

It stopped him short; he sent her a startled look.

"Oh, please," she said, tipping over to annoyance. "You're a furnace."

He ducked his head. Okay then. He might have a possessed blade and a mission and a life pretty much hanging in the balance, but Gwen had a temper—and he was pretty sure this round went to her. The burn of the healing went to his bones.

"An hour," she said. "Ninety minutes. We can't just rush out there, triggering off chaos wherever we go while that man looks for us. We have to talk."

There was truth to that. "We do," he said.

"I need to know that you're okay, for starters," she said—and then, before he could say anything, gestured impatiently. "No, no…I mean, obviously not, right? But…relatively speaking."

"It's under control," he said, and meant it. Although, of course he had to add, "I don't know for how long," if he was going to be truthful.

"Longer if you take a moment than if you don't," she pointed out.

"Hey," he told her. "You already won that one."

She tilted her head slightly, looking pleased. "Did I?" she said. "Well, good for me. Let's not waste it." She gestured at the cot.

"You—"

"Get real. I had plenty of sleep last night." That, he knew, was a lie—the strain of the past several days showed in her face, the faint bruised look around her eyes and the pallor beneath her scattered freckles. Even her bright pink hand bandage had begun to fray around the edges. "Besides, you need it worse."

That, he knew, was no lie at all. He eyed the cot—its knit throw, its narrow stretched canvas—and Gwen laughed, if just a little bit. "Nice try," she said. "Too small for both of us, I'm pretty sure."

"C'mere," he said, and didn't have to reach far in this tiny room. Her uncertainty showed as he pulled her close, but as before, he simply held her—maybe a little too tightly, maybe with a bit too much intensity—and after a moment she returned it, stroking his back in an unconscious gesture.

Then he pulled back, took her face between his hands and kissed the hell out of her.

"Wha—" she said when she drew back, looking as dazed as he felt.

He still managed to say, "Something to remember, going into this."

"I had plenty to remember already, if you want to know." She touched her mouth with her fingertips, sent him a thoughtful look. "Although I suppose there can never be too much of that particular good thing."

"My sentiments exactly," he said, and took himself over to the cot.

She touched the pendant, where she'd habitually tucked it beneath her shirt. "We really need to talk," she said, and then clearly had no intention of telling him just what that meant—pointing at the cot instead, and waiting as he lowered himself down, hunting sleep.

*—want and need and demand and blood and pain and PUNISH PUNISH—*

"Shh." A voice in his ear, a hand on his face. Lips on his mouth. "Shh. Sleep."

He slept.

Mac woke with Gwen's hand draped over his chest and her cheek on his hand. Even as he took the first deep breath of waking, she lifted her head.

"Hey," she said, revealing the seam of the cot imprinted on her face.

"Hey," he said and lifted her wrist to check her watch. His, it seemed, had been a casualty of the past few days. It probably lay in pieces on the hotel floor.

"Not all that long," she told him. "Ninety minutes. Feel better?"

"Better," he affirmed. And he did. The blade had calmed, leaving him with nothing but a trickle of feeling—an awareness of the unrest in the city without the unceasing demand to be part of it, to imbibe of it.

"Good." She climbed to her feet, a weariness in her movement. The cot wasn't quite jammed against the wall; she swung her leg over it and sat on his thighs. No seduction there…just the comfort factor of their bodies in contact. He pushed up on his elbows to regard her, brow raised; listening. She placed a thoughtful hand flat on his stomach and made a face. "Here's a thing you need to know—I did that—there, in the diner. When things were about to go really bad. I stopped that."

He hadn't expected that. Hell, no.

She read his expression easily enough. "I mean, what I did was make the feeling go away. That man's bad mojo, or however he spreads his nastiness. Or maybe I put a double-rainbow force field around the place. *Something.* You know I'm just making this stuff up as I go." She touched the pendant again.

"You... *That?*" He nodded at it. The blade knew of its presence...rested in silent resentment of it.

She nodded. "It's changed these past couple of days. Maybe it was being with you...maybe it was the blood it soaked up. As if metal could actually do that, right? Maybe I woke it up by pitting it against your blade. I have no idea." But her features had gone pensive... words not quite said. "The point is, I did it. Or *it* did it. And that means it might be useful again." She took a deep breath, looked right at him. "I really need to know more."

"Yeah," he said, looking at the pendant outlined beneath her shirt. And, "Yeah," again. "But don't ask me how to find out. Or when we'll have the time to do it."

"Maybe we should run," she suggested. "Get out of here, away from that man. Figure out what's going on." She hesitated, then added, "Together, I mean."

He couldn't help the grin. "Liking the sound of that," he told her.

She watched him a moment longer, then shook her head. "But you don't think so."

He could wonder when she'd learned to read him so well...but he didn't. Several days or a lifetime—it didn't matter. They'd already been revealed to one another, whether they'd meant to or not. So it wasn't hard to look up at her and say, "He'd find us." And then, more seriously, "Gwen, I don't know how it'll go with me. I don't know if I can hold out, and I need to deal with him while I still can."

Her fingers flexed against his stomach, as if she could hold on to him with pure will; she looked away, blinking. But if her eyes grew shiny, her determination didn't fade. "I know," she said. "But it was a nice dream." She looked down at him from her perfect viewpoint. "I see that some part of you liked it, too."

"Honey," he said, "your sexy ass is sitting on my thighs. I can't even imagine the time when that wouldn't get my attention."

She tossed her head. "I'll remember that." And then she clambered off. "Let's go then. Do our thing. Whatever it is."

"Circle the city," he said promptly. Standard approach tactics. And now that he knew what he was looking for, he sat up, swinging his legs over the edge of the cot to stand, all in one motion. "Triangulate in on him. It's time for us to call the shots."

*It's time for us to call the shots.*

More than that. It was time for Gwen to come clean—to let him know what she'd learned about the pendant...and how she'd learned it. She even opened her mouth to do it—but she could sense his restlessness, and his concern for the diner.

They'd been in one place for too long.

They emerged through the kitchen—closed down—and into the diner, now straightened and shining, as the waitress did a final wipe of the tables. She stopped to regard Mac and to nod to herself. "Better," she said.

"Better," Mac agreed. "Let me leave a donation to help pay for the damages."

She scoffed. "Did you make those boys crazy?"

He dropped a handful of bills on the counter. "It made *me* crazy to see that they had Gwen cornered like that. I could have handled it differently."

Not likely. Not that it would have mattered, with that man spreading his hatred. But Gwen stepped between them, providing distraction. "I'm Gwen," she said. "And really, it's all my fault. I've had good luck with that line before, but the way things are around here right now…"

"Gala," said the woman, introducing herself in return. "Will you really try to do something about… *this?*" Her face said it all—that she couldn't understand what they faced, and she couldn't understand how they could do anything about it.

Then again, she didn't have the image in her head of two men with gleaming blades engaged in battle, impossibly swift and able. Gwen wished she didn't, either—even if her imagination had provided it wholesale.

Her imagination had plenty to work with on that score.

Mac merely said, "We're going to do our best."

Gala's lips thinned. "Well, then, you'll need food. And we had plenty of it waiting on the grill. I packed some up for you." She looked at Mac askance. "I saw the way you eat."

Mac's stomach gave an angry growl, and he had the grace to look embarrassed. "You've been kind."

"If you can do this thing, there will never be a way to repay you. And there's no point in doing it hungry."

So they headed for the Jeep laden with takeout and with Gwen's hand already curling into a bag to appropriate French fries. "Yea verily," she said. "Carbohydrates, the food of heroes." She glanced at him. "We *are* the heroes, right?"

"If you gotta pick a side," Mac said, checking all four tires before pulling the driver's door open. Just in case.

"I definitely choose the hero side," Gwen said, settling into the seat and arranging the food—between her feet, on her lap. "But honestly, I don't see why innocent bystander isn't one of the options."

"In this game?" Mac shook his head, shoving the keys into the ignition and cranking up the air-conditioning. "I don't think that's an entirely safe place to be." He glanced at her. "And I don't think your father left you that option."

"I doubt he knew." Gwen found her chin lifting and had no idea in defiance of what.

Except in the next moment, she did. In defiance of self. All her mixed feelings, all her years of outrunning and outtalking herself. *I am nine years old, and my life has changed forever...* "With someone else, it might have gone differently."

"Of that I have no doubt." And then his gaze caught at the center console cup holder, and she knew instantly what had surprised him there.

"I put your cell on the charger," she said, shifting a

bag aside to see it there, tipped casually into the cup holder. "It was getting— Oh."

Because that wasn't what had caught his attention at all. Or maybe at first, but the bright message indicator on the phone display had caught it more. He reached for the phone. "I've got a week before work starts. No one even knows I'm in town."

Gwen's hand froze in the act of untangling another long fry.

Someone knew *she* was in town. Someone who'd taken a call from her on that phone. "Wait!"

He'd flipped the phone open to frown at the displayed number; now he transferred his gaze to hers, a silent question.

"It might be…" she said. "I mean, the other night… I needed to think."

Wow. That tongue of hers sure had lost its glib.

"Listen," she said, desperate as understanding flickered across his features. He went still, waiting. "I went out for a walk. After we… You fell asleep. And I needed a little space. And she found me there."

"She," Mac said, "who?"

"Natalie!" Gwen blurted. "She was watching the hotel. She's with the man who dumped on us that first evening. His name is Devin. They have blades—"

"Like mine?" he said, every bit of him going hard and dangerous. "All these years, and suddenly those things are everywhere?"

"She said they could help you! Us. And her blade has a *name,* Mac. She said she had some sort of truce with it, or control over it, or—I don't know. Something.

And she saw my pendant, because when she came to the—" oh, that was so not how she'd meant to tell him this, but now the word was in her mouth, even if it immediately trailed away "—warehouse…"

He took it in—understanding immediately that she'd seen Natalie not once but twice—and immediately putting the rest of it together. Natalie's message on the phone, his number harvested when Gwen had called her to the warehouse.

Nothing to do now but get it all out. She'd done what she'd thought was right, hadn't she? Done the only thing she could think of at the time? "I was terrified at the warehouse," she said. "I thought you were going to kill yourself. Or that the blade would kill you. So yes, I called her, and she came. And dammit, she made me wait outside, just like you said."

"What I said," he told her—softly, dangerously "—was to run."

"She's got some sort of research mojo, because she'd looked up my pendant. And listen to me, Mac—it all makes sense. It's supposed to be able to sever the connection between blade and wielder."

He did listen, thoughtful even in his anger. "We've seen that. We've also seen the price."

"That's because I don't know what I'm doing!" Gwen said. "And besides, it's different now. It's… awake. It has a name, she says—it has a history." She reached blindly under the seat, groping for the folder she'd jammed there just to have a place to put it. The food bags rustled, obstructing her efforts, but finally she pulled it out and thrust it at him. "And I haven't been keeping this from you, not any of it. You've been out of it or sleeping it off or fighting or—"

"Yeah," he said tightly, taking the folder. "I get the picture."

"Mac," she said, her hand lingering in place even emptied—wanting to reach for him and feeling the emotional barriers he'd flung up. "She said they could help. She didn't ask anything of me. She took the dog to the vet. She helped me deal with what was happening to you. And you *know* she could have taken control of things while you were chained inside that warehouse."

"So did you, when you called her," he said, flipping through the pages—not long enough to absorb anything, but long enough to see the veracity of the materials within. "What were you even *thinking?*"

Ohh, that just crossed the line. "I was *thinking,*" she told him, "that you were going to die, and that I didn't want it to happen! I was thinking that I had this pendant coming alive and no idea what to do about it! I didn't tell her anything she didn't need to know—she wasn't real happy about that, either—but what I did tell her was *mine to tell.* Are you hearing me, Michael MacKenzie? This isn't just about you. Some parts of it maybe aren't about you at all!"

As if she'd expected him to back off. But she hadn't expected him to reach for her—to stop, pull his hand back and fist it at his thigh. To say, "If she'd taken you, Gwen Badura, it damned well would have been about me."

Her mouth hadn't expected it, either, already bursting out with, "Just because you—"

And then, "Oh." She looked at his fist, white-knuckled as it was; she looked up to his face and his eyes gone dark and his gaze latched on to hers. What he'd said, what he'd meant…how deeply he'd meant it. "Oh."

And then, because he still seemed caught there in the very agony of the thought, she said, "Kiss me, dammit!"

Oh, yeah. Right there across the middle console, quick enough to startle her—he grabbed her shoulders and kissed her right to instant flashpoint, hard and not a little bit rough and just exactly what she wanted, a growl stirring in his throat.

She startled as the sweet tension curled fast through her body, thrumming into an unexpected echo—she jerked with it, a surprised little cry trapped between them. Mac stiffened, his hands tightening on her shoulders—and when he drew back from her, his eyes had gone huge and wild, his control tipping and his breath hard and fast.

The blade. The pendant. It had to be.

She opened her mouth to ask—but he only shook his head, cutting her off. And when he could speak, it was only to say, "I don't know. I don't— God, Gwen. I don't know."

Gwen sat heavily against the seat back, just a bit of an uncomfortable squirm there. "I wonder," she said, finding her own breath again, "if that hotel room is safe yet."

A hint of his wry amusement returned. "I wonder if we would survive it, regardless."

"Oh," she breathed. "But what a way to go…"

And then she sighed, straightened the bag on her lap and peeked within it. "Smashed burger, anyone?"

"Anything," he said, fishing for the phone. "I'm hungry enough to—" His gaze caught hers. She stopped breathing again, and he let slip that little twist of his mouth. "Eat anything," he said, finishing the words.

In practical desperation, she shoved a hamburger—indeed somewhat worse for the wear—in his direction. And then when he reached for it, she caught his wrist—just for a moment, passing her eyes over the fading bruises, the healing skin. She shook her head but didn't say anything.

Besides, she was hungry, too. She fished a wrapped burrito out of the bag and spread a napkin in her lap. "Because," she said, feeling absurdly fussy, "I hardly have any clothes left to spare at this point, do I?"

He flipped the phone open again, hitting the voice mail, thumbing in his password and activating the speaker. In moments, a woman's voice issued from the phone—he glanced at her, as neutrally as she imagined he could make it.

She nodded. Yes. Natalie.

*"Gwen, listen. I'm digging up some information on the other blade involved. Believe it or not, I really didn't need you to tell me there's someone else involved, and that you're tangled with him—and it's not good. It's a strong blade, and there are indications that it's created a bond of unusual properties. This man has been building his resources for longer than any one lifetime. Gwen, if he learns about you, he'll*

*stop at nothing to get what you have. I really wish you would—"*

And something interrupted her, or the voice mail system cut her off, but it didn't matter.

"She wanted me to go there." Gwen shifted her weight to pull the business card out of her pocket and display it to him. "She keeps saying they can help—"

Mac took the card from her fingers, dropped it onto the drink holder console, and put the phone on top of it. "*That man* offered to help, too. He offered all sorts of things. They all have their own reasons, Gwen. You heard what she said—he'll stop at nothing to get what you have. Do you know this woman well enough to be sure she's not exactly the same?"

Gwen sucked in a breath.

She didn't, did she?

She remembered the look on Natalie's face when she'd let it slip that she'd used the pendant, however awkwardly—that she'd wrung Mac a temporary separation from it. And then she remembered the quiet manner in which the woman drove away afterward, knowing Gwen hadn't told her everything, knowing Gwen had the pendant and that she had Mac. She let the breath out again. "I've got uh-oh alarms. She didn't set any of them off."

"Neither did I."

"That's different," she protested. "With you it was… it was…" *Way to paint yourself into a corner, Gwen.*

"Love at first sight?" To give him credit, that dark humor came gently.

She lifted her chin. "Not in the least. You scared

me. But you…you caught me, too. Maybe," she added, resting the burrito on top of the bag from which it had come, her appetite momentarily gone, "that's what scared me."

He snorted. "Or maybe you were just smart."

"Look," she said. "Maybe they're not totally safe. But they're not that man, either. If we have to choose between the two—"

The look he sent her held a fierce defiance she hadn't expected. "Who says we have to choose at all?"

She sat back in the seat, momentarily and unexpectedly silenced as he balanced his burger on his lap and shoved the Jeep into gear. Who says?

Except in her heart, she knew the grim truth of it. Natalie and Devin, they belonged here. They had resources. They were positioned to deal with this situation. And that man…he didn't seem to belong here, but hell, yes, he had resources. And power.

She and Mac had a vehicle, a few suitcases, and a compromised hotel room. Mac's blade had made him wanted…and Gwen's pendant would make her wanted. And neither of them truly knew what to do with what they had.

# *Chapter 15*

Mac drove the circuit around Albuquerque with hands tense on the wheel—the burger leaden in a stomach that still demanded more, the impact of what he'd heard lying heavily upon him.

He'd been drawn here; he knew that much. Gwen had been drawn here. And now he faced not one but potentially two enemy adversarial camps that might have had a hand in it.

Except if Natalie was telling the truth, she hadn't known about the pendant and still didn't know much about it. Subdued as she was, Gwen had devoured her burrito, picking through the folder with fingers she kept licking clean. Defining what she could for him—the name of the thing, the purpose of it, the vague genesis of it. But she didn't know, and Natalie apparently didn't know, how to use it.

Or Natalie and Devin could simply be playing them and doing it more subtly than the man at the warehouse.

Not subtle at all, that one.

*Go.* The thought surfaced unbidden. *Run.* Just as Gwen had suggested. If they'd been drawn here, then maybe leaving here would be enough.

Except he didn't believe it for a moment. And he wasn't about to risk Gwen. Not when, as she had so aptly pointed out, it suddenly wasn't about just him anymore. Him and the blade.

"Wow," Gwen said. "Look how fast those clouds came up."

He followed her glance out the windshield, north and west and up, and found towering late afternoon clouds tumbling high, white above, dramatic shadowing below. "We should have checked the weather."

"Oh, but this area can surely use the rain."

He couldn't help a smile—mundane conversation, a Northeastern woman come west. "No doubt. But if I'd known we were about to hit the front edge of monsoon activity, I'd have found time to get us slickers today."

"Huh," she said. "Before the battle for sanity or after?"

"Before," he said firmly, reaching for the bottled water propped between his thighs. "If it rains, you'll see what I mean. What else do you have in those bags?"

She dug in, offering him the ketchup-smeared remains of boxed fries. As he pinched up a mouthful, she said, "Seems quiet."

She wasn't talking about the clouds. And when he answered, neither was he. "So far." The blade, quiescent. The rolling waves of black despair and fury, abated.

So far.

They'd taken the highway up to veer west on Tramway, detoured south to Alameda and across the river to travel Coors south. The rush-hour traffic eased as they headed into the south valley area—not a coincidental choice.

According to the business card Gwen had been given, this was Devin James's turf. And it was time to see how the air tasted here.

Gwen, peering at the map she'd pulled from his door pocket, realized it just as he approached the highway—the highway overpass within sight as he cut east over a narrow road, speed bumps and all, that spilled them out near the Isleta entrance ramp.

North on the highway, and their ninety-minute circuit would be completed in another fifteen, the clouds closing in dark and imminent above them.

"They're here somewhere," she said, looking out over the south valley from the raised highway. "Do you feel—"

"There's something," he told her. Not something he'd have been alert to before these past few days—nothing like the blade's deep obsession with acquiring emotions. Just an underlying awareness as they fish-hooked around the south end of the valley. "You?"

She shook her head. "Maybe it would be there if…" She glanced at him, and he could have sworn that was a blush stealing in on those lightly freckled cheeks. "If you weren't right here."

He smiled to himself. *Okay then.* "Nice to have an impact," he murmured.

"Don't let it go to your head."

At that he only cocked an eyebrow at her, until she heard her own words and laughed a sputtering sound. "Or *do* let it go to your head. But you're on your own with that until we're not driving around looking for trouble."

"And not finding it."

"Bad guys have to sleep, too," Gwen said. "Maybe we can grab our stuff from the hotel."

It wouldn't be the first time he'd lived out of his vehicle. He nodded. "Hit and run."

Although if that man—or even Natalie or Devin— had wanted to get to them through the hotel room, they'd had plenty of opportunity.

Then again, things changed.

Advancing with care at the hotel took longer than hauling down their stuff once they felt safe; checking out took a matter of moments. Mac stuffed the bill in his pocket and joined Gwen where he'd parked beside her little blob of a car, jumper cables at work. "Let's head for the park." He nodded in the direction of the little park to which he'd led them only the day before. "Maybe we can learn something from what's left of the hot spot."

She hesitated as she opened her car door, about to

slide in. "I really wonder if we shouldn't call Natalie. No one else here can help us."

He set his jaw—as much at the anxiety trickling in from her as at the suggestion itself. She thought to hide from him, but couldn't hide from the blade...and he didn't know how he felt about that.

People should, he thought, be allowed their private thoughts and feelings. Even if it benefited him to know them.

Her eyes widened with dismay; her hand went to the pendant. "You're a lot angrier than you look."

He laughed, utterly without humor. "Looks like we're in the same boat," he said. "Is it just me, or—"

"You," she said. "Through the blade, I think. Just like—" She stopped short, biting her lip.

"Just like outside the diner." Yeah. *Damned* intense. "That's what we'll do at the park, I think."

"What?"

He laughed again, this time with true amusement. "That, too, eventually—but no, not in the park. No, I mean this." He gestured between the pendant and the pocket that held the blade. "We need to understand what's happening there. We need to be able to limit it. If one of us gets in trouble, the other one of us has to be able to function."

"Trouble," she said. "Right. Not much chance of *that,* is there?"

But wherever trouble had hidden this late afternoon, it wasn't at the park beneath the threatening rain, thunder now rumbling in the background. A few skateboarders were on their way through; bikers swooped along the walkways while scant pedestrians shared the fast-cooling air. Just a typical park clearing out before dinner time and rain.

"It might not storm," Gwen said, looking over at the clouds. "The hotel clerk said sometimes it just circles around the city."

"The hotel clerk was angling for a look at your excellent ass while you gathered your things from the floor," Mac pointed out. "Not that I'm keeping track."

She shot him a look that might have been amusement or exasperation. "You getting anything from this place? They were right over there."

Mac wandered through the pampered grass, trailing his hand along the picnic table, searching for any visible sign of what had happened here the day before. In the silence of everything but the rising storm gusts and the rustle of leaves, he gave her a rueful look and did that which until now he'd been avoiding.

There was more than one way to run.

He let the blade in.

He did more than that. He went looking for it. Not deep or hard—a mere crack in the wall he'd placed between them.

He barely heard Gwen's gasp through the rush of thunder in his mind, the fierce resentment and craving that curled through his body, wrapping around his bones. It would ease, he told himself, standing stiff and impaled by it…making himself believe.

"Mac—" Her protest held concern—her first inkling of what it was they both asked of him here. Her inward panic and floundering adjustment bounced back at him through whatever had grown between the blade and pendant.

"Now," he told her, his eyes still closed against it all, "would be a good time to see if you can shut it down."

Her fingers found his on the tabletop—the lightest of touches, full of acknowledgment and *I'm here*.

Slowly, his sense of her floundering receded; her panic turned into an underlying determination...and then diminished. Not gone, but...not crashing into him any longer.

The blade, too, receded, its tsunami of resentment easing back to what had become normal between them, while some part of him numbed itself to the consistency of that background noise.

He took a deep breath, rotating his shoulders.

"Better?" she asked.

He nodded, not yet opening his eyes—because now he had work to do. But he murmured, "That was good, what you did. The calm, before you stepped back. Remember that feeling."

*That feeling* nudged against him, a little caress of calm; he turned his hand palm-up and gently captured her fingers—as much in warning as in response. Because yeah...now he was going hunting.

Loosed with his intent behind it, the blade swept out to scour the park. *Hunger hunger hunting free!*

And Mac swept out with it.

Gwen shivered and looked up at the sky—the wind gusting up high, lightning strobing, thunder hard on its heels. "Mac," she said, and not for the first time.

But he just stood there, swaying slightly—his eyes shut, his face closed, his attention turned inward.

She could feel it, in a strained and distant way—the intensity of the blade's hunt, Mac's willingness to go along with it.

Saving his effort for a more critical juncture, she thought.

But still. The first drops of rain splattered against her, huge and startling and bringing out instant goose bumps. A glance around the park told her they were alone, other than a couple now hurrying for their car. Gwen eyed her own car with a certain wistfulness. "Mac."

He made a noise deep in his throat. Not a particularly responsive one.

The scattered drops turned steady; Gwen hunched to receive them. Definitely too far away, those cars. She eyed the nearest overhead shelter, measuring the distance. "Mac," she said, raising her voice above wind and rumble. "It's raining."

And the skies opened up. Water fell upon them as if poured from a bucket; Gwen gasped in shock and outrage. This wasn't rain! This was inundation! "Mac!"

His eyes opened suddenly, gratifyingly wide in startled surprise. They were instantly soaked to the skin, his T-shirt clinging and his hair dripping. His mouth formed a curse—she couldn't hear it—and he grabbed her hand and pulled her toward the shelter.

When he stopped beneath it, she ran right into him and then stayed there for warmth, oh-so-grateful when he put his arms around her. Whatever either of them might have said was lost in the battering sound of rain against the metal shelter roof, and she didn't even try. She shivered, and she thought of his earlier remarks about the monsoon, and she decided even the most encompassing slicker wouldn't have kept out *this* rain.

He didn't shiver. If anything, he had warmth enough for them both, and the realization of it made her glance up at him, understanding. The blade had seen his chilled condition as it would any kind of hurt or illness, and had addressed it.

*Okay, demon blade. For this, you get points.*

But only until his eyes flared briefly wide, just enough warning so she didn't fall when he abruptly jerked her around behind him. Not that she didn't stumble, her soaked pant legs grabbing at one another, her feet squishing in her sport sandals. So disorienting, the rain slamming the roof overhead, the lightning flashing strobe imprints against her vision.

It took her a moment to realize they were no longer alone.

Two young men stood at the edge of the shelter, dripping and panting and still regaining their balance—but already sneering. Only then did Gwen realize that in the middle of this sensory pounding, her instincts had gone into overdrive—even if the only evident weapon was a baseball bat. She grabbed for Mac's shoulder, a warning—and realized he already knew.

Of course he knew. He'd shoved her back, hadn't he? And now he stood like some wild thing, braced for action, water dripping off his hair and clothes and the blade—the Bowie—in his hand, a reverse grip held low. A flush of the blade's delight trickled through to her, shocking her with its beguiling nature.

All that had been warm suddenly turned cold.

This? This was what he had to fight from within?

The two men sorted themselves out, breath and physical composure regained. Hair cut short slicked down dark; olive skin gleamed wetly. Their clothes were neat and well-fitted and on any other day, in any other moment, she would have given them both a second glance of appreciation. But what she saw in their eyes...

It wasn't sanity.

*That's not fair. It's quiet out there!*

And it was. It still was. But inciting hatred had been sweeping over this city for days, and in these men, it seemed to have lodged.

The rain slacked a notch—enough for raised voices and loud conversation. One of the men stepped forward, hefting his bat. "What? You don't want to share your shelter with us?"

Mac's words came steadier than she ever would have believed, knowing what raged inside him. "The shelter is for everyone. The baseball bat doesn't need to come any closer."

"Why?" asked the man. "Are you one of those? The people who think every Latino should go home even when our families founded this city? You look like one of those."

"Dammit," Gwen said, very much in spite of herself as she realized what the second man, his eyes glittering in silence, held in his hand now that he'd tossed his ball glove aside, "Does everyone in this city carry a knife?"

"The shelter," Mac repeated, voice carrying over the rain with a grim determination that told Gwen he was clinging to control, "is for everyone."

She reeled, caught up in the blade's despotism— and then grabbed on to the sudden, grounding realization. Opportunity.

They'd needed practice. She'd needed practice. She needed to know if she could block this out, and if she could control the flow of it, and if she could reach back to him in return, even through this. More than just a moment of calm, but a domination of what tried to engulf her.

Maybe of what tried to engulf *him*.

Poor hubris, to aim so high when she had no experience, no practice—when years of dealing with the blade had given Mac both, and he still now faltered before it.

But he was tired, and she wasn't. He was worn, and she was fresh.

She hadn't yet learned what she couldn't do, and sometimes that made all the difference.

Being able to concentrate…that was another thing altogether.

"Yes," the man was saying, as the rain—so strong and sudden—retreated just as abruptly. "We think *you* should go home."

Mac hesitated there—looking nothing but ominous, even as Gwen felt the common sense of Mac versus the bloodthirst of the blade. The *emotion* thirst.

Given time, she thought he would win.

She didn't think they had time.

She gathered her calm.

"Okay," she said, interrupting the confrontation. "We will. We're leaving now."

"No," the second man said, gesturing with the knife. "You don't understand. *All* the way home."

"Mac," Gwen said, low enough to make it private. "Let's just go. They won't follow us. There's nothing active here."

When he hesitated, she knew it didn't come from him. That the blade pushed him.

So she pushed back. Just a little. Just enough to let him know she was doing it—the calm. The confidence in him. A quiet, centered feeling that she took from within herself, finding it there amid her own growing confidence, and spread to him.

Not to mention a little common sense. "These guys aren't the ones we want."

He blinked. For a moment, the turmoil roiled even more loudly within him, the bare nuances of it reaching through to her—and then it quietly gave way before her. He shook his head. "No. They aren't." He eased back a step, looking out on the park—glistening grass and landscaping, instant puddles everywhere, water still trickling off leaves and the shelter roof to create a symphony of soft percussions. To the east of the city, the Sandia Mountains dominated the skyline—and the dark clouds still dominated the Sandias.

"Whatever was here yesterday," she said, "it's long

gone. *That man* is sleeping, or eating, or watching the news."

He nodded, flipping the blade up to catch it—a closed Barstow pocketknife all over again. To the men—to their scowls and barely restrained anger—he said, "It's all yours, fellows."

Gwen let her breath out, resting her hand on his back, soaked pink bandage and all. Feeling the tension still living there under soaked cotton—and realizing anew how wet she was, too. She glanced down at herself; it might have been a mistake.

Wet, and more than a little see-through.

She thought she'd just stay here behind him. And maybe he read her mind, or maybe she just distracted him, for he did what she thought he would never have done without her interference...he turned his back on the men, blocking her from their view...protecting her.

She knew instantly from their faces—it had been a mistake. "No!" cried one of them. "You do not turn your *back*—" his movement created a strange punctuation in emphasis "—on...*us*."

Mac shoved her—shoved her hard. He ducked and threw himself to the side as she went down with a cry, skinning palms and shooting pain through her injured hand; the baseball bat slammed down on the table with the resounding clang of weighted metal against wood. Gwen twisted wildly, scrabbling away even as she tried to orient—untangling the visuals of three men in the eerie post-storm glitter of water and oblique new sunlight.

Two men with bats.

No. Mac with the Iroquois war club, meeting the man's next blow with swift power—sending the bat flying, slipping away from the slashing knife, whirling around to slam the man in the ribs with a blow that had to be pulled, its potential metered into just enough so the man ended up on the ground not far from Gwen.

Not far at all.

He pressed against the ground, lifting his head… finding her. She didn't need the warning cry of old instincts—and she didn't need Mac's help. She popped him one, right in the nose, and when he fell back on his shoulder, she lashed out with her sandaled toes pointed and fierce.

By the time she scrambled to her feet, he had one hand over his nose and one over his crotch, and the flare of warning had faded to nothing but adrenaline aftermath.

She found his knife not far away; she acquired it.

When she stood, brushing herself off—a futile gesture for one who was now covered in sandy clay mud and wetness—she realized she'd closed Mac out entirely. And when she looked at him, she realized what a mistake that had been.

Or maybe not. She probably wouldn't have been able to function at all had she not kept to herself.

Because now the club was a saber, sweeping and sharp with the faintly unearthly sheen of light running along its edge. And now the single man still upright stood frozen, his irrational anger—a mob mentality gone so badly wrong with only two mob members—

now utterly dissipated in the face of Mac's own lost sanity.

Not to mention the sword.

If the man ran, he'd die. If he blinked, he'd die. If he didn't run...

Maybe he'd die then, too.

Gwen didn't dare even say Mac's name. Not so much as a soothing sound. Not the way he trembled on the edge of explosive violence.

In desperation, she returned to the calm.

Oh, it wasn't easy—not with her own adrenaline reaction zinging along her nerves. But she'd found it before—a subtle, budding confidence in not just the pendant, but also in the way her life was coming together. The way some things suddenly had meaning. What she'd experienced as a child, what she'd grown to in the aftermath. How the wound from her father's blade had left its indelible impression, the gift of warning she had taken half a lifetime to master.

So from the inside out, she touched him. Just a whisper. But a confident whisper, growing with the understanding of what she could do.

His awareness came in the merest shift of his shoulder; the blade's awareness came in a slap of annoyance. Gwen stiffened—found herself offended as much as hurt by it. *Screw you. You can't have him.*

She went back for more. Just enough to let him regain his own grasp of himself—buffering, calming. The blade snapped at her again, a sharp sting of retribution; she pushed past it, lifting her gaze to that of the man who stood frozen in wise fear before them. "You know," she said, "we really were happy to share." She hadn't expected to see the flicker of acknowledgment on his face—or the regret.

She dared to rest her hand on Mac's back. "I think it's safe. Go while you can."

The man didn't hesitate. First things first—he squirted out of range, squelching audibly; only then did he circle around for his friend. By then Gwen could feel Mac breathing more deeply under her hand; she dared to do more than touch him, rubbing a gentle circle over his back.

The man scooped up their baseball gloves—the bat was a lost cause, deeply dented even at a glance—and pulled his friend up, that latter still trying to choose between stanching his nosebleed and comforting his privates. The man caught Gwen's eye, and he was, suddenly, what she'd seen upon their arrival—a well-presented guy out for a session of fielding balls in the park with his friend. "Resentment builds," he said, "but you didn't deserve… I don't know—"

Gwen shook her head. "It was on the wind," she said, the only one of the two of them who knew the near-literal truth of it. "It's in the city. We fought it together, in a way." And then she made a face, a wince, and said, "I hope I didn't break his nose."

"Better that," the man said, "than the other."

Gwen couldn't argue with that.

Or with the deep release of a breath that Mac let go as they left, easing back his ready stance. He looked down at his hand; the blade settled into the Barstow—

still flipped open, keen and wicked and gleaming. "That was too close."

"In all ways," Gwen told him, seeing the self-retribution dark in his eyes. "They made their choice, too. What if you *hadn't* had the blade? How do you think things would have gone for us, your basic average couple sheltering from the rain?"

He cast a startled look at her, still easing down from his alert—she knew that, too, from the faint echo of the blade's turmoil. "Chivalry compels me to mention that you could never be basic average."

How silly was it to feel a little leap of pleasure at those words, here in the middle of what must now be the world's most hostile park, hair and clothes still dripping and the driving culprit of a storm still lumbering along the shoulders of the Sandias?

"Ooh," she said. "I have to stop everything and preen for a moment." But not too much of a moment. She glanced across the landscaping to the parking lot, a narrow strip edged by a curving cemented arroyo on the far side. The Jeep sat gleaming next to her little Bug. "I really think I'd like to call—"

He made a strange sound, a kick-in-the-gut noise. She didn't have to ask why; she felt it. Even as she grabbed at him, slowing his descent to the concrete, she understood exactly where that slashing pain came from and why.

The blade, having its temper tantrum. It had wanted blood and fear; they'd stopped it. And now Mac was pale and stricken, his mouth tight—yet shaking his head. "It'll pass," he said, barely managing the words. "It'll— *Damn*—"

"Stupid blade!" Gwen found herself in a fury. "Worse than a two-year-old!" She glared down at it. "I'd kick you if I could!"

And couldn't she?

Until now, when she'd reached out, it had been to Mac. Her desire to protect him and the unconscious results, then her deliberate attempts to soothe him, to offer him just enough space that he could catch his own emotional and physical breath.

This time, she didn't go for Mac. She looked for something *other*. Blindly groping, no idea what she was looking for other than what it wasn't. She slipped into that head space quickly enough to be frightening, successfully enough so she didn't have time to think about it. She found herself in Mac's muffled pain, slicing claws of temper and retribution…human pain and human struggle and the deep, rich presence underlying the very essence of the man beside her.

But there. Oh, *there*. The stench of super-heated metal and acrid charcoal and singed flesh. That wasn't Mac. Or human.

*I see you,* she told it. And, on impulse, *Who are you? What's your name?*

Learning Demardel's name had changed things for her. If this blade had a name…maybe it would change things for Mac.

But the blade lashed out at her, filled with fury and…*fear*. The strike raked through Mac on its way to her, twisting the rich essence she'd only just found and wrenching a cry from him.

*Me. I did that. I'm doing that to him!*

She fled from it. Found herself clutching him, found him clutching her back, both of them panting and astonished.

And the blade fled, too. Shocked and quiet. Not as before, when the pendant had shut it down, but simply hiding.

For the moment.

Mac, his eyes still wide and wary, said, "What the hell did you do?"

She shook her head, suddenly overwhelmed by it all.

*I am nine years old, and my life will never be the same...*

*My father had a demon blade. He found this pendant. He gave it to me for safekeeping so he could finish his hunting—for those who killed my mother, for those like her. But he waited too long, and he was about to lose his fight with the blade, so he came after it...and me.*

*He wounded me. He left me with the pendant and a healed-in sixth sense about those who would hurt me. Or hurt others. And now the pendant has brought me to this place, this time, this man...*

*I am twenty-seven years old, and my life will never be the same.*

Mac rolled to his knees, to his feet. "What?" he demanded.

"I want to call them," Gwen blurted, climbing to her feet beside him. "I don't want to make the same mistakes my father made. I want to know what's going on!"

She didn't have to define who she meant. Mac bit back his snap of a response, a visible effort. He closed his eyes and took a breath and she couldn't help but be amazed even at that, that he could think at all.

But in the end, he shook his head.

"Don't you understand?" She barely stopped herself from shouting it at him. "I felt it! I *scared* it! If Natalie's found any more information, maybe it's enough. Maybe I can free you from this thing!"

*Free us from this thing.*

But she didn't say it out loud, because it felt presumptuous. Three days of absurd intensity, of an astonishing physical connection and sexual release—maybe that was all it would ever be. She could free herself simply by walking away.

Except she'd felt that deep essence, and she'd tasted that rich, solid, amazing presence that made the core of him.

She knew what stood before her, and what it meant to her.

Mac, however, was not in mind-reading mode. Mac only shook his head. "This blade is the only chance we have to stop that man."

*That man.* It had started as something of a joke, to refer to him that way. Now it was second nature, and suddenly so startlingly unreal. "No," she said. "No, it's not. We don't have to do this by ourselves. My father tried to do it by himself, and look where it got him! Look where it got me!"

He astonished her with the instant fierce tenderness of his response—stepping in to hold her close and tight, to sweep her up, two damp, hurting people under storm-racked skies. She was just as surprised at how tightly she returned the embrace.

"Where it got you," he murmured into her ear, "is right here. And I'd have been lost days ago without you."

She rebelled against that, stiffening in his arms. "Don't say that. It's not true. You're stronger than that. I've felt it."

"Stronger," he agreed. "But tired. And I had no idea it would react like that." He pulled back, touched his forehead to hers, and closed his eyes, taking a deep breath. "Now I do. And you're right. I can't do it alone. So make your call."

# Chapter 16

Devin James paced before the expansive office windows, scowling out at the grounds of the estate. A warm plate from the kitchen sat untouched on the corner desk; Anheriel sat in his pocket. It purred, if a knife could be said to purr.

That was the thing, wasn't it? Not truly just a knife at all. A demon blade, and fully aware of the rising turmoil in the city. Not only that, but fully anticipating the part it would play.

Anheriel would drink deeply this day, Devin had no doubt.

Natalie stood by the worktable, its broad surface covered with papers, copies, notes, and several of the most fragile books from the blade room. She also had a plate—fruit and yogurt parfait, a special treat from

Jimena, the estate's cook, who had been through hell with them not so long ago and who now split her time between the estate and Sawyer's new Alley of Life Restaurant project.

Sawyer Compton had had ulterior motives for that one, using it as a front for his own nefarious deeds—but the idea itself had been too good to lose, and Natalie had kept it alive even as she researched their blades.

And now, Demardel.

"Okay," Natalie muttered. "She's obviously activated the thing, whether she's gotten it to reach its full potential or not. I can find mention of the blood, and earthy stuff like sex never hurts."

"Sex never hurts," Devin agreed. "You're sure they—" He fielded a *look* from her and subsided. "Okay, yeah. Sex never hurts."

"I just can't tell if it matters that she didn't know its name. Names are such a big deal with these…" She hesitated, looking down at the blade on the worktable—it had turned itself into a delicate surgeon's instrument once she started using it to slice up photocopies.

Devin had the suspicion it was amused.

Natalie had apparently made up her mind to avoid making up her mind. "*Entities*. Names are such a big deal with these entities."

It was closer than Devin had ever gotten to defining the complex nature of the blades. Fallen beings, seeking redemption, incorporated into metal, forged into weapons from which they could both influence and act. "It may be enough," he told her. "Look how long I handled Anheriel before even knowing it had a name. I didn't get the impression our new friend knows his blade, either."

"Michael MacKenzie."

"Yeah, yeah. Mac." Not that he hadn't known it. He just hadn't liked the fact that he had a reason to know. "Do you think it matters? I don't see this guy ditching the blade. Didn't seem like the type."

She looked up from the notes she'd just made. "Do you even hear yourself? Two days ago you wanted to take him down. Now he's a good guy?"

"*Didn't seem like the type* doesn't necessarily lead to good things." Devin resumed his prowl along the window wall. "I'm completely secure in my consistency."

"Uh-huh." Natalie shot him amusement and let it stand, but she sobered quickly enough. "Why it matters is that we really don't *want* them to sever that bond right now. Things are too unsettled—we still don't understand what's going on out there. We don't need a loose blade in the middle of it, or a brand-new wielder dealing with it all."

"We don't need this guy attached to the blade if he's about to hit the wild road, either."

She didn't respond right away. She'd been there when *this guy* had made it through the late morning battle with the blade; she better than anyone knew how close he was. Finally she said, "I hope he can do it. I think we need him."

Devin sent another scowl out to the grounds, proxy for the entire city and its turmoil. "I wish I could disagree. Whoever's out there…he's got power."

"As well he should, if we're right about how old he

is and how long he's been with his blade." Natalie set her pen aside as her cell phone rang, reaching for it with an alacrity that told Devin how much she'd hoped to hear it ring.

"Natalie," she said, straightening—startled. "Oh. Mac. Nice to, um, meet you." She drifted closer to Devin; he could hear the deep timbre of another man's voice. "Well, we've figured out some of it. Not the medallion—no more than I gave Gwen earlier. But the thing we're up against—" A nod, a glance at Devin. "Yes. Old. Creepy. Powerful. That about sums it up. Hold on a moment." She moved the phone away from her face, but not so much that Mac wouldn't still be able to hear her. "They're in the city—Kirtland Park near the airport. They can use some backup."

Devin took a breath. This added up to so many places he hadn't wanted to go.

But so far Natalie had been one step ahead of him on this one...her research brains over his gut instinct to protect this turf. So he nodded. "I'm good with that. It'll be about half an hour before I—"

Anheriel grabbed his inner ear, clutching at his thoughts, whispering of violence and blood and sated thirst, reflecting a gleeful dark and roiling power— one that reached into the very roots of this city. One that poured through its people in footprints of violence.

Devin shook himself out of it and found Natalie gone pale—feeling something of the same, if never yet quite as directly. She pulled the phone back to her ear. "Mac? Are you still—yes! We're coming!"

By the time she flipped the phone closed and

snatched up Baitlia, he knew well enough what had happened.

And that they'd be too late.

Mac dropped the phone into the Jeep's front seat. Not panicked, not hasty...but deliberate. Stepping away from the car, putting himself between Gwen and the van just now pulling into the parking lot.

Its passengers disembarked with the air of those exiting a limousine. The driver didn't wear a uniform and cap, but managed to give the impression of it in slacks and a snug polo shirt. The same height as Mac and his six-feet-plus-change...a good fifty pounds beefier.

Not that it mattered. Mac didn't intend to get close enough to bring that muscle into play. And he suspected the man in the limo didn't intend for things to go that way, either. Otherwise, the guns each of the several disembarking men carried would surely be in stark evidence instead of implied threat.

The driver opened the van's sliding door and stepped aside, and a man stepped out.

*That* man.

Mac didn't have a moment's doubt. Not even though the man's appearance surprised him—not a big man, not even a particularly imposing man. Moderately dressed in department store slacks and shirt, his hair a thinning, washed-out brown in a bland style, he stood beside the van and regarded them with a somewhat amused and proprietary air.

"Wow," Gwen said. "I thought you'd be wearing one of those Phantom of the Opera masks. Or a brown paper bag. Or *something,* after that whole warehouse drama."

He smiled. "That was an initial indulgence." Unexpected, that cultured, controlled voice coming from his unprepossessing self. "I needed to feel out your friend. I've done that, don't you think? That particular indulgence would be a little too conspicuous under these circumstances, in any event."

Mac couldn't help but snort. "As if anything you've come here to do is likely to be inconspicuous?"

The man inclined his head. "There is that. Of course, I think you'll discover that most people will be too busy to care." At Mac's frown, he added, "You won't be feeling that just yet. I sent it in other directions."

No longer behind him, Gwen raised her hand like a schoolgirl. "Oh," she said. "Me! Me, call on me!"

Mac wanted to snatch her up and throw her back into the Jeep. Did she not see the guns? Did she not truly understand what this man would do to her if he realized what she had? The value she could be to him?

For Mac himself had watched it happen—the deepening of the bond between Gwen and that pendant. She might not understand it fully yet, but soon enough, she would. And once she truly controlled the pendant, she could affect any wielder she encountered.

He didn't even breathe a sigh of relief when the man chose to be amused. "Now that you've seen what I can offer you—or what I can do to you—now is the time to answer your questions."

Gwen didn't hesitate—and she didn't stay behind

Mac, either, even if she did stand closely enough to brush up against him. "Where did you come from?" she asked. "And how old are you? And what's your name? Although that one's not so important if you don't mind being called *that man*. It's worked for us so far."

*That man* chuckled. "You are indeed charmingly forthright." And while his hired muscle shot startled reactions to that chuckle, Mac watched the hired muscle.

He could take them. He'd take damage, too—but he'd heal. They wouldn't. He just needed the right moment.

And the right moment was coming, presaged by an early summer sunset against a monsoon sky. Once that sun slipped under the horizon, there'd be no lengthy desert twilight. That man could see in it, he suspected, just as Mac could. And by then, Devin James would join them. If Mac and Gwen had been right to call him, he'd help. If not...

Well. One thing at a time.

"Where I started is irrelevant. I come from everywhere." There was no particular pretension to the man's words. "I've been around the world often enough to have lost count. I have a stake in every nation, and I know the roots of them all."

Gwen frowned. Boastful words for any man; surprising words for the man before them. The unprepossessing form and presentation, the singular lack of drama now that he'd abandoned the conceit of the screen. Even then, he'd been matter-of-fact about it;

simply not ready to reveal himself, and quite obviously aware of Mac's ability to pierce the darkness.

The man from which the hatred came. Completely unconvincing. If it weren't for the muscle…

But the muscle was there. And the muscle watched Mac as he watched back, ever monitoring the area—quiet park around them, the hum of cars beyond the cement arroyo, Gwen's quick shiver as she moved up against him.

"You may," the man said, and smiled, "call me Rafe."

There, finally, at the edges of the smile—that was the man Mac had heard in the warehouse. That was the man behind the sweeping tarry hatred. Barely showing through—but showing through, he was.

Rafe said, "As for my age…old enough to have seen the rise and fall of cultures and leaders and countries." Again, his smile was not nearly so benevolent. "Old enough to have had a hand in some of those events."

"The blade," she said, and her reaction trickled through to Mac as she absorbed Rafe's words. As she believed them.

He hid his reaction to her; hid it fiercely. If Rafe even suspected what she had, what she could do, he would stop this jolly little pretense and he would come for her. He'd find a way to use her, and if he couldn't, he'd simply kill her and take the pendant for himself. Never mind the man's obvious penchant for control—Demardel could take him down outright, severing him from the blade he'd exploited so well.

If only they knew how to use it.

"Got it," Mac said out loud. "You're older than dirt. You travel. You like causing trouble. What I want to know is why here?"

Rafe's amusement glimmered with the same hinted darkness as his smile. "Did you think it was for you?"

No. Until these past few days, he'd believed his blade to be one of a kind—but now there was not only Rafe, but also Devin and Natalie.

"I felt a call, just as I'm sure you did." Rafe slipped a hand in his pocket and pulled out a palm-sized blade, a triangular thing gone stout at the diminutive guard and sheathed. Even as it cleared his pocket, it glimmered, flashing into the uncovered sweep of an Arabian dagger. "Before I leave, I'll know what's going on—and I'll make sure there's no threat left in it."

Right. And where was Devin James? The man who called this city his turf? What had he known about the call?

Natalie, Mac thought, had not told nearly enough of their secrets.

"The truth is, had I known of you, I would have come anyway." Rafe shrugged at Mac; beside and behind him, his men shifted—knowing him well enough to read something into that gesture. "You're a prize, no doubt. That blade of yours…similar to mine, in many ways. It feels. It grows strong on those feelings. And," he said, smiling, "it shares them."

The men shifted again—and Mac got it then. Especially as Gwen pressed back against him, a shiver rising from within her that had nothing to do with their damp, chilly clothes or the rising gloom of the soaked park. She felt their intent; she fairly vibrated with it. *Shh,* he thought at her, pushing through the knife—hoping it would stay only between them.

For he, too, understood. Rafe was playing with them for his blade. Trying to wring out the stress and tension of it, even as he pushed at Mac's self-control—and tried to push his buttons.

And did so with total success—if not in the way that he imagined.

*You can't have her. You can't have me. And you can't have this blade.*

"You mean," Gwen said, the strength of her resolve stiffening her entire body, "you're a parasitic leech."

"Ah." Rafe's eyes glimmered with quick anger, a peremptory expression that didn't belong on that unprepossessing face and its nondescript features. "As I said, charmingly forthright. But in this case, so very far from correct. I give as well as take—or hadn't you noticed?"

"You give in order to take," Gwen corrected fiercely. "To destroy!"

The strength of her reaction coursed through Mac twofold—through the blade, reaching eagerly for such purity of emotion, and through the link they'd so recently explored. He drew back from it—drew himself up, jaw hard and nostrils flared and trying to keep it from swirling through his concentration. Trying to keep it from Rafe, lest he see the clarity of their connection and come to understand it as more than just the effect of the blade.

"Think bigger," Rafe advised her. He caressed his

own blade, fingers running lightly over glimmering metal. Behind him, the sun crusted the edges of the lowest clouds, offering a brief, final slash of light across the glowering Sandia thunderheads.

Lightning flickered, ever more apparent in the failing light; the local car headlights had become few and far between, here in this city where people had quickly learned to stay inside at night. "Fear is the most powerful human emotion we have. Fear drives everything we do. Fear controls us—and can be used to control others. Fear does not destroy...fear builds. It changes nations." He looked at Mac, a direct challenge. "You can be part of that."

Mac snapped back a response—and then didn't. He clamped down on it, unwilling to risk Gwen's reaction should it slap through their ever-clearing connection, and kept his voice even. "You mean like the Ku Klux Klan? Like Hitler's Germany? Like the Crusades, and the people who picketed this very park today?"

Satisfaction gleamed in the man's expression. "Not like those things."

Gwen reached back for Mac—found his hand and held on. "You," she said. "You had something to do... with all of it? Those horrible things?"

"People who fear are so very easy to exploit." Rafe held his blade up to what remained of the light. "People who fear can so easily be guided to hatred, and shaped into weapons."

*Sociopath.* Mac realized it with a slap, drew a sharp breath at it. The perfect marriage of blade and human; the creation of an ultimate evil.

*No. You can't have her. You can't have me. And you can't have this blade.*

"Come, now," Rafe said. "I've given you this time to think—to understand. I've protected you from the influence the rest of the city feels this night, these past moments." He took a deep breath, his chest lifting and his eyes closing—right there before them, soaking in the emotional storm of the entire city.

Gwen made a noise, realizing it, too. Feeling as he did—the indecency of it. The lurid nature of it.

Rafe opened his eyes with a snap of motion, looking directly at Mac. "But my patience has come to an end, and frankly, you're boring my men."

The first trickle of it nudged in at him—the first nauseating wave of churning darkness.

*No*— The blade's protest whispered in his mind, its remembrance of pain. And at the same time—*yes oh yes deep rich agonies, fears and oh WANT but let me LET ME oh SHOCK give me PAIN WAIL*—

Mac must have made a sound. He must have stiffened or sucked air or gritted out a curse, understanding it now—that the blade's pain, his pain, came from more than just the overwhelming emotional swamp. It came from Mac's rejection of it—of what the blade craved and what Mac denied.

Gwen whirled to him, alarm over her paled features, eyes gone dark with fear and straining to see him in the deep dusk. "Mac!"

*No! You can't have her! You can't have me. And you can't have this blade!*

Where the *hell* was Devin James?

## Chapter 17

Devin climbed out of his car with the Rio Bravo highway entrance ramp in sight and stood within the open door, scowling down the long double rows of motionless headlights. Horns blared all around; to his left, a fistfight had broken out. Without looking, he dipped into the center console of the battered old truck and pulled out his phone.

A glance gave him the number Natalie had programmed there before he'd left the estate; he dialed it. Up ahead came the screech of tires and the profound slam of metal into metal as someone rear-ended a car on the other side of the overpass, scattering shrapnel and parts; Devin winced. "Dammit," he said into the phone. "Pick up the—"

It clicked over to voice mail and he heard the brief

grumble of a masculine voice, the details of it lost in the background noise.

Devin swore more resoundingly, made as if to toss the phone—and at the last minute pulled it back. A moment later, he had Natalie.

"Devin?" she said—uncertain, as she might well be, with the horns and chaos that greeted her before his voice did.

Not to mention the strangely dangerous feel of the city around them.

"See if you can get through to those two," he said, without wasting time on preamble. "I'm stuck at the Rio Bravo entrance. It's out here happening again—"

"I can't hear—what?" she said, raising her voice in sympathetic response to the chaos at the bridge. "Devin, be careful— Can you feel it?"

"I'm okay!" he shouted into the phone. "Stuck in traffic! Call them! Keep calling them! I'll get there when I can."

This time, he did toss the phone back into the truck, standing beside it to stare down the road...more thoughtfully this time. A fight or two on the other side of the overpass, cars jammed up at the entrance ramp as if everyone had made the turn at once and no one had given way.

Anheriel tugged at him—a blade eager for the action and far too aware of the currents flowing through the night. Excited by them—energized by them. With hours of practice behind him, he instantly shifted his attention to the smell of wet asphalt, the faint chill of the breeze against his face…the feel of his toes in enclosing shoes.

Anheriel subsided, leaving behind a righteous little grumble. It was, after all, trying to earn redemption. It was *supposed* to be drawing his attention to situations in which he might prove useful.

"Don't worry about it," Devin told it, letting his gaze linger on the fast-fading sunset glimmer of dark violet and bruised blue clouds. "There's plenty of action where we're going."

*If we ever get there.*

He saw easily through the gloom, past the confusing shine of headlights off water—straight to the heart of the vehicular mob—a monochrome jumble of metal and violence through blade-given night vision. Gridlock and brainlock. These people weren't going anywhere.

He pulled the truck keys, reacquired his phone, slammed the door with the extra oomph necessary to make it latch and left it locked in the middle of the bumper-to-bumper traffic. Two hundred yards of walking between abandoned vehicles and those harboring terrified, huddled occupants, and he reached the tightly jammed underpass. He barely hesitated in his stride, bounding to a trunk, a roof, a hood…boring through to the problem intersection itself.

And went beyond it to the first interlocked row, while the violence roiled behind him and Anheriel whined to join in. He backtracked two rows, chose a vehicle, and helped himself to the keys still in the ignition, cranking the wheels hard. The car jerked, hanging up on the bumper of the car ahead of it, and then broke free with a brief crunch of metal and glass, heading over the road shoulder to the raw desert.

No one noticed when he floored the accelerator, shooting up the entrance ramp. "On my way," he muttered, as if Mac and Gwen could hear him.

Gwen turned on the unimposing man who called himself Rafe. "Stop it!" she cried as Mac slowly sank to his knees. "You're a monster!"

Rafe tipped his head in acknowledgment. "But a successful one." He eyed her up and down, his eyes lingering on the wet cling of material at her breasts and backside. "If he turns, will you go with him? If he dies, will you go with me? Because there is something about you…and, quite frankly, I can't have you running around as a loose end."

"Get real," she snapped at him. "What am I going to do, call the police? And tell them what exactly?"

Rafe gave an eloquent shrug. "There's someone else here—another blade. I haven't had time to track it down, but I suspect it is the very blade that called us each here. It is a power come into its own—and it might well use you against me. I didn't live this long—which, as I've mentioned, is very, very long indeed—by being careless with loose ends."

"Maybe you've lived long enough." Gwen's fury left her mouth completely unfettered.

Rafe smiled, and the coldness of it in those bland features slapped her anger down hard. "Would that you were entitled to an opinion."

Mac grabbed the Jeep's bumper, then the fender—hauling himself back up to his feet, completely focused on Rafe. "You," he said, grinding the words out in a voice Gwen didn't recognize. "Son. Of. A. *Bitch*."

Rafe regarded him with something akin to fondness. Sick, sick fondness. "I really wish you'd accept the situation," he said. "You would be a great asset to me."

Mac's grin was as dark as they came. "There's an *ass* in that word, in case you thought I wouldn't notice. Not my thing."

Rafe flipped a dismissive hand at them. "Die, then," he said, making it a casual command. "In agony, while you're at it."

Gwen's breath stuttered as Mac made a gargling noise, his eyes rolling back; he slid down the side of the Jeep. She wanted to dive after him, holding him, turning the pendant on him.

But that would only leave them both vulnerable.

She took an involuntary step toward Rafe, hands fisted, so full of anger—overflowing with it, unfamiliar and debilitating, clouding her thoughts, changing her intent—

And realized that it came to her through Mac.

That her connection with him flared strong again.

Recklessly, she reached for it, thinking of calm and cool as he pushed against the wet ground, on his knees. Thinking of her hand in his, thinking of her mouth on his. Forging past the chaotic agonies still beating against her thoughts…giving him something other than hate and fear and pain. She gave him a quiet current, imbuing it with what they were together and what they'd had together.

"Gwen—" he said—as if there should be more to it, but he couldn't quite manage it.

It sounded like a warning.

"Is that it, then?" Rafe stepped closer, his features coming alive with interest. "Is that the key to you? Your one last chance, Mac. Your Gwen goes free—and you become mine. You give over to the wild road and join me, and no one ever touches her. Permanent asylum. She can stay with you, or she can go back to whatever life she had before she met you. Lady's choice."

The thick, scraping flow of imposed emotions faded—Gwen felt it through Mac, and felt the dim echo of it through herself. Mac lifted his head—his expression terrible and strained, his gaze latching on to Rafe's.

"That's it, isn't it?" Rafe said so softly. He took a step closer, crouching with one hand resting over his knee, his own blade so casually held there. "You'll do it. For her, you'll do it."

"Wait," Gwen said. "Wait, wait, wait. What? He will not! Mac, no! You will not!"

But Mac wasn't looking at her. Mac, his jaw set and his face still tense with the battle, looked only at Rafe. His voice held a grim desperation. "You'll leave her alone."

"I'll leave her alone." Rafe's smile spoke of victory, tipping over to smug.

Maybe it was that smug look that did it, triggering Gwen's temper. Maybe it was the look on Mac's face—

the despair, in this moment he so obviously intended to be a goodbye. She looked at him aghast and more than a little annoyed. "Are you *kidding?*"

It was hardly the grateful response of a rescued damsel in distress, and maybe it was all wrong, but so was *this*. "Mac, once you cross that line, you'll be like him! You won't care what happens to me!"

He shook his head. "If I die here, I can't stop him at all. This way, there's a chance. And then…maybe someone will stop me." They both knew who he meant. Devin James, the man who was supposed to have been here. Supposed to have helped them both.

*I am twenty-seven years old, and I'm about to lose the man I love.*

"Screw this," she said. "I know you. *I know you.* Do you hear me? I've *seen* you. I know you can do this. I know *we*—" She stopped talking. She reached deep inside where the pendant gave her access to him. And she reached through him—finding that taste of the blade.

Making it up as she went along, yes—but also following what she'd already learned, and her growing ability to touch the blade—prodding it, listening to it, even shutting it out.

But shutting it out wasn't what she wanted.

She wanted its name. This blade had a name, too, whether Mac knew it or not.

Names mattered.

Names meant control.

*I see you,* she told it, finding the blazing alien heart of it within him. *I want to know you.*

It startled; it shied away. It struck out at Mac, daring

her to hurt the one she loved. And while Mac jerked with surprise, a strangled noise replacing the words in his throat, Rafe drew back in pure astonishment. "What?" he said, not the least bit suave—and then the surprise turned to pure avarice. "What is this?"

And Mac said, "Don't—he can *hear*—"

But Gwen had seen their only chance, and she dared to hurt the one she loved.

*Keska.*

The word blazed through Mac's thoughts, branding them from the inside out—blinding him to all else, as the blade spasmed in reaction to its forced confession, spitting fury and fear and resentment. It struck, then—pushing and shoving, stealing time and breath—and yet somehow leaving enough of both to howl, a ragged voice expressing both the blade's fury and the man's agony.

*Keska.* Merely a whispered reminder at the edges of awareness, nudging him. *You are not me. Your feelings are not mine. I am in control of me and mine.*

*I am in control of* you.

But it wasn't as easy as that, with days of a siege riding him, leaving him worn and battered.

Mac ignored his body, letting the white-hot slashes of pain streak across his mind's eye without touching the core of him. He'd felt the blade's retreat. He'd felt its need for recovery. It, too, needed an end to this. Gwen knew it; Gwen buoyed him.

But the blade Keska said *no.* The blade said *I won't.* The blade said *no* and *hurt* and *die.*

And the blade had nothing to lose. Because while Mac needed to stay alive, the blade was what it was. Weary, it could hang on for one moment longer than he. It could afford to strike out; it knew how to wound.

There would be no waiting it out.

For the first time, Mac understood that determination might not be enough, no matter how much of it he had. Keska fought back, striking hard; Mac lost the sense of his body, his sense of Gwen.

Until she screamed. Loud and piercing and furious—never anything demure about Gwen.

It shocked the blade, too, enough so Mac found himself momentarily free on the asphalt, fingers bloodied from clawing at it, cheek throbbing from where he'd gone down, body aching—Gwen's cry still echoing in his mind. He lifted a heavy head to find her in the grip of two of the muscle men—stretched out between them and still twisting to kick at them, not quite having the distance.

"See that she's not hurt," Rafe said sharply. His cheek bled from a trio of deep scratches; he didn't seem to notice.

Gwen had made her play, all right.

Rafe turned his attention to Mac. "Ah," he said. "There you are. Deal's off, I'm afraid. She is, it has become obvious, one of a kind." He smiled thinly, with a mean cast behind it. "I can make another one of you, once the blade finishes you off. I appreciate the show, by the way."

"Bastard!" Gwen spat, still struggling in the parking lot light. It was full dark now, with the lightning more dramatic than ever behind her, a constant flutter and rumble. Unidentifiable sound muttered in Mac's ear—he counted it a trick of the blade.

The blade floundered in what had turned to defeat. Mac had it now—he had its name and he had his focus. Thanks to Gwen—to that scream, to the anchor she'd given him.

Rafe turned his head to the man behind him. "Get the abduction kit. I want her tranquilized."

"You *what?*" Gwen cast a desperate look at Mac— and it became even more desperate when she found him looking back, drawn by her need. "Mac—you were right, what you said earlier—when you wouldn't let me—when you had to stay this way—" A frantic glance at Rafe, and Mac understood. *When you wouldn't let me separate you from the blade. When you refused to make things okay for us, okay for you, in order to take this man down.*

"Yeah," he said. "I know. I'm working on it."

The mutter of sound in the background had escalated—not a trick of the blade at all, but now a rush and tumble roar. *The storms. The concrete, urbanized arroyo.*

Gwen didn't seem to notice it. She gave a token jerk against the men who held her, doing no more than annoying them. "But if—if—" The irony of her struggle for words wasn't lost on Mac, even if she'd gone so far into the moment that she didn't realize it. "If things don't—"

And then she stopped altogether so as not to say

things that neither of them wanted to share with the enemy.

"Yeah," he said, and caught her gaze—holding it, the best he could, in this light, not sure how much she could truly see. *Not enough.* "I know."

She took matters into her own hands, doing that which she'd only just learned to do in the first place. She lifted her chin—even if it trembled—and she stared back at him with an unexpected defiance—and in that moment the blade Keska gave a startled little leap, welcoming the subtle warmth of emotion. *I know you* and *I love you* and *I'm with you.*

Mac's throat tightened down completely. "Yeah," he managed again, and sent her a poor excuse for a dark, wry smile. *Me, too.*

He didn't know if she'd catch it; she was the one who knew how to reach out...he'd only ever received. But he thought from the way her chin firmed—from her faint hint of a smile—that she had. And then as Rafe's personal muscle man approached, syringe in hand, her head tipped back in that shorthand gesture of defiance—and damned if he didn't see it coming. Gwen, ready to go for it in spite of the odds.

Damned if he was going to let her do it alone.

The blade leaped in eager response—gratified to soak up the cruel flat intentions of the muscle man, happy to flood Mac with the quickness and strength that flowed so familiar between them. *—hurt kill drink—!*

"Yeah," Mac muttered. "He's all yours."

A sparking nova of metal, heat here and gone

again—a familiar pain, and one he finally embraced. The Civil War sword extended his reach as he lunged off the ground, driving up with purpose and exacting control.

They shouldn't have counted him out of it.

Rafe's man paid with his fingers. The syringe went flying; so did the fingers. And when the injured man cried out, aghast and recoiling, Gwen didn't hesitate. The moment her two human restraints reacted, she jerked herself free from one and went after the other. No skill there, just a frenzy of determination—clawing at his eyes, slamming at his balls, teeth bared and active. Rafe's man recovered enough to clench his hand into a protective fist and come for Mac, but Mac ignored him for the third man, the one now reaching to haul Gwen off his buddy.

—*no*—! The blade, as obscure and demanding as ever. —*mine*—!

*In a minute,* Mac thought at it, nothing more than a distracted push of intent—until his injured leg gave out from under him, a blast of heat and inexplicable failure, and he suddenly understood—the blade had been claiming *him*. Claiming its turf in the presence of the intruding blade that had just taken him down.

He clawed his way back up, dragging the leg and ignoring Keska's territorial snarl. His form turned choppy—he slashed out with the saber, overreaching to close the distance. The blade sliced diagonally across the legs of the third man, flaying muscle and tendon as he grabbed for Gwen. The man went down;

he could do nothing else. Not even yet realizing the extent of his injuries, his cry more angry than pained.

Mac sprawled full-length, stretched to make that attack—and when he would have rolled aside, springing up to face those who remained, the dead weight of his leg dragged him down. Rafe's man slammed him with a kick.

He lost his grip on the blade—just out of reach, stretching for it—*almost!*—and it reached back, just brushing his fingers as another kick lifted him off the ground and sent him rolling away.

He knew well enough that the blade could be used against him. Remembered with vivid clarity the moment it had first found his hand, taking the life of its own erstwhile partner.

But that man had been lost to himself—lost to the wild road without understanding it or working it. And Mac wasn't.

In that moment, Rafe stood over him—wrenching, with no delicacy at all, at his own blade—the one still sunk deeply into Mac's thigh.

Mac cried out with it, lost in a moment of retching agony. Gwen echoed it with a cry of frustration and quite suddenly slammed to the ground beside him— winded and still fighting mad. She caught his eye, and it came through to him in a flash as Keska gloried in her intention to fight, her spirit running hot and high.

He pushed back. *No,* he thought at Gwen. *You run, dammit. You protect yourself. You protect what you have from this evil.*

It slapped at her, reflected in eyes wide with sudden

doubt—and just as sudden realization. Understanding, for the first time, the true price of carrying something bigger than she was.

She'd hardly had time to get used to it at all.

Only then did she see Rafe, backing up a step and glaring at them with annoyance but no concern; only then did she see Mac's leg, a dark and rapidly spreading stain. She may have even felt it; her fingers twitched toward her own leg.

*I'll buy you time.* Dammit, surely she could understand the gist of it, if not his exact words. He pushed at the blade, pushed toward her. *You run like hell!*

"That," Rafe said with profound disgust, "was a complete waste of time and of my staff." The only uninjured man among the three knelt by his bleeding buddy.

*"That,"* Mac grunted, "would be a matter of opinion. I think it went pretty well." *Work on that leg, Keska.* He sent it out not as a request but a command— to work it hard and fast, whatever patch job would do, whatever the price. And then he barely contained a startled gasp as the blade, fired up by action and blood, sprang to work—a lightning bolt stitching flesh from the inside out. His face flushed against the chilling night, sweat dotting out along his temples.

Rafe only smiled—understanding as no one else could. "It won't be enough. You're too young, and you know too little. But you've impressed me. I might give you a second chance—if you walk the road with me now."

Mac didn't relent—pushing the blade, pushing at

Gwen, and pushing right back at Rafe. "You mean I just took out the two men you had chosen for my blade."

A one-shouldered shrug. "That, too." Rafe held up his own blade, watching as Mac's blood soaked into the gleaming metal. "Our thirst is endless. You decide."

Gwen hesitated at his back—he felt it more than saw it, knowing she'd finally understood him through the blade and pendant. Feeling from her the wild hope that he could do what needed to be done and somehow live through it...and then find her again.

Because she was going to run—she and the pendant.

Mac grinned, a dark, wry thing full of self-awareness—he knew his odds here, even if he'd obscured them from Gwen. Warmth filled his leg, spreading the length of the long muscle so badly damaged—and it filled his hand, forming to a grip not quite as familiar as most but nonetheless welcome.

The frontier tomahawk. Cruder than most of the blade's forms, but just as thirsty, just as keen-edged... and as accurate in the throw. Even without the time or space to set his feet, line up the throw...straight back, straight forward, release.

The blade couldn't turn a wild throw straight. But it could make a straight throw fly true against the odds.

Rafe frowned at this evidence of Mac's intent, annoyed and just wary enough to be smart. Rafe's muscle man hesitated.

A man had only so many fingers to lose.

Gwen turned tense and trembling, hovering on the moment, and Mac said, "Yeah. Decision made." He rolled to his feet, favoring the injured leg and compensating with balance and determination. "I've decided not to die today."

He eyed Rafe's muscle man, ignoring the gun. "How about you?"

Rafe snapped, "Your continued existence is no longer your choice. It's mine, and I've made it."

*Go, Gwen. Go!*

He wouldn't hold them both for long. And as soon as the uninjured man gave up on his buddy...

"Really?" he said to Rafe's man, eyeing the gun, letting his skepticism show. "With your off hand? To protect a man I bet you've never seen take on someone who could fight back."

From the flicker in the man's eye, he knew he'd hit target. From the anger on Rafe's face, he was certain of it.

"Lifetimes," Rafe said, his speech no longer quite as clear. "I have *lifetimes* of survival. You haven't even made it through one."

*Go, Gwen. Go NOW!*

Gwen spurted away in a scrabbling run, hands as much as feet until she gained a stride or two—and then Rafe's man was on her, eschewing the gun to throw himself bodily across her with an impact that squeaked all the air out of her body.

"Wrong," Mac said, "decision." Swift as his movement, the tomahawk glimmered into war club, slamming down across the man's shoulders—breaking flesh and bone with an audible crunch that left the man in paralyzed shock and Gwen cursing beneath his weight, clawing to pull herself out from under him.

Mac hooked the man's side with his club and flipped him over, halfway freeing Gwen—and that was all he could do, as blade shimmered back to tomahawk and he pivoted around, all one motion, to release the throw as Rafe finally came for him—finally goaded beyond endurance to physical action.

No surprise that Rafe blocked the blow—he'd had too much time, too much space to do it, his blade a stout scimitar that showered showy and improbable sparks through the night as it parried Keska away.

It didn't matter. Because as Mac dove for Keska—knowing it would find his hand more readily than he ever truly thought possible—Gwen scrambled free from the weight of Rafe's dying muscle man and sprinted away.

Rafe cried out in wordless outrage, standing with legs splayed and arms spread—completely open, if Mac had only been in a position to do something about it. Not that he had any compunction at all about whipping the tomahawk around into the shallow angle of Rafe's back, but *damn* if that leg hadn't given out on him, just enough to lose the moment.

Rafe didn't even notice Mac, all his attention on Gwen. "No!" he cried, honest horror in his voice. "Watch out!"

Because Gwen ran straight for the concrete arroyo. Gwen, who'd only been in this city a matter of days and who'd never experienced the violence of a monsoon storm. Gwen, who probably hadn't even realized what the arroyos *were* or that the noise behind them was six feet of water rushing along at a startling speed.

"Gwen!" Mac cried—but no, he'd *told* her to go, he'd pushed her with everything she had. She wouldn't stop now.

Still, she jerked around—just for an instant. Just before her foot hit that first step on a steep wet concrete slope.

She went down with a startled cry; it turned terrified as she plunged out of sight, and then it cut short with a splash, barely audible over the rushing water.

Mac saved his breath on a curse, bolting forward—a lurching, awkward run that took him to the edge only just before Rafe made it there, both of them stricken. But if Mac was wild with it, Rafe quickly turned to cold fury—watching the dark rush of water, foam and rapids and debris churning along faster than the average man could run.

*I'm not average.* For the moment, Mac forgot he was on one-and-a-half legs and forgot he stood beside the man he was sworn to stop. "Gwen!" he shouted out over that roiling water, a deep notch of concrete draining straight to the Rio Grande. "Gwen!"

But he heard nothing in response…not so much as a distant cry. Deep within, a jerk of thought slapped up against him. *Rafe. Right here beside me.*

The man he had to stop. The one from whom he'd thought to save Gwen, at the cost of his own body.

He hadn't done that—hadn't kept her safe at all. But he damned sure wouldn't let it be for nothing.

As if Rafe hadn't figured that out.

Even as Mac turned on him, the man's blade sliced air, aiming to cut him through. Mac stumbled back—fell as the leg went out yet again, but rolled more nimbly this time, barely off his feet and up again, Keska striking out in a cutting sheen of metal—coming back at Rafe fast enough so the older man swore and slapped at the blade, a clumsy move.

*Oh, yeah, it's been a while.* For how many lifetimes had the man been living by proxy, sucking down the emotions of others—evoking what he wanted, manipulating the results, watching the agony and sorrow of his own making and then profiting from it? Never putting himself out there, never facing direct retribution.

But Rafe struck back, a flurry of blows—his form strengthening, his movements growing more fine and subtle, his blade slowly straightening to match the sweep of Mac's saber.

Not long enough, apparently.

And Rafe wasn't already winded...wasn't already bleeding...wasn't already exhausted from days of battling an unknown foe along with his blade.

He smiled with grim satisfaction as Mac missed a parry from low to high guard, his blade skipping along the outer edge of Keska to nick Mac's arm, then flicking down to slash shallowly across his thigh while Keska chased its shadow, not quite there in time.

"Lifetimes," Rafe reminded him as they stood apart, Mac panting and stung, his thigh burning deeply and his heart still shouting after Gwen, "which you cannot defeat." He raised his blade-sword, a ceremonial gesture, and spoke to it, reveling in the moment. "You may take them now."

Oh, no. No, no, no. That was the whole point. It was why Mac had refused to be parted from the shackles of his own blade, why Gwen had let him go—why she had fled to protect the pendant. *Because you don't get to win.*

But the man's dark blade was right there. And it knew how to spew hatred, up close and personal. It knew how to ooze through to Mac's soul, flooding in through the blade to swamp them both, looking for the slightest echo from within Mac.

And Keska gave way.

Mac staggered back as the blade's connection snapped shut, leaving him only what he was: a man sorely tried, sorely wounded, with dead dull metal in hand.

*Keska!*

In response, only the merest flicker through their bond. Not a blade separated, not a blade destroyed... but a blade overwhelmed. A blade in complete retreat.

Mac sucked in a deep, ragged breath, taking a two-handed grip on a sword not meant for it—braced and waiting even as he reeled. Rafe might have taken him down right then—that moment, with a long sweep of slashing metal that Mac could no longer evade.

But no. Rafe stopped. He took the deepest of breaths—satisfaction of the most profound nature, nostrils flared and standing with proud arrogance, the storm's pounding flicker of light the perfect backdrop.

And through the thick, pounding nature of horror,

Mac felt it. A feather-light touch, no more than a whisper. *Keska. Be strong.*

More than that, Rafe felt it. He stepped back, jerking around—looking for it. *I see you...I taste you... Halgos...you are known.*

"Halgos," Mac said in the wonderment of it—the hope of it, glimmering through the overriding swamp of heavy, pounding despair and darkness. Demardel?

He didn't have time to think about it. Rafe whirled, came crashing down on him with metal and fury and no small spark of blooming fear. "It," he said each word distinct and growing in emphasis. "Won't. *Work.*"

Mac staggered back away from him. Rafe's final remaining man abandoned his sorely wounded comrades to snap foolishly around the edges of the fight and Mac pivoted to him with blade extended, driving him away and bringing the point back into guard just in time to keep Rafe from plunging at him. Metal clashed; Keska sparked back to life. —*halgos*— it murmured, intrigued. —*keska. be strong. strong*—!

*Halgos,* said the trickle from outside them all, growing stronger. *I see you. I can deny you.*

"No," Rafe said, a harsh whisper from between clenched teeth. "No one can take what we have! And you'll die trying!" He pressed a quick flurry of attacks and Keska surged to meet him, offering Mac a renewed strength and quickness for which he would later pay.

*Halgos. You may NOT.*

And all the hatred fell away. The deep inner attack, the imposed hatred wrapped around keen fear wrapped around gibbering insanities. It fell away and it left Mac clear and sharp, reflecting only Keska's normal trickling mutter of satisfactions—and with those, he was well able to deal.

Suddenly it was Mac pressing the attack. Suddenly it was Mac pushing the older man back.

Suddenly it was Mac, having quietly closed the distance between them, moving just inside Rafe's guard without notice, allowing small hits to embolden Rafe into taking the bigger strike. It would have impaled Mac through the heart had he let it, giving Keska no time to heal him at all.

But he didn't; he lured the strike in and he parried it away. And suddenly it was Mac, the sword buried deeply in his side and grating on ribs—stuck there, for the merest instant—while Mac returned the favor. A clean strike, up beneath the breastbone, up through the heart…right on through as they both fell heavily to the ground.

And it was Gwen, soaked and dripping all over, who yanked Rafe aside without regard to his dead and glazing eyes, and who yanked out the blade Halgos—and who threw herself down on Mac. And then—in the nicest possible way—she said, "That was the worst plan *ever*," before she planted her hands at the side of his face and kissed him senseless.

Violence lingered in Gwen's thoughts. Clashing images of fear and peril, the bruising grip of water—the slam of her body up against the inexplicable lip of concrete to which she had clung. The water tugging viciously at her—tearing away her sandals, stretching her shirt.

But she'd latched on, pounded by sensation—the noise, the cold, the battering pain—and she'd nonetheless sent her focus elsewhere. Reaching out. Not to Mac, but to the blade in Rafe's hands. Halgos.

She hadn't been strong enough to sunder them apart; she hadn't known enough. But she'd sure as hell distracted them. And she'd frightened Rafe…and it had been enough.

She just hadn't known if it had been in time for Mac. And she hadn't known if she'd survive to find out—not until an unfamiliar form slid down to join her, hauling her away from the outflow pipe against which she'd lodged and boosting her out of the concrete arroyo with impersonal hands placed by necessity in personal places.

Disoriented, uncoordinated and staggering, she nonetheless found Rafe dead and toppled over Mac, hating the very touch of that heinous blade as she flung it away—then finding Mac and that dark wry grin… *kissing* him.

But he wasn't so much kissing her back any longer. And while she'd forgotten to feel the soaking cold, Mac was the one who now shivered.

"Hey," she said, running her hands over him. Dark blood stained his pants, his shirt, now his chin. "Hey." She groped to find Keska—not quite retreated to its neutral pocketknife form, but lingering as the frontier trade blade, all glimmering Damascus-like metal. It lay on the ground behind her, exactly where she'd so recently shoved Rafe's body.

Where Rafe no longer lay. Nothing. Nada.

No body. No body parts.

She sucked in a breath. He'd been dead—she'd been so *sure* he was dead! But she'd heard nothing, seen nothing…

And he wasn't there.

"Mac," she said—only a whisper because could he even hear her? She'd never felt quite so alone, kneeling on the asphalt beside one shivering, wounded and unconscious man.

On impulse, she shoved Keska into Mac's cold hand, forcibly wrapping his fingers around it. She chafed his arms—quite suddenly feeling her own sodden clothes and her own very close call with death. "Keska," she said, out loud and concentrating hard, "you better do something here. If he—"

Okay, maybe *out loud* hadn't been the best idea, because she suddenly choked on the words. She swallowed against the big knot in her throat and tried again. "If he dies, things aren't going to turn out well for you. You can't take me, and I'll make damned sure you don't get a chance at anyone else."

Maybe, just maybe, the blade glimmered slightly in response.

Squishing footsteps came up behind her; water splatted the asphalt, merging with the spreading puddle of water and blood. "Hell, that poor bastard." The voice was unfamiliar, and a little rough with swallowed water.

Surreptitiously, Gwen reached for Keska—not knowing if the blade would allow her to use it at all.

But the man just laughed. "Who just pulled you away from an outflow pipe and boosted your ass out of that arroyo?"

"I have no idea," Gwen said, closing her hand around Mac's with Keska, finding it warm again. "But I'd really like it if you weren't close enough to drip on me."

He laughed again, short but amused, and moved to the other side of Mac, his hands low and away from his body in a gesture of peace. "Devin James," he said. "I think you were expecting me."

It fired her up all over again. "Damned right we were! 'We can help,' Natalie kept saying. Well, where the hell were you?"

"Caught in traffic," he said easily and cocked his head slightly, looking at her with enough scrutiny that she finally made a face at him. He nodded slightly. "Natalie was right about you two. I'm sorry I didn't see it sooner. Let's say I was...distracted." His dark expression left no doubt about his meaning. *That man.*

"Rafe!" Gwen moved closer to Mac—protective again, and realizing that the warmth had spread to his chest and shoulder...that he no longer shivered. That his face, an odd, pale cast in the parking lot light, no longer looked quite as ghostly pale. *Go, Keska, go!* "He was here. I swear he was dead. And his blade—"

Devin's amiable expression fell away, and Gwen found herself suddenly looking at the same man who'd first accosted them in the street, dark and dangerous.

"If I'd been a little faster…" He shook his head. "The blade is gone—one of Rafe's people. He and another guy took the van. There's a third one over there, looking pretty dead."

"But Rafe—" She looked again to the spot where she'd shoved him, so close that she'd surely have seen if he'd…

Surely.

Devin grinned, a quick and generous thing, all the more startling for the contrast of his dark demeanor. "The blades clean up after themselves." He nodded down at Mac, whose clothes seemed notably drier, whose bleeding had stopped. "It's how they fuel themselves."

She made a face. "How gruesomely convenient."

"Nothing about the blades comes without a touch of darkness," Devin said, absently enough so the words hit home even harder than they were probably meant to. What they'd done to Mac…what wielders like Devin and Natalie lived with every day…

What *Mac* would live with every day…

Unless he chose not to.

Her hand went to the pendant.

Devin's eyes narrowed. "I'd really like to know what happened down there." He flicked a gesture out, encompassing the rushing channel of water behind her. "You only had a few more moments of hanging on left—and you weren't even trying to get out. People who take those arroyos lightly tend to die."

She frowned at him. "Like I even know what a concrete arroyo is? In the dark?"

Mac made a deeply disgruntled and incoherent sound of protest. To Gwen, it was a sound of beauty. "Mac!" she said, pressing her hand against his shoulder. His eyes flickered, didn't open. No, not quite yet.

Not that Devin was done with her. "And then there's what happened up here—there's no way your guy beat out that man with that blade—he's been one foot from the wild road for days. And I know what it looks like to commune with one of these things. I know how damned dangerous it is, too—for everyone!"

Her temper flashed. "I did what I had to, and it *worked,* didn't it? And even if Rafe's little minion got away with the blade, he doesn't know what he's doing. We can find him. I know that blade now—*I* can find him."

"Ah," Devin said, brows raised. He appraised her for another long moment. "Demardel chose well." And, looking down, he gave Mac a gentle nudge with his toe. "You, too, fella. Though I'm guessing it'll be a while before you realize it." He reached down, offering his hand to Gwen. "Come on. Let's get you both somewhere warm."

# *Epilogue*

Mac stumbled at the threshold of the little casita and caught himself on the doorjamb.

"Hey," Gwen said, catching up under his shoulder—fitting nicely there. "No hurry. Let's not have any more fainting."

"Passing out," Mac said through gritted teeth. "And seriously, at the park? That was more of a trying-not-to-die thing."

"Yes, dear," Gwen said, slipping through the door to pat the back of the couch not far from it. Nothing was terribly far from anything in this small guesthouse on the former Sawyer estate—and it was theirs to use for as long as they needed.

Or wanted.

Mac growled at her cheerfully patent disbelief.

"Bring it on," he said, leaving the security of the door-way to swoop in and lift her up.

She clung to him in self-defense, legs wrapping around him and expression full of alarm. "Mac—*Mac*—I give, I give! There was no fainting! Just put me down before—"

Wisely, she didn't say the words *you fall down*.

Wisely, Mac wasted no time getting to the kitchen, where he set her delectable bottom down on the counter. He didn't mention that his vision had greyed or that he couldn't quite hear clearly or that his thigh had seized up.

Keska had done its job these past few days. Week. Whatever. Having Gwen by his side hadn't hurt—napping with him, forcing the estate cook's good food on him at every opportunity, holding his hand when she thought he was asleep and murmuring truly naughty things in his ear when she thought he was awake.

But in the end, nothing took the place of time…and he still needed it.

His new employer—thinking he'd been in a car accident during that mysterious rash of trouble in the city—had regretfully replaced him; Devin had already hired him on and then immediately put him on sick leave.

When he was on his feet, he'd start by protecting the city alongside Devin. But as they peeled back the layers of Demardel, he and Gwen would also have a new mission—using Keska and Demardel. *Find the others.* Those unknown blade wielders out there, lost and alone and still trying to make it on their own.

*Before* they turned into Rafe. Or Sawyer Compton. Or the thing Mac had almost become.

Because Natalie was right—she and Devin had the unique resources to help them all. They had a powerful primary blade; they had Compton's library.

And now they had Demardel.

They'd already started teaching Mac the exercises that would give him more control over the blade than he'd ever dreamed possible.

Gwen's eyes had narrowed; her legs locked tightly around his hips, jerking him close and to attention. "You can't fool me," she said. "And no, I am not cheating." Not peeking through the connection they'd forged. "This," she told him, sending him a rush of sensation, "would be cheating."

He jerked again. And swore.

She laughed. "I practiced that."

"Prove it," he suggested, though it didn't come out with the confident demand he'd planned. Too breathless for that. And his eyes were too close to rolling back in his head.

"Mmm. I don't know if I should." Her hands rested at his jeans snap, fiddling slightly.

He narrowed his eyes at her flowery skort and decided they'd be no impediment at all. And then, when his cell phone rang, he said fiercely, "Ignore it."

"Men," she told him. "Can't you multitask? Besides, I emailed this number to Sandy this morning. You know, my friend? Who went to Vegas? When

I didn't? And who probably just found out I'm not coming back to work?" She fished the phone from his pocket, flipped it open...and slipped a smooth, wicked hand down the front of his jeans. "I'll keep it short."

Not that he could answer. Not that he could do anything other than clutch the counter. He barely heard her say, "Hey, Sandy. How was—yeah, yeah, okay. What happens in Vegas..." Jeans unsnapped, hand stroking around his clenched butt cheek and back again. Mac made a noise. Couldn't help but make a noise. "What? I didn't hear anything...and no, I'm really not coming back. I got a better offer on my walkabout." There, her hand—just *right*. And he'd found the buttons on her shirt, and she laughed again, more breathlessly this time, and at the feel of her in his hands he made a rough, low noise and Gwen said, "Hey—yeah—I really gotta go. I'll email, okay? I'll be back to pack up my stuff, so...yeah...what?"

And then she laughed outright. "Hey," she said. "What happens on walkabout, stays on walkabout."

She flipped the phone closed and put it aside. Mac put his hand over hers and interlaced their fingers. "Permanent," he said. "That walkabout. You and me."

Gwen stilled herself to hold him tight—to let what they had swell between them and only them. Not through the blade, not through the pendant. Just man and woman, controlling who they were and what they were—if each for the first time in a long time. "What happens on walkabout..."

*"Stays,"* he told her—and held her gaze, grey-blue

eyes gone dark and deep, that wry set of his mouth gone completely and utterly kissable.

So she did, and it was answer enough.

* * * * *

*A sneaky peek at next month...*

# NOCTURNE™

BEYOND DARKNESS...BEYOND DESIRE

## *My wish list for next month's titles...*

In stores from 18th October 2013:

☐ The Keepers: Christmas in Salem –
   Heather Graham, Deborah LeBlanc,
   Kathleen Pickering & Beth Ciotta

☐ Siren's Secret – Debbie Herbert

In stores from 1st November 2013:

☐ Twilight Hunter – Kait Ballenger

Available at WHSmith, Tesco, Asda, Eason, Amazon and Apple

## *Just can't wait?*

# *Special Offers*

Every month we put together collections and longer reads written by your favourite authors.

Here are some of next month's highlights— and don't miss our fabulous discount online!

On sale 1st November    On sale 1st November    On sale 18th Octobe

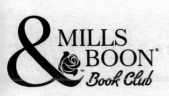

**MILLS & BOON®** *Book Club*

# Join the Mills & Boon Book Club

Want to read more **Nocturne**™ books?
We're offering you **1** more absolutely **FREE!**

We'll also treat you to these fabulous extras:

- ❧ **Exclusive offers and much more!**
- ❧ **FREE home delivery**
- ❧ **FREE books and gifts with our special rewards scheme**

*Get your free books now!*

visit **www.millsandboon.co.uk/bookclub**
or call Customer Relations on **020 8288 2888**

# The World of Mills & Boon®

There's a Mills & Boon® series that's perfect for you. We publish ten series and, with new titles every month, you never have to wait long for your favourite to come along.

---

## Blaze.
*Scorching hot, sexy reads*
4 new stories every month

## By Request
*Relive the romance with the best of the best*
9 new stories every month

## Cherish™
*Romance to melt the heart every time*
12 new stories every month

## Desire™
*Passionate and dramatic love stories*
8 new stories every month